HIS GOOD DEEDS

A KATE REID NOVEL
BOOK 13

ROBIN MAHLE

HARP HOUSE PUBLISHING, LLC.

Published by HARP House Publishing
May 2021 (1st edition)

1

The asphalt streets seared under the noonday sun in Downtown Pittsburgh where the rivers converged in an area known as the Golden Triangle. The "triangle" appeared to have been stitched together in this City of Bridges, like wounds that hadn't yet closed. Nearby, in Market Square, well-dressed businessmen and women with an air of self-importance hurried for a speedy lunch inside one of the many restaurants and cafés.

"Rats in the maze," Danny whispered, sweat forming a ring around his collar in the summer heat. From across the street where high-rises loomed, he peered at the café under the stale guise of sunglasses and a baseball hat. Still, no one took notice, most with their heads buried in phones while they navigated the city streets.

Rob Delaney sat in a booth inside the café across from friend and colleague, Gwen Madura, while the two finished lunch. Through Danny's shaded lenses, Rob appeared to be enjoying her company, though he looked awkward around the beautiful woman. Rob was single and so was Gwen. They worked together at TriState Financial. Danny knew all this because Rob updated everything he did and everywhere he went on his social media.

"Hey, buddy, watch out!" A man in a shirt and tie brushed by him but not before glancing over his shoulder with a smirk. "You undercover or something, pal?"

Danny pulled down his ballcap and drew back under an awning, out of the path of on-comers, but hadn't taken his gaze off the café window. He learned that Rob, at 34-years-old, hadn't had many serious relationships. It seemed the ladder of success took precedence. That all changed when Gwen, the 30-year-old with light brown hair, shiny, curly and just at her chin, had been hired.

"Can I get you two anything else?" The waiter stood at their table wearing a wide smile with impatience behind his eyes.

"Just the check, please. Thanks." Rob quickly turned to Gwen. "Unless you wanted a refill or something?"

"No, I'm good. We should probably head back to the office anyway." She turned up her chin at the waiter. "Everything was delicious, though. Thank you."

"Of course. I'll be right back with the check."

When he disappeared, Rob cleared his throat and fidgeted with his fingers, casting down his gaze for a moment. Finally, with a deep intake of breath he peered up at her again. "So, this was really nice."

Wearing a demure smile, Gwen dipped her head, and her cheeks flushed the palest of pinks. "It was."

"So I was thinking maybe we could get together, like tomorrow night or something? Grab some dinner or whatever."

With a long, slender finger and perfectly manicured nail, Gwen tucked a full swath of light brown hair behind her right ear. "Sure, I'd like that."

His shoulders pulled back, Rob sat up with confidence. "Great. Okay. That's awesome. So dinner, tomorrow night."

The waiter arrived holding the leather folder. "Here's the bill whenever you're ready."

Rob had his credit card in hand and noticed Gwen retrieve her own card. "I got this."

"Are you sure? You don't have to."

"I want to." He handed the card to the waiter.

Gwen waited until the man was out of earshot. "I'll buy you a drink tomorrow night, then."

Rob revealed a gleaming white smile. "Perfect." He stood from the table and tucked the receipt into his wallet. His hand extended toward her. "After you."

Gwen started toward the exit and emerged beneath the bright sunlight. "First day we haven't had rain in a while. It's nice to see the sun." She brushed up against his arm and smiled.

"Summer has arrived." He shoved his hands in his pockets and started toward the street to his silver BMW parked along the curb in a metered spot. "You sure you don't want me to walk you to your car?"

"No, please. It's fine." Gwen swatted away the notion. "I'm only around the block. I didn't get lucky enough to get a good spot like you."

"If you insist." With his phone in his hand, Rob pressed on an auto app to unlock his car. "We could've driven together, you know."

She retrieved her keys from her purse. "Next time. Hey, I'll see you back at the office."

"See you." Rob walked to the driver's side door and slipped onto the black leather seats. He watched Gwen turn the corner and sighed as she disappeared.

From across the street, Danny reemerged from the shadows. Sunglasses on, he pulled his cap low on his head. Sweat beaded along the sides of his smooth cheeks now. He smacked his lips to moisten them while his clammy hands made holding onto the device a challenge.

From inside his car, Rob placed his phone in the center console cup holder and pressed the ignition. When his phone lit up, he peered at the screen. With a furrowed brow, Rob saw his own face on the screen. His camera had been activated. "What the hell?"

A thunderous boom, like a jet breaking the sound barrier, rattled nearby windows, including the café. Bystanders were blown back from the surging wave of blistering hot energy. The BMW became engulfed inside an inferno. Flames and black smoke reached the sky. Metal debris propelled at a great speed, threatening to impale anyone within 100 feet.

Car alarms shrieked and people screamed. From around the corner, Gwen ran toward the noise, and thrust her hands over her mouth. The muffled sound of horror contained, she squatted low. "Rob!" With trembling hands, she fumbled for her phone and dialed 911. "A bomb. A bomb!"

"Ma'am, emergency services are on the way. Are you hurt?" the operator asked.

"No. But my friend. Oh God. My friend's car. It was his car. Please, hurry!"

THE PITTSBURGH POLICE cordoned off two blocks of Fourth Avenue. News vans, reporters with cameras, and crowds were held back outside the barricades. Inside, patrol cars with swirling lights, ambulances, and fire fighters lined the street. Rob Delaney's 2015 silver BMW M3 was reduced to charred metal. And he was still inside.

At last count, 10 injured, no one else had died. A stroke of luck. ATF Agent Chris Stallard stepped out of his SUV and walked to the middle of the road. The smell of burned rubber and burned flesh assaulted his senses. No matter how often he'd been exposed to the stench of death, it always turned his stomach.

At 5 feet 8 inches, Stallard was overall a fairly average guy. Dark hair, slightly thinning on top as he reached his mid-forties. He was an everyman in every way, except for a remarkable knowledge of explosives and a sharp sense of humor. His hands on his waist, he peered left. Yellow police tape flapped in the breeze near the barricade. He turned to his right and noticed the debris on the sidewalks and in the street. Broken glass, café menu signs split in half. In front of him—blood. Stallard squatted low and eyeballed the approximate radius field of the blast. "50 yards, at least."

"Hey. You're ATF?" FBI Agent Grant Tillis, wearing his signature windbreaker approached.

"That's what the jacket says," Stallard replied. "You must be FBI."

"That's what the jacket says. I'm Agent Tillis." He offered his hand. "Looks like we're going to have to figure out who the hell is in charge here. Pittsburgh Police is over there. Come on, let's hash this out." He started across the street toward the BMW. "The lieutenant's talking to a friend of the victim now."

"I heard 10 injured. Anyone critical?" Stallard asked.

"Just the driver." Tillis approached the lieutenant. "Lieutenant Crenshaw, sorry to interrupt. ATF is here."

"Great. Welcome to the show. I was just speaking to Ms. Madura. She's a friend of the deceased and had been having lunch with him before this happened." The lieutenant turned to her. "Ms. Madura, why don't you show these gentlemen what you just showed me?"

Gwen's eyes were red, and her curly hair clung to her cheeks where tears had dried. She retrieved her phone. "After I called

911, I held my phone in my hand and stood back and just watched him burn."

"Ma'am," Stallard cut in. "There's nothing you could've done for your friend. Trust me."

She shrugged off the comment and continued. "I don't know how long I stood here. Seconds? Minutes? But my phone vibrated in my hand and I thought it was 911 calling me back or something, I don't know. I looked at my screen and saw a Facebook notification from Rob."

"He's the victim?" Stallard asked.

Gwen nodded. "Anyway, I opened it." Her voice faltered and tears streamed down her cheeks again.

"The lieutenant placed his hand on her shoulder to offer comfort before he eyed the agents. "Apparently, for just a few moments right before the blast, Mr. Delaney, the victim, was live streaming."

"What?" FBI Agent Tillis pulled back in confusion.

"He didn't appear aware of it," the lieutenant replied.

Gwen opened her phone and held up the screen. "It's still here."

The agents watched as Rob's brow furrowed when he glanced down at his phone, seemingly unaware it had been recording.

"It went out shortly after the blast, but not before everyone saw him..." She turned away.

"For Christ's sake. They watched him burn." Agent Tillis tossed a glance to Stallard and started walking. When Stallard and the lieutenant joined him, he continued. "We can rule out any ideas that this was a random attack."

Stallard glanced over his shoulder at the still-smoldering vehicle. "You got that right. Mr. Delaney was targeted by someone. And this someone had access to his social media, his car, and knew exactly where he would be." He turned back to the other men. "Are we calling this terrorism or good old-fashioned murder?"

~

SENIOR UNIT AGENT Cameron Fisher eyed the box of toothpicks as he pulled out his pencil drawer. He picked it up and tapped the end of it like it was a pack of cigarettes, until one shook out. "That was the hiring board." Fisher stuck the toothpick between his lips as he studied Special Agent Kate Reid.

The 48-year-old former NYPD detective now ran this operation. BAU-4 at Quantico specialized in violent killers...serial killers, and other violent offenses against adults. He used to work alongside Agent Reid but was now her boss. He watched her grow anxious with anticipation.

Kate Reid sat on the edge of the chair. The 34-year-old, who'd been with the Bureau going on six years, waited for the news. After new-hire Jonathan Surrey pulled himself out of the running for Noah Quinn's old job and recommended Kate for the position, she'd been waiting for the Board to reach their decision. It would mean she would be the lead profiler and a Senior Supervisory Agent.

Her elbow leaned on the armrest; she shook away a few rogue strands of brunette hair from the low bun at the back of her neck. "And?"

"You got the promotion." Fisher stood from his desk with an outstretched hand. "Congratulations. You're our lead profiler and our newest Supervisory Special Agent."

The weight fell from her shoulders and she stood to accept his hand. "Thank you, Cam. You have no idea how good this feels."

"Oh, I have some idea. You deserved this, Kate. It should've been yours a long time ago, but..."

"Protocol. Yeah, I get it. I also have Surrey to thank for this."

"I'm not sure you do." Fisher released her hand and pulled the toothpick from his mouth. The wrinkles around his eyes grew deeper as he raised his lips into a grin. "He said you were the most qualified, sure. But we all knew that already. I'm just sorry the whole Quinn situation put a damper on your career."

"I don't have to worry about him anymore," Kate replied. "Well, I should get to work packing my things and moving offices."

Fisher shoved his hands in his pockets. His brown eyes bored into hers like a concerned father, though he was scarcely 15 years her senior. "You let me know if you need any help. Congrats again, Kate. We're all excited for you. Now get to work."

"Yes, sir." She smiled before retreating into the hall, knowing the first stop was to see Levi. His office was only steps ahead and she stood in front of his open door.

Levi Walsh was as close to Kate as a brother. An only child with few friends in her life who were close enough to consider family, Levi was among them. Dwight Jameson from her days at the Washington Field Office, and Sam Hansen were among the others. Oh, how Kate wished Sam could be here for this. She would've never believed it. But Sam's life had been taken by a man who nearly destroyed Kate more than once. The childhood friend was always in her heart and never forgotten. Kate's guilt also made sure of that.

"Agent Reid. Do we have news?" Walsh peered up from his desk. The forty-something military man from Alabama had piercing blue eyes and the kindest face she'd ever known. Former Army Intelligence, he could read her like a book and the look on her face must've spoken volumes.

"We do." Kate sauntered inside. Her slender, petite frame was defined by black dress pants and a fitted black blazer. "Fisher got off the phone with the hiring board. It's a go."

He stood. "You got it. Well, son of a bitch. I knew you would, SSA Reid." Levi walked around his desk, his stocky build accentuated by his rolled-up white Oxford shirt and tailored dark blue dress pants. He pulled her into a gentle embrace. "Good going, kid. I knew they'd come around."

"Thanks, Levi. I'm not sure I believe it just yet. Maybe after I move into Quinn's office," she replied.

"*Your* office." Walsh pulled back from the embrace. "I'll bet Scarborough is happy."

"I haven't told him yet. I just walked out of Fisher's office with the news. I'll call him in a minute."

"Good. Hey, we should celebrate. Let's see if everyone's up for drinks after work," he added.

"I won't turn down drinks." Kate spun on her heel.

"Let Scarborough know, would you? It'd be nice to see him," he called out after her.

"Sure thing." Kate's smile faded as she returned to her office. It would be nice to get the gang back together. It had been months since Nick's transfer to Unit 2. As the Senior Unit Agent for that department, he still worked to overcome the water-cooler talk that he hadn't deserved the promotion after being demoted in Unit 4. That he didn't have the background to work in Unit 2, but Nick had a long and storied history with the Bureau dating back more than 10 years. He had friends in high places, like Unit Chief Cole. He couldn't bear to watch Nick's talents be wasted. Still, in the few months that he'd been in Unit 2, the situation had improved. She knew once he displayed his leadership, they'd back him.

Kate sat down at her desk, still in a euphoric daze. She hadn't spoken yet to Eva Duncan, her lone female ally on the team, nor had she spoken to Jonathan Surrey. Owing people wasn't how Kate preferred to operate, but there was no mistaking, regardless of what Fisher said, that Surrey had played a big part in this move. He deserved some credit.

~

THE OLD HENRY PUB and grill was only blocks from the Quantico compound. The BAU Unit 4 team gathered around two tables that had been pushed together in the center of the room. Dark panels adorned the walls and wood details surrounded the place. It was as close to being inside an English pub as one could find in D.C.

Cameron Fisher sat next to his subordinate, who also happened to be his live-in girlfriend, Eva. A force to be reckoned with, Eva Duncan grew up in Chicago. In her mid-thirties, she wore her wavy caramel hair down past her shoulders and was built like an elite athlete. Their relationship had gone dark since Fisher took over as Senior Unit Agent. It was as if the situation had been swept under the rug. Don't ask, don't tell. Regardless, it was no skin off Kate's teeth. Hell, she'd dated her boss before he became her husband for years. Had it been a problem at times? Yes. Yes, it had. There were many reasons why Nick Scarborough now worked in Unit 2.

Levi tossed back a long swig of beer. He lived in an apartment not far from the pub. Divorced for several years now, he lived alone and had no children. His work was his life. Whether that had been a choice, Kate hadn't known.

Then there was Jonathan Surrey. Mid-thirties, Kate's age. Polished. Slim, moderately tall. Never saw him in anything other than a bespoke suit. Initially hired on to replace Noah Quinn after an incident that saw Kate censured, he was learning to fit in with the elite group. His style was to leave everything at the office, or so he claimed. Take nothing home. He'd learned that the hard way after his wife left him with his kids. It seemed he never looked back at that life he had in Denver.

Senior Unit 2 Agent Nick Scarborough was the last to arrive. Kate waved him over and stood to greet her husband with a kiss. "You're late."

"Sorry. I had a hard time getting out of the office." He turned to his former team. "Hey, guys. Long time, no see."

"Scarborough! Man, it's about time you showed your face." Fisher was on his second beer and wasn't a big drinker to begin with. It showed. "How's it going, brother?"

"Good, man. Unit 2 is treating me well." Nick sat down.

Kate leaned into his ear and whispered. "I ordered you a Coke."

"Thanks, hon."

While it had become common knowledge that Nick was a recovering alcoholic, Kate felt a strange sense of secrecy about it. Perhaps dealing with her father's drinking for most of her life forced into her a belief that it was something to hide, something of which to be ashamed. After all, it was never discussed in her family. Nick had quit drinking more than a year ago, then relapsed during the team's investigation in Rio. That was how Kate remembered it.

Nick was a few years older than Kate, at 41, but kept fit with a trim waist and broad, muscular shoulders. His hair started to grey, but she didn't mind it.

Fisher cleared his throat and prepared to speak. "Okay. Now that we're all here, I'd like to raise a glass to Senior Supervisory Agent Kate Reid."

The waitress returned with Nick's Coke and he raised his glass.

"I can't tell you how proud I am of the work you've put into this team," Fisher added. "And after everything you've had to face down recently, I'm even more impressed."

Kate glanced away with some embarrassment. She still blamed herself for letting George Lehmann get the drop on her and take her hostage back in the spring. The nightmares hadn't abated.

"And now you'll be the one we turn to as our lead profiler," Fisher continued. "Those sons of bitches don't stand a chance."

Scattered laughter sounded from the rest of the team.

"So, congratulations, SSA Reid. Your star shines bright at the Bureau. Cheers!"

The team held their glasses high and let out a resounding, "Cheers."

As the evening wore on and the drinks flowed, Kate pushed back her chair and leaned into Nick. "I'll be right back."

Nick pulled his attention from a conversation with Walsh. "Okay."

She started toward the restrooms and stopped at the bar to glance at the television screen above. "Oh my God."

The bartender turned to her. "Crazy, right?"

"Yeah." Kate's eyes were fixed to the screen as she watched the burnt remains of a vehicle in the distance and a whole city block cordoned off. "Where is this?"

"Pittsburgh, I think. You want me to turn it up?" he asked.

"No. No, that's okay. Thanks." She spotted the ATF and FBI agents in the distance. Several local police vehicles were positioned inside the barricade. The scrolling words beneath captioned the scene. "Car Bomb Explosion goes Live on Facebook."

2

L ight from a bright moon diffused around the bedroom curtains when Kate rolled out of bed. Nick appeared undisturbed as she padded through the hall and into the kitchen of their Woodbridge condo. Standing at the sink, she turned it on and peered out into the darkened living room. It took a moment before she realized her glass overflowed beneath the running water.

Kate took a sip. Her eyelids were heavy, her body was tired, and her mind was besieged with thoughts of George and Richard Lehmann. One who took her hostage. The other, she murdered. So many questions lingered. Chief among them was who had sent her the message from a dead man's phone? *See you again*, it had read. It all pointed back to the Mercy Killer. The case that saw her team on the hunt for a man who killed those who needed help the most.

Theo Bishop, the Mercy Killer, was a madman and his mother, Carol Whitman, aided in his escape to Mexico. But she hadn't acted alone. Someone inside the Bureau had helped. And when

Kate received a text message from Richard Lehmann's phone after his death, it hadn't taken long for her and Nick to realize the Bureau insider who helped had issued a threat. Pay the price for what she'd done to Richard Lehmann or stop looking into Carol Whitman. Those were her options. She still hadn't picked one.

"Hey."

Kate jumped and spilled water from her glass as she looked at Nick, who had appeared from nowhere. She placed her hand over her heart. "You scared the hell out of me."

"I called out to you. I guess you didn't hear me." Nick stood at the breakfast bar. His hair disheveled, rubbing his eyes, he stood bare-chested and carried unease on his face. "What are you doing up?"

"Couldn't sleep. I didn't mean to wake you." Kate set down her glass on the counter.

"You didn't. I woke up and checked the time before noticing you weren't there. And not for the first time this week. Not for the first time in a while, actually." He walked around the bar and stood next to her. "Like I've said to you before, I'm here if you want to talk."

"I know. I appreciate it, but I'm fine. Really. It's just the promotion. I guess I'm nervous I'll let everyone down."

"First of all, you could never do that. Secondly, the Board wouldn't have okayed the promotion had they not read the count-less letters of recommendation and interviewed you themselves." He placed the crook of his index finger under her chin and guided her eyes toward him. "I don't think this is about the promotion. Kate, it's only been a few months since all that..."

"That what, Nick? Since I killed someone? Since I was taken hostage? I'm fine. I told you that. You're going to have to give me some space here, okay?" She pulled away. "Let's just go back to bed."

NEVER BEFORE HAD Nick felt so vulnerable where Kate was concerned. No longer could he watch over her; make sure she stayed safe. It was part of the deal when he chose to leave the BAU-4 team. It was always in Kate's best interest. But now, after watching her cope with the fallout of her actions, the suffering she denied experiencing; to him, it looked eerily like PTSD. He could do nothing except find the one whose threat still loomed. And there was no mistaking, it had been a threat. When and where this individual would choose to reveal his intentions was unknown. And Nick was never good at waiting.

"Thanks for coming over to my side of the compound." He offered his hand.

"I don't mind slumming it once in a while," Walsh replied with a hearty handshake.

Nick returned to his desk chair. "We keep plenty busy here. I bet there are more money launderers and hackers than there are serial killers."

Walsh chuckled and dropped down onto the guest chair. "I wouldn't take that bet. In all seriousness, man, I'm glad you found a home here. These guys are lucky as hell to have you. And I'll admit, things aren't quite the same in Unit 4. But Reid, well, we all know she's going to kick ass in her new job."

Nick grinned. "I couldn't agree more, which makes this all the more important."

"Yeah. I get that."

Nick leaned over his desk on his elbows. "We both know someone helped Theo Bishop flee to Mexico. We already know the ties his mother's family had to the Bureau."

"Top brass who was seriously connected on the inside and out," Walsh replied.

"You got it. That message from Richard Lehmann's phone. I'm striking out all over the place. Can't get a lead on anything. It's taking a toll on her and has for a while now. I know you gave it your best before. What I need to know now, Levi, is will you help me see this to its end?"

Walsh pulled in a deep breath. "I did root around a little bit when this all came about, as you know."

"Right."

"And I got about as far as you have. That was before the Richard Lehmann message. Nick, I have to think someone has dirt on Kate. I don't know what it could possibly be or how they got it, but whoever it is must believe she did something wrong in the whole Lehmann debacle."

"She killed Richard Lehmann in self-defense. No one can prove otherwise. Surrey, himself, insisted that had been the case. He would've been killed too."

Walsh raised his hands. "Yeah, I get that. But someone believes otherwise, and we have no idea who it is or what they have. The driving factor here is that this individual realizes we know more than we should about Carol Whitman and her son. And it scares them. So, you want me to get into the muck with you on this one? You need to know that it could come crashing down on us hard. The likes that will bury us forever, you hear me?"

"I hear you," Nick replied. "So, you in?"

Walsh raised the corner of his mouth in a crooked smile. "Hell, yeah."

FOURTH AVENUE in Downtown Pittsburgh looked exactly as it had before the horrific car bomb just days earlier. The only reminder was a black burn mark on the asphalt that looked like a firework had been set off. A really big firework.

The charred BMW sat inside the FBI's warehouse while the local field agent, Grant Tillis, labored to uncover more details about the murder of Financial Analyst, Rob Delaney. He stood before the car, examining it when he turned at the sound of his name. "Agent Stallard. Thanks for coming down."

Chris Stallard was ATF and was on the scene after it happened. "You guys get all the good stuff." He surveyed the warehouse. "Makes me wonder why the hell ATF exists."

"Someone's gotta arrest the bootleggers," Tillis replied.

Stallard laughed. "Sure. Bootleggers. Big business in these parts." He folded his arms and widened his stance. "Where are we at with this heap of scrap metal?"

"That's why you're here," Tillis added. "I have my team hitting it hard on who had access to the victim's social media. Autopsy is still pending. We've talked to his colleagues, family, and friends. We just aren't making the kind of headway we should've made by this point in the investigation."

Stallard rubbed his square chin as he walked around the BMW. "No enemies?"

"None we've been able to find, or who would admit to it," Tillis replied. "The guy was basically an accountant. Worked a 9 to 5, single, no kids. I mean, you couldn't get any cleaner than Rob Delaney."

"But we know this wasn't random." Stallard stopped at the front of the car and squatted low. "We know the device was placed on the mudflap, front driver's side. Used clay adhesive. Pretty basic. Gasoline from the tank was the propellant. This didn't happen on the fly, though. Whoever installed the bomb would've needed a window of opportunity."

"Someone who knew his schedule, possibly where he lived,

and planted the device when he had enough time," Tillis replied. "Okay. So how was the bomb detonated?"

"From what my team has learned, it was remote detonation. Which means the bomber knew Delaney had returned to his car."

"He was being watched?" Tillis asked.

"Watched. Maybe. Or..." Stallard glanced at him. "Have you pulled anything off the victim's phone? Data, messages, whatever."

"No dice. It's beyond repair. They pulled the SIM card, but it was melted. We have a request in for the carrier to provide the records. Should have that in our hands now, actually."

"According to the friend," Stallard added. "She said Delaney used an app on his phone to unlock his car. Makes me wonder if the bomber received some sort of notification from Delaney's phone that the car had been unlocked. Maybe the bomber didn't need to be there—watching. It's not a leap to assume someone hacked into Delaney's Facebook account and livestreamed just before the bomb went off. One guy on site, one guy behind the scenes. We could be talking about a two-man operation."

Tillis pursed his lips as he appeared to consider the notion. "Someone with explosives knowledge and another who can hack their way into social media giants' fortresses. But why Delaney?"

"Hell if I know. Maybe he owed money to some folks. That's up to your people to figure out," Stallard replied. "I just need to know how they got the materials, where they got the materials, and if they plan on doing it again."

JONATHAN SURREY STOOD outside Kate's new office a moment before walking in. "Place is starting to take shape. Looks better than when it was mine."

Kate glanced up at him. "You hardly had a chance to unpack."

"Oh yeah. That's right." He smiled and nodded. "Seems to me you swooped right in and snatched the best office on the floor." Before she could defend herself, he raised his hands. "I'm kidding, Reid. You know I'm kidding. Hey, sorry I bailed early on your celebration the other night."

"No problem. I'm just glad you could be there for a while. Sit down. What's going on?"

He took a seat opposite her desk and surveyed the room. "Just wanted to see how you're settling in. Looks like you've done a good job so far."

Kate narrowed her gaze. "That's it? That's all you wanted to do? I haven't measured for the drapes yet. You could help me out with that."

"I might still have the measurements written down somewhere." He chuckled. "Besides, can't a colleague check in on his newly promoted co-worker?"

"Sure, but I think I've learned enough about you to know you couldn't care less about this office. So, what is it?" Kate pressed on.

"Well, if you must know, since it looks like I'll be sticking around for a while, I wanted to get your thoughts on where a new guy in town might think to put down some roots."

Kate pulled back in surprise. "Put down roots? You want to buy a house?"

He shrugged. "I was thinking about it. I'm in a small apartment now. It's nice, but I prefer a little more space. And now that it looks like I've found my new role and my new home here at Unit 4, I guess I'd like to make things more permanent. It'd be nice for my kids to have their own rooms when they come visit. Whenever their mom allows it, that is."

Surrey had, so far, kept himself at arm's length from the rest of the team. Never revealed much about himself. Didn't express opinions unless it was about a case. So it surprised her he'd come to her for advice, even mentioning his kids. Maybe he was looking to open himself up a little bit. Make friends, stick around a while. More importantly, he'd turned to her as a friend. Kate didn't have many friends.

"Scarborough and I live in Woodbridge. It's just a condo. Well, it's Nick's condo, but we like it. It's fine for now. I had rented a house in Woodbridge for a few years before that, just as soon as I arrived from San Diego. Great little house. Backyard. I don't know if it's available or if the old lady's son sold it, but I could find out."

"I'd appreciate that, Reid, thanks. Yeah, I think a small house would suit me better than an apartment. Never really been an apartment kind of guy." Surrey stood.

"I'm not much of an apartment person either. And I do remember what it was like being the new guy here."

"Sure, but the team leader was your boyfriend," he replied.

Kate's smile faded as she cast down her gaze.

"Hey, Reid, I didn't mean anything by that." Surrey gripped the back of the chair as he wore regret. "I just meant..."

"Don't worry about it. I'll see if that house is available. You'd like it."

He nodded ruefully. "I'm sure I would. See you later, Reid."

At 22, Danny King had never intended to be sitting inside the Department of Economic Security in Pittsburgh. He shook away his blonde curly hair and shifted in the hard plastic seat as he checked the clock on the wall. 4:35pm. He looked at his ticket. Number 432. The next ticket to be called was 417. Danny sighed and his shoulders dropped. It wasn't looking good that his number would be called before the government office closed. If that happened, he'd have to ask for another day off work to sit here and wait. All he'd wanted was to find out why his sister's check hadn't shown up this month. He needed that money, and he needed his job. One would suffer if he wasn't called on today.

A heavy-set man appeared from the staff entrance door and gazed out into the waiting area. "We'll be taking up to number 431 today. The rest of you will have to come back in the morning. Good news is, keep your number. We'll start at 432."

The waiting area was chock-full of people who let out a collective sigh, including Danny. "Seriously? I'm 432!"

"Bad luck, kid." The man next to him patted his shoulder. "Look at it this way, you'll be in and out in the morning." He laughed, seeming to know that was unlikely.

"Yeah, thanks." Danny stood and grabbed his backpack that was on the floor, slinging it over his shoulder. "Fucking government." He pushed through the glass door hard enough to make it snap back on its hinges.

Outside, the sun broke through the clouds as it worked its way west. Danny squinted before putting on his sunglasses. He marched through the parking lot, still muttering obscenities at the dysfunctional bureaucratic system before he reached his old white Ford Focus. He unlocked his car and slipped behind the wheel, throwing his backpack onto the passenger seat. "Assholes!" He glared at the building and keyed the ignition. "Bet you'd work faster if it was money you needed."

The rumble of his engine was in no way due to the puny 4-cylinder machine, rather it was the need for a new muffler. Something else he couldn't afford. He slammed on the gas pedal and reversed out of his spot. Shoving the gear shift into Drive, he sped out onto the road ahead.

Danny hated this city more with each passing day. He dropped out of college to care for his disabled sister and wanted nothing more than to leave. Sunny California called out to him.

Warm weather, beaches, beautiful women in bikinis on those beaches. Never mind that a beautiful woman would ever give him a second glance. Danny wasn't unattractive, but some men were smooth around women. He was not. Not ever. He couldn't speak to them without sounding like a fool. Couldn't relate to them. Except for his sister.

Melanie King was 26 and had been born with cerebral palsy. She'd been in a home for most of her life, but when their mother got sick with cancer a few years ago, the money ran dry and forced Danny to quit school and bring Melanie back to their childhood home in East Hills, Pittsburgh.

It was just Melanie and Danny now in that home. Their father, who Danny refused to reference by name, took off shortly after Danny was born when Melanie's symptoms seemed to become more apparent. That was also when the doctors suggested she be moved to assisted living. It was Danny and his mom until a year before she died, then Melanie came back.

Danny pulled onto the single-car driveway of their narrow 2-story home. He spotted Janie walk through the front door as he stepped out. "Hey. Thanks for staying late."

Janie pulled her purse up over her shoulder and adjusted her scrubs. "You get everything worked out?"

"I wish. I have to go back in the morning."

"For real?" she asked.

"Yeah, can you believe that shit?"

Janie reached for her car keys. "Danny, I gotta work in the morning or else I'd be happy..."

"No, it's okay." He held up his hands. "They tell me I'll be the first in line, so I don't think I'll be gone that long. Mel will be okay for a couple hours. I'll make sure she has everything before I leave."

"You sure?" Janie asked.

"Yeah. I got it. Thanks for doing this. It means a lot. Have a good night." Danny walked up the steps and onto the front porch.

"You too, Danny."

He pulled open the screen door and walked inside. "Mel, it's me. I'm home." The staircase lay directly in front of him and on the right was a small living room. Beyond that was the kitchen and laundry. Danny walked through to the living room where Mel sat on the faded blue sofa and watched television.

He walked up behind her and kissed the top of her head. "You doing all right, sis?"

"Yeah, I'm fine." Melanie didn't suffer from extreme cognitive decline and had tested just above the baseline for severe impairment. Mentally, she functioned at a roughly middle-school level. Physically, she used a walker but could get around on her own. Stairs were a problem, so Danny helped her to her room every night. God forbid should there ever be an emergency that would require him to get her out quickly. They'd probably both suffer.

"What do you want me to make you for dinner?" Danny asked as he walked into the kitchen and opened the fridge. "I think we have some stuff for burritos." He glanced into the living room. "You want burritos, Mel?"

"Sure."

"Burritos it is." He pulled out a can of beans and a block of cheese. He set down his phone on the kitchen counter and spotted a notification arrive. A brief glance and he picked it up, swiping open the screen to view the message.

"Your six-digit access code required for two-step authentication. Do not give this to anyone."

Danny raised the corner of his mouth. "No. Of course not. Wouldn't want to do that, now would we?"

3

_____

Grant Tillis was a decorated federal agent who had worked at the Pittsburgh field office for three years. A West Point graduate, he'd spent four years in the Army with the intent on being a career officer. A roadside bomb in Afghanistan had other ideas when it exploded and sent shrapnel flying through the air at record speeds. Some of it eventually lodged itself into Tillis' neck, chest, and upper right arm, shredding his shoulder to the point that the military sent him packing. He was done and so was his career. Or so he thought. Two years of intense physical therapy while he worked as a civilian at the Bureau and he was given the okay to apply for the Academy. His shoulder essentially rebuilt, Tillis passed the physical demands of Quantico and while he had finished almost dead last in that part of his exams, he still passed. It was his excellent academic scores that carried him over the line.

So here he was, a federal agent who now stared at pages upon pages of phone records of the deceased Rob Delaney. And something might have finally opened.

A solid 6 feet tall, the 31-year-old agent rubbed his eyes to clear them of their fatigue. He needed to be sure what he was looking at was real. "Something's definitely off here."

Another agent popped her head into his office. "Are you talking to yourself again, Tillis?"

He eyed her. "Hey, Geisler. Come in. Yeah, I'm talking to myself." He shuffled the papers. "You mind taking a look at something for me while you're here?"

"Sure. I was on the way to the breakroom when I heard you. What do you have?" she asked. Her short brunette hair was cut into a straight bob and tucked behind her ears. In her mid-thirties, Geisler had worked some of the worst corruption cases in the city and had a nose for things that seemed 'off.'

"The car bombing. These are the victim's phone records. Take a look at this and tell me I'm not crazy," he replied.

"First of all, you're not crazy." She laughed. "Seriously, though, what am I looking for here?"

"This guy was just some mid-level finance guy. Worked downtown. Young and single," Tillis began. "Take a look at these phone records from the past month. Tell me you don't see some weird phone calls on there."

Geisler studied the pages, flipping one after the other. Her brow furrowed at times and raised inquisitively at others.

"You see it?" he pressed on.

"Give me a second. I'm still looking." She didn't take her eyes off the pages for another few minutes until finally, she looked at him. "You want to know what I think?"

"Please. Yes. I know what I think, but I wouldn't mind some backup on this." Tillis leaned back in his desk chair and laced his fingers behind his head. Slight armpit wetness revealed his diligence.

"Looks to me like this phone was cloned."

He pulled upright again and slapped his hand on his desk. "Thank you! I knew it. I frickin knew it."

"Yeah..." she looked down at the pages, flipping through them again. "You have some crazy international calls on here. Then you have charges. I mean, did this guy even look at his bill?"

"He probably hadn't gotten the bill yet. This was pushed to us by the carrier through a subpoena. The previous month's bill wasn't like this. It had some unusual calls on it, but..."

"So it must've been cloned around the end of the previous billing cycle. The victim didn't notice and then..."

"Kaboom," Tillis replied. "Exactly."

"What are you going to do with this? You're working with ATF and Pittsburgh Bureau?" Geisler asked.

"Yep. It's one big party right now."

"It can't stay that way," she replied.

"Nope. I'll let the boss give PBP the bad news that it's going to have to be us and the ATF."

Geisler stood from the chair. "Good luck with that, Tillis. They really hate it when we squeeze them out like that." She turned on her heel.

"Don't I know it. Thanks, Geisler."

"Anytime." She waved her hand as she left.

Tillis let his gaze wander around his office. "A cloned phone. Pretty tough to do unless someone has physical access to it. A friend, maybe?" He shook his head. "With friends like that..."

KATE OPENED the door to the condo and noticed the soft glow of candles burning. Her lips drew up into a smile as she set down her carrier bag and placed her car keys on the hook beside the door. "What is going on here?"

Nick emerged from their small kitchen holding a bouquet of roses. "I thought we could celebrate your promotion privately." He stood in front of her and gazed into her eyes. "I'm so proud of you, Kate."

She took the flowers and inhaled a deep breath, her nose buried inside the petals. "I can't believe you did all this. When did you have time?"

He unveiled an impish grin. "Despite what you might think, Mrs. Scarborough, I can be quite the romantic. I also took the liberty of making dinner and I opened a bottle of wine."

"Well, I'm starved. How about I put these in water before we eat?"

"Let me. Sit. Have a glass of wine." Nick returned to the kitchen. "You're all moved into Quinn's old office, huh? How did that go?" He filled a vase with water.

"It went." Kate slipped off her low-heeled shoes and pulled out a chair. The bottle of wine rested inside an ice bucket and she poured a glass. "No, it was good. Weird, but good. Oh, and you know what? Surrey came to me today asking for advice on where he should live."

Nick turned to her with the flowers inside the vase. "Live?"

"Yeah. He says he's in an apartment and that he's not an apartment kind of guy, so he asked for ideas on where he could find a house."

"That's funny. You're not an apartment person either." He returned with plated food.

Kate eyed the dish. "Did you cook this?"

"Hell no. If I had, you might end up with food poisoning. I have to confess that I did cheat and ordered this in. Put it in a nice plate, and there you go. Dinner served."

"It looks amazing, Nick. Thank you."

"Good. I'm glad you think so." Nick sat down. "I just wanted to do something nice for you. I know these past few months haven't been easy. You haven't been sleeping well..."

Kate held the glass of wine to her lips while her eyes raised slightly over the rim to meet his.

Her intent didn't appear to be lost on him. "Maybe this isn't the best time to talk about this, but I hate to see you suffer, that's all. When we first met..."

"It all feels very déjà vu, doesn't it?" she cut in. "But know that I am handling it, Nick. I promise you."

He reached for her hand. "You've seen me through so much. I want to be there for you as much as you've been there for me. I know you'll overcome this. And the promotion? This is your golden ticket. You will be able to go anywhere inside the Bureau. Move up as high as you want with this job in your back pocket. You might one day be the next Unit Chief Cole."

Kate chuckled. "I doubt that. And I don't know if that's what I want but thank you for having that kind of faith in me." She took in a breath and closed her eyes for a moment. "I won't lie. What happened with the Lehmanns; it did a number on me. But I won't let it define me."

"I know you won't. And I promise you, no one will ever get to you like that again. I know you won't let it and I sure as hell won't either."

Kate peeled off a piece of the grilled salmon on her plate. "What about the message?"

"I'm still working on that," Nick said. "You don't need to do anything. I have it under control. Your only job is to find a way through what happened and be the best lead profiler you can be. And I have no doubt you'll do just that."

Her eyes glistened as she blinked away the welling tears. "I love you so much, Nick. Don't you ever forget that."

He raised the corner of his mouth in a cock-eyed grin. "I won't if you won't."

~

WITH A HEADSET OVER HIS EARS, Danny King sat in the corner of his kitchen at a folding table that was pressed against the wall. Two monitors were lined up, side by side, and he kept a keyboard in his lap. "Like I said, ma'am, you'll need to restart your laptop and then we can figure out where the problem is. So, just turn it off." He closed his eyes. "Yes, ma'am. That's it. Now, press the power button again and give it a minute to boot up." He grabbed his mic that was attached to the headphones. "Boot up, not boom up. It has to have time to load the programs first." *What the hell?* Danny mouthed as he rolled his eyes.

Next to him on the table was a plastic in-box with several cell phones inside. One of them illuminated with an incoming notification. Danny snatched it and peered at the notice while a smile arose on his lips. "Now it's on." He was pulled back into the moment. "No, ma'am. I'm sorry. I was talking to someone else. Just wait another minute and I'll walk you through it."

It took almost half an hour to get Mrs. Filmore's laptop up and running again. "No problem at all, ma'am. You have a nice day. Be on the lookout for a survey asking how your experience was." Danny pressed the end call button and ripped off his headset. "Holy shit. What a fucking idiot. What's wrong with these people?"

"Danny? Are you okay?"

He turned at the sound of her voice. "Fine, Mel. Sorry. It's just work. Go back to your show." As much as he loved his sister, this life was hard and getting harder by the moment.

Danny stood from the table and headed through the living room. "I'll be upstairs in my room for a few minutes."

"Okay." Melanie kept her eyes fixed on the TV.

He made his way upstairs and down the narrow hall to his bedroom. The worn carpet beneath his feet was dark green. His double bed was shoved into the corner to give the small room a sense of space and had a plaid green quilt covering it haphazardly. Danny rarely bothered to make his bed.

He pulled out the chair tucked beneath a small desk he'd had since grade school. The desk's top displayed various carvings he'd done over the years in addition to ring marks and other stains. His family had always struggled financially, and it seemed Danny had continued the cycle. Never mind he got a 1400 on his SATs and could've stayed in college. Apparently, that wasn't the life he was meant to have.

As he turned on his monitor, Danny placed the headset over his ears and opened the website. His eyes glazed over as he stared at the screen, transformed to another place. It was a dark place where the people he watched burned. Horror masked their faces while they cried out in agony. Death and destruction were everywhere. Fire, smoke, ash. This was Danny's inspiration.

As a child, he'd always been obsessed with fire. His mother often caught him with matches in his room where he would flick them away while they burned. The holes in the carpet were still there. But it wasn't so much the look or feel of fire that enchanted him. It was the destruction it caused. A house could be in ashes on the ground in minutes. A forest could be nothing but charred twigs in days.

He thought he'd grown out of it when he was in college. His interests diverged into better, but still destructive behaviors, like breaking into the school's computer and changing his buddy's grades. He had straight A's, so there wasn't much point in altering his own.

In the end, it all seemed childish when he was forced to come home and care for his ailing mother and disabled sister. But as the years passed and pressure mounted, a light went off in him. He began to see society as a problem, the "system" as a problem. Not him. Danny wasn't the problem.

When he tired of watching the videos, he picked up one of several cell phones. "Let's see what you're up to today, Heather. Heading to the gym? How about some yoga? Maybe drinks with the girls?"

The type of skills Danny had would've lent themselves well at some Silicon Valley tech company, but those options were no longer available to him. Instead, he was forced into the life of an old man. Working day in and day out to support his family. Taking care of children who weren't his. There was only one way to fix a broken system.

He logged into Heather's Instagram account and noticed the authentication code arrive on the phone. Danny keyed it in and waited. "Here we are. Ms. Heather Hillcrest. Seriously, did you make that name up?" As he read Heather's posts, the sound of another phone captured his attention. "Oh, great. Tom's back. And where are you at today?" The text message had been sent by a woman. "Having dinner with Denise tonight? I wonder what happened to Laura?" He pulled out a pad of paper and jotted down the address. "Great. See you soon, Denise."

Danny jogged downstairs and swiped the keys from the table. "Janie's coming over soon. She has a key and can let herself in. You sure you'll be all right for a while?"

"I can take care of myself, Danny," Mel replied. "Janie doesn't have to come over."

"I just feel better knowing someone's here in case you need

anything. I'll just be a few hours anyway. Besides, Janie loves movies just like you do. You should find one to watch together. Make some popcorn. It'll be fun." He kissed her forehead. "I'll be back in time to get you upstairs for bed."

"Bye, Danny. Have fun."

"Bye." He closed the door and walked to his car. The ground was wet, and the car was still spotted with droplets of water, though the rain subsided for now.

He stepped inside and turned the engine before double checking the address. "30 minutes, tops. Piece of cake."

The weight of the world fell from his shoulders the farther away he got from his neighborhood. Mel was capable of looking after herself for a while and Janie probably hadn't needed to come over, but it put his mind at ease knowing Mel wasn't alone. If anything happened to her, he'd blame himself for the rest of his life. Danny couldn't protect his mom, but he could still protect his sister.

TOM REVEALED a toothy grin as he pulled out his date's chair. "It's really good to see you, Denise. I'm glad you finally said yes." Velvety-smooth, self-important, and loaded; that was Tom. He sat down at what was arguably the best table in the restaurant, sparing no expense for Denise, whom he'd been after for a while.

"I'm glad I said yes, too." Her blonde hair was in perfect soft curls that rested on her shoulders. Blue eyes that could melt any heart it wanted. And a figure that appeared to step off the pages of Vogue.

Needless to say, Tom never had trouble with the ladies. Not just wealthy, but attractive too and still young at just 35. He could get just about any woman he wanted. The problem was, he knew it. Tonight, he wanted Denise. Tomorrow, it would probably be some other woman.

From outside the restaurant, Danny looked in as he stood across the street. He leaned against a slim tree trunk wearing his baseball hat, shorts, and a Nike t-shirt. The humidity had gotten worse, which meant it would probably rain again soon. Getting soaked was a small price to pay for forcing the kind of change this society needed.

Danny had been following Tom for a while and now with his cherry popped, he had grown confident. Relying on some outside help was necessary, but he was the one who deserved credit. The police, the feds, they'd never figure it out. If Danny had to be the one leading the charge, then so be it. Soon, his message would be heard.

Tonight, it was Tom's turn. According to his social media, he led the perfect life. Wore perfect clothes, drove a perfect car, traveled. Always a different beautiful woman on his arm. The opposite of everything Danny was. Society teemed with people who did nothing but try to make themselves look good online. And for what? Likes? Comments? They were pathetic and soon he would prove that to the rest of the world.

Danny watched as the plates arrived at Tom's table. It was time to get to work. "Enjoy your meal, asshole."

Moving fast and keeping out of sight was key to his success. It was a tough ask in this part of town that was busy with several restaurants and bars. The valet had parked Tom's $100,000 Mercedes AMG in the nearby parking garage. Son of a bitch couldn't drive a regular Mercedes. No, he had to get the fast one that cost more than Danny's house.

He walked around the corner toward the parking garage when two young women walked by. Danny smiled while still wearing his baseball hat low on his brow.

"Dude, you look like a stalker," one of them said.

"What a creeper," the other added.

His smile vanished as he arrived at the garage. "Ugly bitches." Danny retrieved his handy little device, an EMP jammer he learned to build by watching YouTube. The do-it-yourself electromagnetic pulse jammer had the ability to disable any electronic device and scramble the signals of CCTV cameras within a small radius. It would take out cell phones too, so he quickly shut his off. It was a small device with a short-term effect. This was where speed would come into play. The first camera was at the entrance. He pressed the button on the device and in double-time, he walked up and down each row until spotting the shiny black beast, jamming each camera before he reached its purview.

Danny hustled to the Mercedes and unzipped his backpack. Footfalls echoed in the distance along with muted voices.

"I'm sure it was on this floor." An older man dressed in a suit gazed out over the sea of cars.

Danny ducked low next to the Mercedes.

"You've had too much to drink. It's on the next floor up."

He couldn't see who had spoken, but it sounded like a woman. Danny glanced up at the camera several feet ahead that was mounted on the ceiling. "God damn it," he whispered.

"Maybe you're right. I keep pressing the button and I don't see it flashing." The man's voice sounded. Finally, the echo of the footsteps faded.

"Holy shit." Danny let out his breath and quickly jammed the camera again, unsure if he'd caught it before it recovered.

Inside his backpack was the homemade explosive complete with adhesive to place under the driver's side tire flap. The best spot to take out the driver. Danny was finished with two minutes to spare.

Disabling the cameras as he made his way out of the garage,

Danny tugged on his ballcap and headed down the street, ignoring any bystanders along the way. His little white car came into view and he glanced over at the restaurant.

Tom and Denise appeared to be having a good time. "Good for them." Danny stepped into his car. "Hope you get lucky tonight, Tom."

4

The young man's style was elegant, ambitious, and most of all, brilliant. But with his potential cut short through a variety of circumstances that now saw him living paycheck to paycheck, Danny had been forced into what he considered a menial position a monkey could've handled.

A customer service representative who worked from home, he aided clients who could hardly turn on their computers, let alone operate them. Given the available time he had, since he had no other life, this allowed him to perfect his technique for cloning cell phones. For a guy like Danny, the challenge was minimal, at best.

He exploited a vulnerability in cell phone carriers' update protocols. Over the Air, or OTA updates was his ticket inside. He only needed the phone number of his target and that was simple enough to obtain. A binary SMS sent to the target's phone and that was it, vulnerability exploited. The technicalities were a little more involved than that and it had taken some time, but Danny was nothing if not patient.

From that point, it was all straight-forward. Incoming calls and messages diverted to his cloned phone. This included the two-step verification codes sent by online retailers, social media apps, and the like. That was how he gained access to the target's social media accounts.

This morning, Danny would keep his eye on Tom, knowing where he worked, what time he usually left for the day, and where he went on most days. With the explosive device installed on Tom's Mercedes, it was a waiting game. Wait for the perfect time and the perfect place.

He trotted down the steps from his second-floor bedroom after helping Melanie bathe, and dress. She now sat on the sofa eating a bowl of cereal. She liked to play card games and do word puzzles on the laptop, so he queued those up for her.

"I'm leaving now. Are you sure you don't need anything, Mel?"

She turned to him with brown eyes that smiled, but lips that just wouldn't cooperate. "Just go, Danny. I'm not totally helpless you know."

"I know you're not. I'll be back in a few hours. Your phone is next to you here. Call me if you need anything."

"Got it. Bye."

"See ya, Mel." Danny stepped outside to a blast of warm, muggy air and walked to his car in the driveway. He pulled out onto the road and started toward the north side where the rich people lived, where Tom lived. It was Wednesday and on Wednesdays, Tom went to the gym before going into work around 10am. It paid to be the boss.

From what Danny learned, Tom was a self-made man. Ran his own consulting firm. After following him for weeks, Danny still hadn't learned exactly what kind of consulting Tom had done. The kind that charged a lot of money, he imagined.

On the upside, the gym would be reasonably empty at this

time of morning. Most people had to be at work by 8 or 9am. His targets were targets for a reason. Danny wasn't into killing innocent people.

He arrived at the gym that was part of a new stretch of retail shops at the upscale strip mall. Danny pulled to a stop and eyed the Mercedes. "Isn't it just like you to keep to your schedule, Tom." He parked near the edge of the strip mall lot and was out there alone. If someone with even a modicum of suspicion cast a glance his way, he would have to scrap the whole plan. For now, no one noticed his white Ford Focus piece of crap. Danny was invisible to the rest of the world.

He waited in the front seat and hunkered down to avoid detection. The time showed 9:30am. Tom's workout should be wrapping up by now. With his baseball cap pulled low over his blonde hair, Danny peered at the doors of the gym with his phone in his hand. It was a clone of Tom's phone and was ready to go.

He instinctively crouched lower. "There you are. How was your workout, Tom? Must've been tired after getting laid by Denise last night." He watched Tom make his way to his Mercedes and unlock the door.

Tom tossed his gym bag onto the passenger seat, fully showered and dressed for a day at the office. He stepped inside and closed the door.

Danny's pulse quickened. Adrenaline surged in his veins and his eyes widened. His fingers hovered over the phone. He swallowed and the noise echoed in his ears. The familiar turning of his stomach began. Not quite butterflies, not quite nausea. He heard the Mercedes' enormous engine roar to life. The luxury sedan rumbled, and Danny thought he felt the vibrations from where he waited.

The moment had arrived. All the planning. All the scheming led up to this moment. Danny started the livestream and waited until Tom noticed. He watched him buckle his seatbelt, adjust his rearview mirror. "Ahh, there you go. Smile for the camera. Kaboom." He pressed the screen. "See ya later, Tom."

The flash of light forced him to squint, even at this distance, then came the blast's wave of energy. It was beautiful. The fire, the metal. Car alarms sounded; windows trembled.

Danny had but a few moments before people ran out of the buildings. He turned the engine and drove off, peering through the rearview to see the panic and the chaos ensue. The livestream ended and so had Tom.

ATF Agent Chris Stallard arrived in his dark grey Chevy Tahoe and stopped at the strip mall near the scene. The lights on the firetruck flashed as it remained stationed near the site while the firefighters put away their equipment. An ambulance waited with its doors opened. A few feet away, foam blanketed the burnt vehicle and coated the asphalt for several feet.

Stallard exhaled a full breath and stepped out, pulling on his ATF windbreaker. "Here we go again. I knew you weren't done yet." He approached Agent Tillis and offered his hand. "I had hoped our next meeting wouldn't be at another crime scene."

"You and me, both, brother." Tillis accepted his hand. "What are the odds? Two car bombings in less than two weeks?"

"If we were in Northern Ireland, I'd say 50/50, but here in the suburbs of Pittsburgh, PA? One in a million."

"That's what I thought." Tillis moved in toward the scene. "PBP is here. Word came down to the chief that they're here for backup only. Securing the scene and holding off onlookers and the press."

Stallard examined the vehicle. "Looks like it was a Mercedes."

"Yes, sir."

"Nice car, as was the BMW," Stallard replied. "Could be our suspect has something against folks with money."

"Might be. I do know one thing for sure. He has some impressive skills," Tillis replied.

"How do you mean?"

"Damn thing was livestreamed again. Everyone on this guy's Facebook page watched as he blew up into pieces."

Stallard turned away. "For God's sake."

"We've run out the clock on this one," Tillis began. "My boss wants to bring in the experts."

Stallard turned to him. "I thought we were the experts."

He laughed. "Apparently not. No, he wants Quantico in on this. Get the BAU involved before we find ourselves with a mass casualty event."

"The big boys, huh? Does that mean we're out?" Stallard asked.

"From your perspective, no. ATF's focus is on the explosives. This is on my end. I'm not out, but Quantico will come in here and try to get a handle on the type of suspect we're dealing with. I'll be lucky to have a say in anything."

"Sucks for you," Stallard began. "I have seen enough now to figure there's an angle here. The bomber is sending a message. Livestreaming this shit? Are you kidding me? If Quantico can figure out what that message is, good Goddam luck to them."

CAMERON FISHER HELD a file in his hand as he walked through the corridor and arrived at Kate's office. He pulled the toothpick from his mouth. "Knock, knock. You have a minute, Reid?"

She eyed him in the doorway. "Of course. Whatcha got there?"

"Your first test." He dropped the file onto her desk and sat down. "Pittsburgh bomber."

"Car bombs?"

"You're already familiar?" Fisher replied.

"When we were at the bar celebrating my promotion, I caught some of the news story on TV. Something about a car bomb in the heart of Downtown Pittsburgh."

"Yep, well, there was another one yesterday. This one was in the suburbs but looks to be the same M.O. and get this, whoever's planting these bombs also happens to be livestreaming the attack on the victim's Facebook page."

"The victim's Facebook page? How could that even happen?" Kate asked.

"You got me. The friends of both victims were lucky enough to watch them moments before the blast and hear the screams."

"Oh my God." Kate turned away for a moment.

Fisher sighed. "Anyway, the ASAC in Pittsburgh wants this thing squashed as quickly as possible. The media is starting to run wild with the story. Interviewing everyone who was within a mile of the blast sites just for sound bites."

"I see. We both know that'll only add fuel to the fire. Is this a consult or are we aiding in the investigation?" Kate asked.

"Right now, they're dealing with a cross-jurisdictional operation. ATF is investigating the explosives aspect of it and the Bureau is investigating the murders. Pittsburgh Police is essentially out of it, though they're helping to contain the scenes and keep the media away. So, pack your bags. You're taking a trip to Pittsburgh. I want Duncan with you. She's the most educated in cybersecurity threats. The unsub or unsubs are gaining access to the victim's social media.

This is more than just your run-of-the-mill bomber. I want you both to assess the situation. See if you have enough to develop a profile they can use." Fisher stood again. "This needs to happen ASAP."

"You got it." After he left, Kate picked up her phone. "Eva, looks like you and me are taking a trip to Pittsburgh."

"When?" she asked.

"Is now too soon?"

THE TWO WORLDS in which Danny currently lived were at stark odds with one another. He was smart enough to recognize one would have to defeat the other soon enough. Nevertheless, his daily grind to earn money and care for Melanie took precedence over his desire to expose those who abused the system for their own benefit. For now, it was all about timing.

Danny pulled off his headset after the final call of the day. 5:30pm. Half an hour after quitting time. Customers didn't care that it was past quitting time. They only cared to get their computers running again. He took in a breath to level his irritation. There was nothing to do for tonight anyway. Acting too quickly would be his downfall, so he would wait it out for the next opportunity.

Danny walked into the living room where Mel had been for most of the day. He knew she needed regular exercise and that wasn't always possible. But he would make time for her now. "Hey, do you want to go for a short walk before it gets dark? Stretch your legs? I wouldn't mind some fresh air."

Melanie turned to him. "You know I don't like going out there, Danny. People stare."

"I know they do, but like I told you before, you just have to ignore them. They don't know any better. People are ignorant jerks, okay? Your health is more important."

"Easy for you to say." She turned back to the TV. "They aren't staring at you."

He sat down on the sofa next to her. "Mel, I'm sorry about all of this. I wish Mom was still here. I wish I could give you more." He reached for her hand. "You're all I have in this world. I don't give a shit what anyone else thinks and if they start making you feel uncomfortable, just tell me. I'll kick their ass."

Melanie laughed. "Okay. Just a short walk, though."

"You got it." He stood again. "And I'll order some pizza for dinner when we get back."

He hopped up the stairs to grab his sneakers and jogged back down when he spotted her on the floor. "Mel! Mel, are you okay? Oh my God. What happened?" He rushed to her side.

"I tripped over my stupid legs." Tears ran down her face. "My arm. Danny, my arm."

He raked over her with wild eyes to check for blood when he noticed her arm twisted behind her back. "Oh no." He touched it.

"No!" she screamed.

"Okay. Okay, I'm sorry. I won't touch it again. I have to get you to a hospital. Your arm might be broken. This is going to hurt, but I have to get you up, okay?"

"No. No, please just leave me here. It hurts to move," she pleaded.

"I can't leave you here, sis. You're hurt. I can't call an ambulance because we can't afford it. I have to drive you. That means I have to get you up. I'm so sorry." He gently placed his arms underneath to get her to her feet.

She wailed in agony. "Stop. Please, Danny, stop!"

His eyes welled as he pulled on her again. "I can't. I have to get you up. Where's your walker? Never mind. I see it." He reached out but was still inches away from it. "Okay. Here's what we're going to do. I'm going to set you down on the couch and grab your walker. Do your legs hurt?"

She shook her head.

"Good. Okay. One more time." He pulled her up with some exertion. Danny was lanky, hardly any meat on his bones and Mel outweighed him by at least 20 pounds. Their nightly routine of going up the stairs exhausted them both. He got her to the couch. "There. The hard part's over." He walked a few feet to grab her walker and returned. "This should be the easy part. Just don't move your arm, okay?"

"Okay."

Danny placed one hand on her back and another on her waist to keep her balanced while she stood. "Almost. You're almost there, Mel. Then we'll go get in my car."

It took several more minutes to get her outside and onto the passenger seat. Her arm swelled up like a balloon.

"I think it's definitely broken, Mel." Danny keyed the ignition and made his way to the hospital. He knew there was no way he could pay for this, but she needed help. It was a consequence he'd have to deal with later.

"This is it, Mel. We're here. I'm going to pull up to the emergency entrance. Just sit tight. I'll get you some help." Danny pulled onto the circular driveway and parked beneath the covered entrance. He hurried inside. "My sister's hurt. She has cerebral palsy. I need help."

The woman behind the desk grabbed the phone and looked to be calling for help. Danny didn't wait and quickly returned outside. A moment later, two nurses with a wheelchair arrived.

"She's right here. I think her arm is broken."

"What happened, sir?" the nurse asked.

"She fell. She doesn't do well on her feet. Please help her."

As the nurses helped her onto the wheelchair, she peered at her brother with teary eyes. "Danny, don't leave me."

"They're going to take good care of you. I promise. You'll be fine. It's just a broken arm. You'll be just fine, Mel."

She disappeared into the triage unit and Danny peered at the nurse. "Can I go back there? She has to know I'm with her."

"Let us do our initial intake. Someone will come and get you after that. I'm sure your sister will be just fine."

Danny folded his arms and stared into the corridor. "Yeah. Okay."

AGENT GRANT TILLIS stood in the lobby of his field office as the BAU agents arrived. He approached with an extended hand. "Agent Reid?"

"That's me." Kate returned the gesture. "This is Agent Duncan. That must make you Agent Tillis."

"The one and only. Pleasure. Appreciate you clearing your schedule for us." Tillis started ahead. "Let's talk in my office. ATF Agent Stallard is waiting."

5

Night had fallen more than an hour ago and Danny still waited in the hospital. The familiar smell of ammonia and sickness was exactly as he had remembered when he waited with his mother too many times over the course of her illness. She eventually died in this very hospital.

At least one of the nurses had come out to tell him that Mel's right arm was broken, as he suspected. But that came almost two hours ago. His patience wore paper-thin.

"Mr. King?" An older woman wearing a pantsuit approached him.

He stood from the chair. "Yes?"

"I'd like to speak with you for a moment in private. Would you mind following me?" She started on without giving him a chance to answer.

"I'm sorry, are you a doctor? Is my sister okay?" He jogged to catch up.

"Your sister is resting. She'll be fine, Mr. King."

"Then what is this about?"

"Right through here, sir." She opened the door to a conference room where two others were already inside. The highly polished wood table reflected the can lighting above. City lights shone through the windows. "Please take a seat, Mr. King."

"What is this about? What's going on here?" he demanded.

"Mr. King, we need to speak with you about your sister, Melanie." Another suit spoke, but this one offered a name. "I'm Bob Spears. I work for the Department of Human Services."

Danny glanced at the woman who had dragged him in here. "You'd better tell me who you are and why I'm here."

She regarded him with what could have been mistaken for sympathy but looked to him an awful lot like condescension. "Fine." Danny pulled out a chair and dropped down. "Just so you know, I'm Melanie's legal guardian."

"Actually, Mr. King, that's not the case." Spears opened a file. "We understand Melanie had been in a home for the disabled up until about 3 years ago when your mother, Ms. Ellen King, pulled her out to return to your current home."

"Yeah, that's right." Danny folded his arms. "What's the problem?"

Spears glanced at his colleagues before continuing. "Unfortunately, it seems that when your mother passed, there was nothing noted in the department's files that suggested who would be caring for Melanie. You have been receiving the disability payments issued to her, but it does look as though that was an error."

"What are you trying to say?" Danny pressed on.

"Mr. King, how did your sister hurt herself?" the woman in the pantsuit asked.

"I told you, she fell down. She falls sometimes, like everyone."

"Yes, but most people can manage on their own to get back up again. As you are probably already aware, while cerebral palsy doesn't progress with age, it does, in essence, prematurely age those afflicted with the condition. We're seeing patients with cerebral palsy living longer and while that is a wonderful achievement, it has brought with it new struggles. The primary struggle being Melanie's use of her legs. Mr. King, she will continue to be prone to such falls. Possibly, eventually losing her ability to walk altogether. Frankly, you were lucky this time the situation wasn't worse."

"Which was why I was there to help her up," Danny replied. "I'm always there for her."

"Are you employed, Mr. King?" Spears asked.

"Yes. I work from home in order to look after Mel. I also have a neighbor who checks in on her when I'm not home, which isn't often. I have no life outside of caring for my sister."

"But you do rely on the State's disability payments in order for you to provide for Melanie, isn't that true?" he pressed on.

"Yeah. Of course it is. Mel has a right to that money."

"Yes, she does," Spears replied. "We just need to be sure it's going to her in order to give her the best care possible. But let's get back to the point of guardianship."

Danny knew where this was going. Up to now, this had never been an issue because Melanie went to her regular doctors for meds and checkups and nothing had ever happened, until this. "You're telling me that I have to fight to keep my sister at home. Is that right?"

"In a manner of speaking..." Spears continued but was cut short.

"Fine. So what do I have to sign to make that happen, huh? The sooner I can get Mel home, the better it will be for her. And I assume you all want what's in her best interest."

"Of course we do," Spears added. "But according to her doctors and our own evaluation, we believe it is in Melanie's best interest to reside at a long-term care facility where she won't have accidents such as this. Mr. King, there are people who should be taking care of her, ensuring she gets proper exercise, physical therapy, as well as continuing education that will help her."

Danny slapped the table and stood. "You're not letting me take Mel home?"

"Mr. King, please sit down. Don't make this harder than it has to be," Spears replied. "I don't want to have to call security."

Danny's face reddened. "Then let me take my sister home."

"I'm afraid we can't do that. If you wish to pursue this further, you'll need to file paperwork and wait for a hearing," Spears replied.

"How long will that take?" Danny asked.

"Months, maybe longer."

Danny's hands clenched into fists. "You assholes. I'm doing the right thing by helping Mel. And here you are taking her away from her home and her family. You don't want to do this. I promise you."

Spears glanced at his colleagues and returned his attention to Danny. "I'm sorry. It's already done."

STALLARD LEANED against the lateral file cabinet behind Tillis's desk. With his arms folded, he peered at the BAU agents. "So, Agents Reid, Duncan, what do you think? What kind of suspect are we dealing with?"

Files had been spread out on the table in Tillis's office. Kate peered at them again. "Obviously someone with extensive knowledge of computer hacking. Anyone who can break into someone's Facebook page to initiate a livestream of their death is someone who is looking to make a statement."

"A social statement, in my opinion," Duncan added. "The bomb, to me, is the delivery mechanism of his message."

"I agree," Kate continued. "We're dealing with a killer who wants to kill but doesn't have the fortitude to get close enough to do it himself. Either he doesn't think he has the physical strength, though a gun would resolve that, or he doesn't have the mental strength. Murdering someone takes the kind of mindset most people don't have. And to murder using their own physical attributes means that person has an extraordinary ability to compartmentalize."

Stallard pushed off the file cabinet and paced the office. "I don't claim to be an expert in psycho-analysis. That's why you all are here. But I can tell you, the explosives used were pretty bush-league. Whoever it is probably watched videos on YouTube about how to build bombs. They were remotely detonated and the devices themselves weren't substantial enough to do a lot of damage outside the intended targets. Though his use of the vehicle's fuel as a propellant could do extensive damage if it were the right vehicle."

"That could be the goal," Duncan replied. "You had the death of the victim at the blast in Downtown, along with some minor injuries. And no one else was hurt in the strip mall blast."

"That's right." Stallard halted in place. "You could surmise the target was the only one the suspect intended to kill. Placement of the explosive also suggests that. We don't know that yet and it's impossible to say for sure this early in the game."

"Could be the unsub is testing the waters. He knows he's not an expert in that area so he's trying things out for size. Learning from mistakes." Kate turned to Stallard. "Did you find any distinctions in the materials between the two explosive devices?"

"We're still analyzing the second device, but so far, they appear identical," he replied.

"And he's definitely cloning the phones," Tillis cut in. "The first victim's phone records were clear in that respect. We're currently analyzing the phone records of Tom Massena now."

"That's how he's getting into their social media accounts," Duncan added.

"He's following them, both online and in person," Kate said. "He's learning their habits, schedules, then picking just the right time to make his move. Making sure they're alone when the opportune time presents itself. These victims were successful, well-off, right?"

Tillis nodded. "That's right. The first victim, Rob Delaney, wasn't wealthy, but he clearly had some money. Our second victim, Tom Massena, was pretty well-off. But the two lived on opposite ends of town. I have no idea how the suspect would have found these guys."

"One thing I've noticed, Agent Reid," Stallard began. "Is that you keep referring to the suspect as a 'he.' Is that used in the general sense of the term, or are you convinced we're dealing with a male suspect? Could there possibly be two?"

"Serial killers, in general, are male, white, mid 20s to early 30s," Kate replied. "Serial bombers, in particular, are also male. It's too early to definitively state whether we are dealing with a lone serial bomber. Generally speaking, they're a little older, as I'm sure you know, but I won't rule out a younger male suspect based on his knowledge of cell phone software vulnerabilities and social media. Unless I'm wrong about that? You're ATF. You're the bomb expert."

He nodded. "That's the general assumption, yes."

"So, we agree that we're most likely dealing with a male unsub," Kate replied. "That leaves me with developing a deeper profile based on what we know right now. I should say the idea there could be two is possible, though the nature of a serial killer is to act alone. Not always, but usually."

"How soon can you get us something?" Tillis asked. "I don't want another bombing on my watch."

"A couple of days, at the most," Kate replied.

"Will you two be sticking around then?" Stallard asked.

"Tonight only. We have a team back at Quantico who will offer input on our profile," Kate replied. "We would still like to see the sites of both explosions first thing in the morning. Then we'll get out of your way until we can put something together for you."

"Fair enough." Tillis approached Kate. "It was a pleasure meeting you Agent Reid. Agent Duncan. Glad to have the big boys and girls at Quantico on board."

THE SIT-DOWN WAS SCHEDULED offsite to avoid eavesdroppers and it was a good excuse to see Levi Walsh after work and have a drink with him. Nick waited in the booth of the restaurant and sipped on his Coke.

Walsh arrived right on time and stood before him. "Scarborough. How's it going, brother?"

"Hey, man. Doing all right. Thanks for coming down." Nick offered his hand. "Take a seat." He raised his index finger to the bartender and glanced at Walsh. "What can I get you?"

"Draft beer. Doesn't matter what kind." He slipped into the booth.

"Can I get a draft over here?" Nick asked.

"Bud okay?"

"That'll do," Nick replied. "So, how's things going at Unit 4 without Kate and Duncan around?"

"What, are you kidding me? Never been so bored in my life. Those two keep us on our toes," Walsh replied.

"I remember it well." Nick glanced at his soda and hesitated a moment, turning serious. "Listen, I heard back from a buddy in the Boston Field Office. Made a quick call in search of answers without digging too deep."

The bartender set down the pint glass of beer. "Can I get you guys anything else? Wings, nachos?"

Walsh peered up at him. "I'll take some wings."

"Same here. Thanks," Nick added. "So, anyway, he says only two people had access to Richard Lehmann's possessions, which included his phone."

"And?" Walsh asked.

"And at the time Kate received that text message, no one from that field office had signed in to view Lehmann's personal property. In fact, as far as he knows, no one from his office had gone down there until the next day."

"So a big goose egg, huh?" Walsh tipped the beer to his lips and wiped away the foam.

"For now. I'm not sure what I was hoping for. Whoever it was isn't going to make this easy for us. I've learned that much over the past few months," Nick replied.

"That doesn't mean it wasn't someone who decided to take a stroll into Evidence and had some fun with Lehmann's phone. Someone higher-ranking. Someone nobody would question as to why they didn't follow protocol and fill out the proper paperwork. What do you want to do now?"

"We go deeper," Nick said. "Gustafson, Carol Whitman's father was highly influential at the Bureau in his day."

"And I've tracked down everything I could find about him. His record was extraordinarily clean. No ethics complaints, no censures," Walsh said.

"And he passed away, what, 10 years ago?" Nick stopped speaking when the bartender returned with the food. "Thanks very much. I'll take another Coke too, please." When he walked out of earshot, Nick continued. "We need to find out everyone he was in charge of during his tenure. I have to think it's someone who worked under him. Admired him. Got close to him."

"And that person must still be with the Bureau." Walsh picked up a chicken wing and dipped it into the blue cheese dressing. "It'll take some time and will be a little tough to do without raising any flags. You got any idea how to go about that?"

Nick glanced through the window. "Can't make a records request. We might have to go about this the old-fashioned way."

"Physical files." Walsh nodded. "It'll still be tough, but I can think of something that'll appear innocent enough. Research into the old man. Bureau history. Whatever."

Nick took a drink again. "So long as you steer clear of it. You're too high-profile. It'll have to be someone we can trust who's lower on the food chain. Not an agent."

"Civilian staff. That means we have to tell someone else what we're up to."

"Not if it's under the pretense of research, like you said. Let me check with Cole's office. He's got some grunts who would be more than willing to do a favor for a senior agent," Nick replied.

"What happens if they're questioned?" Walsh threw back a swig of beer.

"All they'll need to do is give Cole's name. No one will ask anything further."

Walsh wiped his mouth with a napkin. "That's a risky proposition, my friend. One you'd better hope Cole doesn't learn about."

6

Fear and confusion shrouded Melanie's face the moment Danny revealed she wasn't going home. It was as if the trust she'd placed in him all these years vanished in an instant. They let him drive her there while they followed.

From behind the wheel, he tendered a desolate gaze. "It won't be like before, Mel," he assured her, glancing at the home where she had been years earlier. "I will come see you every day this time." He ushered her inside and helped get her checked in while the social workers filled out the paperwork.

It hadn't been Danny's choice to keep Mel in a home until his mother could no longer afford it. It had simply come down to a financial choice. If Mel was home, his mother would've had to stay home with her. The resulting money issues would've been unavoidable, much as they were right now. And when Mel finally came home, Danny had both his mother and his sister to care for. Mel's life improved, his had not. However, he had accepted his fate.

Now, having returned home alone, he threw open the front

door and marched inside. Rage churned in his gut as he slammed the door and paced the living room, desperate for a way to fix this. Danny snatched a glass from the coffee table and threw it against the wall, shattering it into tiny shards that landed in the carpet. He gave voice to his rage with a guttural moan before dropping onto the sofa.

After spending hours at the hospital only to be denied his rights, Danny was helpless to do anything. Just as he had been when his mother died. And how his sister was in the same shithole he'd gotten her out of only a few years earlier.

With is elbows on his knees, his leg twitched, and his mind raced. His laptop lay on the coffee table and he opened it. The loss of control sent him reeling and he did the only thing that would return his sense of power.

Danny spent a great deal of time online, but not where ordinary people operated. He was drawn into the darkness where the wicked dwelled. And now he sought the advice of those who had offered it before. He logged into the private group. *"I have more to offer. Just tell me how best to do to them what they've done to me. My resources are endless."*

Guidance was offered for a steep price and Danny readily paid that price. Now, he knew what he had to do. His choice had been taken from him and so it was time to take away theirs.

His palms pressed against his thighs, Danny pushed off the sofa and walked into the kitchen. Standing at his folding table where he had spent too many hours, he stared at the phones in the small black tray. There were five now. He placed his index finger on each one. "Duck, duck, duck...goose." He picked up one of the phones and pressed the screen to illuminate it. "When your number's up, it's up."

Sienna Page was a 23-year-old Instagram Influencer and in Danny's eyes, was nothing more than a fraud. Famous and rich for doing nothing but peddling products made by desperate companies, she was the epitome of everything wrong with this society.

He pulled out his chair to sit down and scrolled through the messages. He hadn't checked in on her in a few days. Perhaps now was the time for an introduction. Only the most deserving caught his eye and Sienna had proven herself worthy.

Within minutes, he'd learned her location. Danny swiped his keys and started away once again. This time, to a trendy bar in a trendy part of town. That was where Sienna Page was with two of her friends. Stupid bitch told the world when and where she was every moment of every day.

He drove through the darkened streets until reaching the spot near Downtown. It was ladies' night and the bar appeared busy. Music pounded through the walls of the building when Danny stepped out of his car parked several yards away. As he approached, he checked Sienna's posts once again just to be sure she was still here. "Perfect." He returned the phone to his pocket and stood near the edge of the building, away from the entrance. The bar would close soon, and Danny would ride it out. One last test before deciding Sienna's fate.

He lingered nearby while people began to emerge from the bar, stumbling over each other, laughing like insane hyenas. Making fools of themselves without a care in the world. They were nothing like him.

Finally, he spotted her. Sienna Page walked out of the bar with two other women at her side. All three appeared perfect, even in the early morning hours after a night of drinking. Danny pulled back his shoulders, making himself taller, and started toward the entrance. He watched Sienna eye the men who followed, teasing them with her gaze. She might as well have fluttered her eyes at them like they did in the old movies.

When the three neared the sidewalk, he moved toward them.

His gaze cast down, Danny lurched forward, appearing to stumble into Sienna.

"Hey." Her brow knitted as she looked at him in disgust. "Watch it, man." Sienna grabbed hold of her friend to help steady her. "You ran right into me. What are you drunk or something?"

Words failed him. His tongue tied into knots. For a moment, he forgot why he was there and why he'd just rammed into this admittedly beautiful woman. "Sorry."

"Come on, Sienna. Let's go." One of her friends took hold of her and the three marched on, but not before the friend looked back. "Asshole."

Danny regained his composure and eyed them as they stepped into a car with Sienna behind the wheel. He suddenly remembered why he was there.

THE WHITEBOARD HAD ALWAYS BEEN Kate's best friend. It was how she visualized her profiles, a technique she'd learned through years of working alongside Nick Scarborough. Other, more sophisticated, tools were at her disposal, but staring at that board sparked her thoughts in a way nothing else had. And so she peered at it now as it sat on the easel inside her office.

What she knew about the Pittsburgh bomber, written in bullet points on the board, was just a starting point. Computer expert. In his 20s. May have a grudge against people with money, which suggested possible financial struggles. Aims only to kill the one he targets, as evidenced by the type of explosive device used. "Not a mass murderer," Kate said as she chewed on the cap of the black Sharpie.

"Not yet." Eva Duncan stood in the doorway and made her

way to Kate. "Looks like you're jumping right in. I think you might be forgetting one thing."

"What's that?" Kate asked.

"The unsub is finding his victims somehow. The two dead so far lived on opposite ends of the city, but both worked near the center," Duncan added.

"Coincidence? I'm not sure this guy is trolling Downtown Pittsburgh in search of targets."

"Why not? People who work in the area have good jobs in the financial sector, most likely. Then we have to remember that in order to clone a cell phone, he'd have to get pretty up close and personal with his victims. Walking the streets, running into people. I don't know, but I think it's worth considering."

Kate leaned back against her desk as they continued to study the whiteboard. "It's almost impossible to get physical access to someone's phone without them knowing about it."

"With my limited knowledge of cloning phones, I'd agree with you. It would, however, make it easier to gain access through the victims' social media this way. That could be how he's doing it. Might be a good idea to consult with Unit 2 on this. They're the cybercrime experts."

"Yep. You're absolutely right," Kate replied. "I requested CCTV footage from the immediate perimeter around the bomb sites. Tillis assured me his team scoured it already in search of new details, but I thought it might give us a better idea of how the unsub operates."

"I'm sure that went over well," Duncan replied. "I have a feeling we weren't Agent Tillis's first choice. But hey, I'm all for utilizing a second set of eyes."

"Yeah, I don't think we're his favorite right now. But according to ATF, the bombs were remotely detonated. The bomber had to be around somewhere. He knows his victims get into their cars. He knows that they're alone. Neither bomb went off until after the vehicles were started. That means he must be watching them, waiting for the precise moment to initiate the livestream and then...boom." Kate's fingers flicked away for illustrative purposes.

"I'm not arguing your point. We'll just have to take a look. Has ATF viewed the footage as well, or just the Bureau?" Duncan asked.

"I don't know. Stallard has been fairly non-committal. I think he's waiting for results from his own team before he takes a position."

Fisher appeared in the hall and stopped in. "Hey. You two just get back?" He glanced at Eva. "I haven't heard how it went, but I see you're already hard at work."

"Pieces of a puzzle," Kate jumped in. "We gathered a lot of detail from the field office and the ATF agent, so we're trying to assemble these pieces now and see if something starts to click into place."

Fisher walked inside and studied the board. "You might want to think about pulling old case files for reference or get with the ATF agent and ask him to pull relevant cases. You need guidance on the type of bomber you're dealing with. Maybe someone who's following in the footsteps of Kaczynski, McVeigh, or Rudolph. There's a lot of precedence to study. Especially when you consider the motive could be that he thinks he's leveling the playing field."

"Kaczynski could serve as a role model based on that theory, but the other two were looking more for mass carnage," Kate added. "I just don't see evidence of that here. These attacks were highly targeted. He was after those men and I think the only way to know why is to learn more about who they were. That's how we'll figure out who he is."

"Let me know what resources you need," Fisher replied. "We'll get it done."

Kate waited for him to disappear into the hall and looked at Duncan. "Why do I get the feeling he's holding back? It's not like him to nod and walk away."

"He's the boss now. I don't think he wants to be accused of keeping his thumb on the team. Cam's still finding his footing and with you getting the promotion, he's looking to you to take the lead on what you do best—profiling."

"He may want to leave it up to me, but I'm finding my footing too." Kate turned her gaze back to the trusted whiteboard. "I'd like to bring the team up to speed and get some input."

Duncan started toward the door. "Let's get it on the books."

THE INFORMATION HAD BEEN PRESENTED to the team and now Kate waited for guidance as she stood at the head of the conference table. "Anyone have any thoughts? Any holes in my theories that need to be plugged?" She looked at Surrey, who had been quiet throughout and appeared unwilling to offer suggestions.

Instead, it was Levi Walsh who chimed in first. "Do you know if the field agent has spoken to either of the victims' co-workers?"

"From what Duncan and I were told yesterday, interviews with the Delaney victim's co-workers were nearly finished. The most recent victim ran his own business. I don't know if they've interviewed his staff as of yet. What are you thinking?" Kate asked him.

"Just wondering if anyone noticed anything unusual going on around the victims in the preceding days. If they'd had unexpected visitors. Anything that might point to a suspect," Walsh added.

"Nothing so far stood out to Tillis based on the first round of interviews. I'm not sure what he asked, but he didn't seem to think anything was out of the ordinary," Kate replied. "But Duncan thinks the unsub could be hunting for his victims in the downtown area. The financial district."

"That would line up with your theory the unsub is looking for retribution, or fairness, as it were. Good luck with that, right?" he added

Surrey raised his index finger. "They won't find any connection to the victims or the companies they worked for or owned."

Kate regarded him. "You seem sure of that."

"It's debatable as to whether this is personal for him," Surrey added. "To me, it's a statement against, well, to make a generalization—capitalism. What I think is that the unsub is targeting the wealthy because he isn't among them. Whether he had once been remains a possibility. He could've lost money in the stock market. Lost a business. Hard to say at this point. He has a remarkable understanding of cyber security, cloning, hacking."

"He's educated," Kate replied. "I would agree with that."

"There are still a lot of unknowns right now," Fisher cut in. "Feels like we're spit balling, but that's the name of the game. Give them what you have. See where it gets them. I know I'm not alone in the assumption that this unsub won't stop at two. Reid, you'll take point if this thing hits hard. Two bombs in two weeks. He's not done. Livestreaming the event shows you he wants attention. He wants people to stand up and take notice of his work."

Agent Grant Tillis tossed the file onto the ASAC's desk. "This is it. This is the best the BAU has to offer. A generic profile we could've done here in our own office. Nothing we didn't already know or discuss with those agents two days ago." He paced

the floor. "What the hell, sir? What are we supposed to do with this?"

"Just calm down, Tillis." Assistant Special-Agent-In-Charge Neil Garofalo leaned back at his desk. "It's thin, I'll give you that. But what we gave them was thin. We don't know shit about this suspect or his motives. Getting the BAU in here early was the right call. ATF hasn't done anything for us except tell us how the suspect made the bomb. They did their own profile and came up with not much more than those guys at Quantico did. This entire investigation is light on details and heavy on sensationalism. That is exactly what I wanted to avoid." He pulled up at his desk. "Did you see the news last night? Lead story...'Downtown bomber wants to make the rich pay.' Seriously. That was their tease. They're already branding him as some sort of damn Robinhood. How do you think that's going to go down with the mayor, the governor?"

Tillis stopped and looked at him. "Rob Delaney wasn't a rich man. More than the average Joe, but not wealthy by any stretch of the imagination."

"Yeah, well, tell that to the 6 o'clock news anchors," Garofalo replied. "Look, just do your damn job, Grant. That's all I can ask of you. Take the file, learn as much as you can from it. Use those guys at Quantico. Pick their brains. That's what they're there for— us. Okay?" He closed the file folder. "And find this son of a bitch before he blows up someone else."

"Yes, sir." Tillis grabbed the file and marched back to his office. So far, he'd been juggling the Pittsburgh police, the ATF and now some profiler with the BAU. And yet with all these so-called experts, a bomber was still on the loose.

He returned to his office and sat at his desk. With his head in his hands, he heard his name and glanced up. "Yeah?"

"Agent Stallard is here. Wants to see you," the man replied.

"Yeah, fine. Send him back." Tillis pulled up in his chair and waited for the agent to arrive. "Stallard. I hope you come bearing gifts."

"Not the kind you want." He entered the office. "Listen, I think…"

Another agent hurried inside, brushing by Stallard. "Excuse me. Tillis, there's been another bomb. PBP is heading to the scene now."

Tillis stood and grabbed his keys. "Where?"

"Duquesne Heights, Emerald View Park," the agent replied.

Stallard shot a look at Tillis. "That's not Downtown."

Tillis started ahead. "No, but it's not far from it. Let's go."

NOT A CLOUD HUNG in the sky as the agents raced toward Emerald View Park. Patrol cars, fire trucks, and ambulances were already on the scene on their arrival.

"Looks like we're the last ones to the party." Tillis rolled to a stop and jumped out with Stallard trailing. "I see Lieutenant Crenshaw ahead. Let's see what he knows."

The lieutenant spotted their approach. "Well, well, well. Look who decided to show up. A day late and a dollar short, by the look of it."

"Spare us. Who's the victim?" Tillis asked.

"Victim is Sienna Page, 23 years old. Some kind of social media influencer."

"I'm sorry. What?" Stallard cupped his ear as though he hadn't heard the man properly.

"She was an influencer. Someone on social media who gets paid to basically advertise and make it look like she lives a desirable life," the lieutenant replied. "That's what I was told."

"A desirable life." Stallard nodded. "Right. Okay. Female victim. That's a first." He placed his hands on his hips. "What kind of car was it?"

"She leased a Lexus sports coupe. Red."

"Giving off the appearance of money, then," Tillis replied.

"That's how it seems," he added. "I don't know much else yet. We're just now searching for next of kin. Looks like our bomber is still on the hunt."

"We're going to check out the car." Tillis and Stallard carried on toward the scene when Tillis continued. "Jesus. Right here in the park?"

"Wasn't all that busy this morning. Downtown was far busier, but the gym wasn't. He appears to be considering collateral damage, but that's hard to be sure," Stallard replied.

"How much you willing to bet her phone was cloned, same as the others?" Tillis asked.

"I'm not dumb enough to take that bet. How the hell is he finding these people? Had they wronged him in some way?"

Tillis gazed out at the scene. "Couldn't tell you. Right now, it doesn't look like he knew them personally, but then, we haven't asked him."

Stallard chuckled. "Then let's get right on that. Look, I don't know anything about Sienna Page yet, but if the bomber thought she had money, she made for a prime target, just like the others. Doesn't look like he cares if it's a man or woman."

"Money, or wealth, seems to be the only common thread among these victims. And it doesn't get us any closer to learning how he finds them." Tillis picked up his phone. "But I'll give Reid a call and let her know we have ourselves another attack. Maybe she can pull a rabbit out of a hat."

～

KATE RUSHED THROUGH THE HALLS, passing by colleagues with a mere nod. She arrived at Fisher's office. "There was another attack."

Fisher pulled the toothpick from his mouth. "The bomber?"

"Female victim. Alone at a park, according to Agent Tillis," Kate walked inside. "He and Stallard are on the scene now. Duncan and I need to be there. The third bomb and this one less than one week from the last."

"He's speeding up his timeline for whatever reason," Fisher replied. "Go. But I want Surrey in on this too. You'll be running the show, but you'll need them both to back you up. Take the plane and get there as soon as you can. We got to be all in on this one."

"I agree, but what about Walsh?"

"He is our local liaison, but I need him here with me for a while," he replied. "Besides, with you three, the ATF and the local field office, there's enough talent."

"If you say so." Kate disappeared into the hall and hurried back to her office. It was odd that Fisher didn't want Levi to go with them. They were a team, each with their own areas of expertise. So to hold him back meant Levi was working on something important, and Kate could only guess what that was.

NICK SCARBOROUGH GLANCED at his phone and noticed the incoming call from Kate. He pressed the cancel button. "Sorry about that. You were saying about Gustafson?" He had made the drive to downtown D.C. to meet with an agent who had worked for Gustafson, Carol Whitman's father. Through a friend of a friend, and with Walsh's help, the lunch appointment was just getting underway.

"Right. So, yeah, this was years back. I'd just graduated from the Academy and my first post was at the Maryland field office."

"I knew some guys there a long time ago," Nick replied. "I heard nothing but good things coming out of there."

The man nodded and smiled. "We did all right for what we had at the time. Course, technology and all. Shit, all the crazy developments there, right?"

"I hear you. Good thing the young recruits are computer savvy. Otherwise, the Bureau would be screwed." Nick sipped on his Coke as he peered through the restaurant window. "How long did you work for Gustafson?"

He peered up as if considering the question. "A year or so. Then he retired. The guy was a hell of a smooth talker. A requirement around here."

"No doubt," Nick replied.

"But hey, you're here on Cole's orders, huh? A senior unit agent at BAU is no small accomplishment."

"Thanks. It's been a long road. So, what else can you tell me?" Nick pressed on. "And I have to apologize, but this is a project Cole is working on. I think it has something to do with policy, but for now, it's hush-hush."

"Yeah, no. I get it," the agent replied. "Gustafson penned Bureau policy for a long time. He set the standards we still use today. Made a lot of money in retirement on the speech circuit. I hear he even has a building named after him at Georgetown University."

"That's what I hear." Nick sipped on his drink again. "I imagine there are a lot of guys out there still loyal to Gustafson, huh?"

"Loyal, how?" he asked.

"Well, just in the ways he set up. Like you said, policy, protocol. And I'll bet he rubbed elbows with a lot of politicians too," Nick replied.

"A requirement when you get that high up. You'll see, if you haven't already had a taste of that," the man said. "Listen, it's been great talking to you, but I really need to head back to the shop." He stood and dropped cash on the table. "You need anything, don't hesitate to get in touch."

"Will do, man. Thank you for your time." Nick watched the agent leave and picked up his phone. "Walsh, you still around?"

"Leaving the Baltimore field office now. How did it go?"

"Not sure yet. Meet me back at Quantico and we'll compare notes."

"You got it. Oh, and hey, our team's been called out to Pittsburgh. Fisher wants me to stay."

"That must've been why Kate called," Nick replied. "Thanks. I'll give her a buzz and see what's up. Catch up with you soon."

7

The media vans had gone. The late afternoon sun poked through clouds while its rays scattered among the tree-tops. What was usually a busy park lay vacant as it had been cordoned off by the Pittsburgh police. ATF Agent Stallard stood by while the burned-out Lexus coupe was loaded onto a tow truck. Next to him stood FBI Agent Tillis. Both turned at the sound of a car approaching.

"Well, that was fast," Tillis said.

"Cavalry's here, buddy." Stallard patted him on the back. "I'm sure one look at this scene and they'll have it all figured out."

Tillis watched as the three agents stepped out of the car. "Looks like they brought reinforcements. Good. Just what I wanted. More supposed experts telling me how to do my job." He forced a smile as they approached. "You're back. And you brought a friend."

"Agent Tillis," Kate began. "You know Eva Duncan already. This is Jonathan Surrey. Given the circumstances, I thought we could use an extra set of eyes."

Surrey offered his hand to the agents. "Pleasure."

"We're glad for your speedy arrival." Tillis started toward the scene. "As you can see, we're trying to clear all this out as quickly as we can. Public park and all. Lots of interested citizens rubbernecking."

Stallard placed his hands on his thick hips. "Yes, sir. Local news is calling this guy some kind of Robinhood. Except that he's killing the rich, not just stealing from them. Glad to have you all here. How about we show you around?"

"Here's what we know," Tillis began. "Female victim. 23, some kind of social media star. That car, or what's left of it, was a lease."

"She's outside his apparent demographic; the first female victim," Kate added.

"That is how it appears," Tillis replied. "It's safe to assume our suspect is watching these victims' lives through the lens of social media and not real life. Either that, or he'd had some encounter with them, which we have no way to confirm at the moment."

"They're calling him Robinhood, huh? Almost like the media has a thing for him. Admires him for killing people with money," Surrey added.

"Except he got that wrong in at least two of the cases," Tillis added. "I already have my team working on Sienna Page's phone. Unfortunately, it was significantly damaged, as were the others, but they'll do what they can. We'll pull the records, too. Same as before."

Kate surveyed the grounds. "How far is the downtown area from here?"

"Just over the river." Stallard pointed to it. "Right there. A stone's throw."

"He's sticking to the area, albeit still a pretty large area," Kate replied.

"And the explosive?" Duncan asked. "Same as the others?"

Stallard stepped in. "Won't know for sure till I get it back to my lab, but it looks to be, yes."

"Livestreamed too, I imagine." Kate looked on.

"Bingo." Tillis opened his phone. "The parents of this girl are already doing whatever they can to help us figure this out. They sent us the video." He looked to the others. "You guys might want to look at this. Sorry to say, it's a little different than the others."

The team huddled around Tillis when Kate began. "Let's see it."

He started the video. "She's behind the wheel with her phone in the holder mounted on the dash. From what I understand, she often filmed herself driving. Can't for the life of me tell you why." The video continued to play. "She notices it's on right here."

Kate nodded. "She looks like she's trying to shut it off."

"Just wait," Tillis added.

Sienna pulled the phone from its holder and appeared to press buttons to shut it down. "What the hell? Hey, everyone. I don't know what's going on here, but I must've turned on the livestream. Oops!" She laughed. "I'll fix it. Just remember to watch me..." Her eyes widened at the sound of the blast and she dropped the phone to the floorboard, screen side up.

"It's still going," Kate said. "Jesus. Don't tell me he let everyone watch her burn."

"You want to see more? 'Cause that's exactly what happens until the phone cuts out from the heat," Tillis replied.

"For God's sake." Surrey turned away. "End it."

Tillis ended the video. "Yep, that's pretty much how we felt. What do you make of that, Agent Reid?"

"How long does that video go on?" she asked.

"It was a good 90 seconds. But the bomber didn't end it like he did the others. He let it run as long as it could. He's changed his M.O. with this one."

"He wanted everyone to watch her burn like this was personal for him. And why the hell didn't Facebook kill the feed?" she asked.

"I wish I knew," Tillis replied.

"How long since the last bomb?" Surrey pressed on.

"Less than a week ago. Was almost two weeks between bomb number one and bomb number two. This one? About four days," Stallard replied.

"Why did he change tactics? Something provoked him, or someone. Maybe the victim." Kate looked at Tillis. "Any connection between this girl and the other victims?"

"It's a little early to say for sure, but you'd better believe we'll be all over that," Tillis replied. "I've already got a call into my computer forensics lead to check into her social media followers. He might've been one, who the hell knows?"

Stallard peered out over the scene. "My gut tells me he's local. He knows these streets, the community. He knows when places are busy and when they're not. No way an outsider would know that. This isn't just some random social media follower with a vendetta."

"I agree," Duncan replied. "But he does follow his victims. He learns their routines, their habits, and uses it against them. Attacks them when they're the most vulnerable—alone."

"She's got you on that point, Stallard," Tillis replied. "So where does all this conjecture leave us, huh? You guys are the profiling experts. And Agent Reid, I'm sorry to say, your initial profile didn't offer a whole lot of insight. What can you tell us now?"

At least Kate knew one thing about Tillis. He could call a spade a spade. "I don't disagree. However, this victim is different and adds more layers for us to include that will start to fill out the profile. He's exposing his true nature. Short fuse. Quick to act. I don't think he took as much time getting to know Sienna Page as he did the other two victims. Why the hurry? I don't know yet. Maybe he feels as though he's running out of time." She took in a deep breath. "Where are you at on the CCTV from the other crime scenes?"

"We scoured the footage obtained from the exterior of the buildings around the financial district. We're still working on getting the footage from the strip mall. Came up empty-handed on the first go-round. Don't expect that to be any different this time. But who knows? Based on what we've seen today, he wants to make a bigger, bolder statement and he might screw it up," Tillis replied.

"Going back to the victims' phones being cloned," Duncan interjected. "Agent Tillis if you're good with it, I'd like to make a call to a colleague who knows a lot more about them than I do. There could be a shot at determining when these phones were cloned, possibly where they were cloned, too."

"Go for it. Hey, look, we all work for the Bureau. Well, except for Stallard over there. He's ATF."

"The red-headed stepchild of the federal agencies," Stallard chuckled. "But I'm used to it."

"Point being, we're on the same team." Tillis eyed them. "Whatever we need to do to end this, I'm all for. My toes have been stepped on plenty of times and I'm still walking just fine."

Kate nodded. "Then we should probably make some arrangements. Set up shop in your field office. Get a place to stay. We aren't leaving until we get answers for you."

~

A TEXT ARRIVED on Nick's phone and drew his attention. His brow pulled tight as he studied the message and took in a breath. From behind his desk, he peered into the hall. A moment later, he headed into the corridor.

"Scarborough, hey, you have a minute?" Agent Moskowitz stopped him in the hall. He was Nick's second-in-command. The Cameron Fisher of Unit 2, though he was younger and taller than Fisher. "I hear your old team is working those car bombings out of Pittsburgh."

"That's right. How'd you find out?" Nick asked.

"Villanova got a call from one of them. An Agent Duncan."

"Is that so?" Nick folded his arms. "What did she want?"

"Turns out, they're looking for a guy who's some kind of genius hacker. I don't know the whole deal, but she asked Villanova if there was a way to pinpoint when and where a phone might have been cloned. You know anything more about it? Your wife's there, too, I hear."

"She is. They're with the field office and the ATF, as far as I know. Hadn't heard much in the way of details yet," Nick replied.

"I don't know, man. Kind of sounds like something Unit 2 should be handling, if that's the case."

"Looks like we already have fingers in the pie." He glanced at his phone. "Hey, I'm on my way to a quick meeting. Let me dig into this a little and I'll let you know what I come up with."

"You got it, Boss. Catch you later."

Nick stepped onto the elevator to meet Walsh, who waited for him downstairs. The elevator doors opened to the lobby and Nick headed outside. He caught sight of Walsh just beyond the entrance and walked through the glass doors. "You didn't want to come up. That can't be good."

Walsh scanned the area as though he was under surveillance. "We can't be sure who's on our team and who isn't."

"Didn't realize we had more than one," Nick replied.

"Go figure." He pulled Nick aside. "Look, we wanted to know who worked under Gustafson? Well, I learned of at least one person."

Nick fixed his stance and prepared for the worst.

"He worked at Headquarters in D.C. when Gustafson was there, right before the guy retired. Apparently, they were close. I'm working on more details, so I'll spare you my working theories. Just bear with me for a day and I'll have some answers for you."

"Walsh, man, you could've told me this over the phone. Why the cloak and dagger? Something else going on?"

I think it's best from this point forward that we only discuss this outside the compound. The way we're going around asking questions, people might start to talk. Might overhear conversations. And hey, we're talking about the Bureau. Our phones are their phones."

"Point taken. Got it. I didn't get much from my lunch expedition anyway. The usual stuff. We need to find someone who will talk."

"Process of elimination, buddy," Walsh replied. "Whoever threatened Kate, we'll find them before they make good on that threat."

The Rapid Response team inside the Pittsburgh field office set up an area for the BAU to aid in the hunt for the serial bomber, nicknamed "Robinhood" by the media. This was in no way a situation where this guy was looking after the less fortunate. He was a murderer, but straightforward stories didn't increase ratings.

Tillis walked into the room. "This should be everything your team will need, Agent Reid. It's the largest space we have that can accommodate you."

"This is perfect. Thank you. I know it must be hard for you with all of us here. The ATF too. You probably feel like you're being squeezed out," she replied.

"No, no, it's...well, yeah." He chuckled. "It's starting to feel a little claustrophobic in here."

"I get it. We can do that to our colleagues in the field offices sometimes. It's not intentional. We just want to make available all our resources." She thumbed back to Surrey and Duncan. "Those guys... we're better together if you know what I mean."

"Sure. I get it, Reid. Look, we all want to get this guy. I don't have a problem with you being here. I really don't. All I ask is that you try to remember this is still my town."

"Understood."

"Good. Then I'd like to check in on Forensics to see how far they've gotten with reviewing the security footage from the Messena case and have them start gathering any public camera information around the park where Page was killed. Maybe we'll get lucky in that our genius hacker bomber was dumb enough to be seen on video."

Kate revealed a cockeyed grin. "We can only hope." She gathered Surrey and Duncan who had already settled into their spots. "Tillis wants to get an update on the footage they've scoured so far. Whatever they haven't finished, we should jump in and help."

Surrey pushed off the chair and followed as they left the room. "Agreed. We wrap that up, it'll be another thing to check off the list. The best we can do is to narrow down our field of search."

"I'm waiting on a call back from Villanova in Unit 2 to learn if those cloned phones are traceable in any way," Duncan replied. "We might get a hit on something."

Tillis looked back. "This is it, folks. I'll make the introductions.

These computer guys scare easy." He laughed. "Just kidding. They're all good people. Just a little dry if you ask me." He pushed inside. "Fellas! Tell me you got something on the bomber footage. I got the BAU here, so don't let me down."

"Still working on it, Chief." A young analyst eyed Tillis as he approached. "We viewed the footage around the time of the blast in the gym parking lot, turned up squat. So, we're going through the previous two days to see if we pick up anything unusual. Haven't started on what happened today."

"You think he might've scoped out the location?" Kate asked. "Sorry, I'm Reid."

"Right. Agent Reid. I just look at video all day. I leave the detective work to you guys. But if I were to guess, I'd say that no one just shows up and decides to plant a bomb, right?"

"Not usually," Kate replied.

"It requires planning. Especially, if like Tillis says, the bomber wanted to make sure the bomb went off when his location was the least busy."

"Anything we can do to help?" Surrey asked.

The analyst looked at Tillis. "The more eyes on this, the faster it'll go. But that's up to you."

"Might as well put these guys to work right away," Tillis replied. "Send me the details on exactly where you and your people have left off. We'll divide and conquer."

8

___

After Sienna Page, prudence suggested Danny would be better served by keeping out of sight. Instead, he chose to give law enforcement the middle finger by sitting inside a bar, drinking a beer as though he hadn't just blown up someone. The tingling in his spine told him to watch his back, but another beer would dampen the notion.

Danny was a new breed of crusader. He wasn't alone in that crusade, but no one else had taken the stand that he had. Guess it only took the system to kick him while he was down one more time. Now, he felt unstoppable with nothing left to lose. Mel was gone and the uphill battle to get her back would grow exhausting. Just as caring for his dying mother had.

Culling the self-important masses was necessary for society to function for all. Generating fame for doing absolutely nothing to further the greatness of humanity only dumbed it down. All the while, still placing upon a pedestal the vain, hackneyed, beautiful people for their worthless contributions. Danny sought retribution for this flawed system that hurt people like him and families like he had.

An angry fire in him that grew alongside his desperation flourished. Danny threw back the last of his beer and gazed at the television.

The barman approached and braced his hands against the shiny wood top. "Hey, buddy, you need another one? You can squeeze in one more before last call if you want."

"No. I'm good. Thanks." Danny caught sight of a man at the end of the bar. He must've only just arrived. Older than he was, probably mid-thirties if he was to venture a guess. Danny scoffed at the sight of the man scrolling through his phone, utterly ignoring the world around him as so many people had.

The man drew his eyes slowly to Danny. "You all right there, pal?"

"No problem here." He turned his gaze to the TV above the bar but couldn't help casting a side-eye at the man, realizing he still hadn't taken his eyes off his phone. "What a fucking joke."

Finally setting down his phone, he turned to Danny. "What's that now? I'm sorry, do I know you?"

The bartender eyed the exchange and appeared to sense a scuffle on the horizon. "Hey. We have a problem here, boys?"

Danny shook his head. "None at all."

"Good." The barman cast his gaze between the men. "Let's keep it that way."

"I will take another beer, actually," Danny said to him. "Please."

"Sure thing." He grabbed a bottle and opened the top. "Last one, then I gotta close out the bar."

"Thanks." Danny drank his beer and tried to ignore the guy at the end. He'd already caused a scene at the hospital the other night and they'd almost called the cops. Given his recent actions, cops weren't on his list of people he wanted to see.

Danny reached for his phone and casually scrolled through it like all the other lemmings, except that he had a purpose. The software installed on it allowed him to connect to the cell tower that everyone in the bar, and everyone around for several blocks, was connected to. He picked up the signals and now had to filter them. That was the hard part. Hard, but not impossible. With two main carriers in the area, Danny narrowed down the signals. He knew the guy at the end of the bar wasn't using some cut-rate carrier since he held a brand new iPhone in his hand.

Danny sent a binary SMS to the signals coming from inside the bar. Luckily, there were only 4 as it was almost closing time. He relied on the fact that most of the big carriers still used outdated DES ciphers. While the carrier would send back an error message with an embedded cryptographic signature through SMS, Danny could use a simple table to decrypt the message. After that, he could send a properly coded SMS that carried a Java applet. Once the original phone opened the message, the Java applet would install onto the SIM card. Voila! Job done.

To eliminate the other numbers, Danny was going to have to talk to this guy. Sure, he could play the game with everyone in this bar, but the man at the end drew the short straw. "Hey, I didn't mean any offense earlier." He offered his hand. "I'm Danny. It's just been a rough day. I apologize."

The man turned to him, pulling his gaze away from his phone. "Jeff. No worries, Danny. I get it. Happens to the best of us."

Danny returned to his beer. "Good to meet you, Jeff."

KATE BOLTED UPRIGHT in the hotel bed and surveyed the room. *Where am I? Where am I?* It took a moment to register her whereabouts until she spotted Eva asleep in the other bed. Relief swelled in her chest. She padded into the bathroom and quietly closed the door. The harsh blue light stung her eyes and when they adjusted, she saw her reflection in the mirror. Kate's brunette hair was in stark contrast to her ghostly white face. The purple circles under her eyes aged her ten years. Some might call this PTSD, but Kate refused. Just like everything she had faced in her life, this, too, would pass.

It was important that she keep this to herself. She could handle it and wouldn't dare jeopardize her new position. And while Nick had seen her struggles up close and personal, he wouldn't say a word to Fisher. This promotion was too important, and Kate had worked too hard to let the Lehmann situation get in her way.

She splashed water on her face and patted it dry with a hand towel. Calmer, collected, she turned off the light and walked back into the room.

"You okay?" Eva's tone was soft and unexpected.

"Fine. I'm fine. Get some rest." Kate climbed back into bed and closed her eyes. George Lehmann couldn't get to her anymore. He sat in a jail cell and would never touch her again. And as far as his brother, Richard... he was a little harder to forget.

JONATHAN SURREY HELD a cup of coffee while he stood in the hotel lobby, waiting for the rest of his team. When the elevator doors parted and the agents appeared, he raised the cup. "Morning. You two want to grab a coffee?" He tossed a glance toward the café. "It's not half-bad. I'll wait."

"Mind if we hit the Starbucks on the way to the field office?" Kate wore black dress pants with a beige blouse and her hair was pulled back in a ponytail. It looked as though she hadn't suffered a restless night at all.

"Why didn't I think of that? Probably better than this crap." Surrey tossed his cup in the trash and starting toward the exit. "How did everyone sleep?"

Duncan spoke up. "Not bad for a hotel. You?"

"Meh." He pushed through the doors and headed to the parking lot. "Got a text from Tillis a little while ago. He says his team has finished reviewing all the surveillance video."

"And?" Kate asked, trailing him just a few steps.

"Nada. No signs of anything unusual. No cars hanging around, no one scoping out the joints," he replied. "So I guess we're back at Square One."

"We're always at Square One." Kate opened the rear passenger door of the rental car and slipped onto the grey cloth seat. "How did a man who planted bombs on cars avoid detection anywhere near the crime scenes? It doesn't make sense."

Surrey keyed the ignition and pulled out of the lot. "He had to have planted the devices at another location. Another time."

"We already know he follows his victims for days, maybe weeks to learn their routines." Duncan glanced over her shoulder at Kate. "Let me see if Villanova made any headway on determining when those phones were cloned." She made the call. "Hey, it's Duncan. Any news?" She listened and nodded. "Yeah, that's great. Send it over to me, would you? We needed this. Appreciate the help." Duncan ended the call. "Villanova got what we needed. It should help us pinpoint a timeline."

"Finally, some good news," Kate replied. "Something we might also want to consider..."

"What's that?" Surrey asked.

"The unsub might work for a cell phone carrier, given his particular knowledge of phones. Do we know if the victims used the same carrier?"

Surrey eyed her through the rearview mirror. "At this point, it's worth a look."

~

AGENT STALLARD HURRIED inside the Pittsburgh FBI field office. Wearing an ardent expression, he stopped at the security desk. "I need to see Agent Tillis. Now."

Tillis strolled into the lobby as he awaited the BAU agents and spotted Stallard. "Morning. I didn't expect to see you this early. Just waiting on our expert profilers to see what great things..."

Stallard marched ahead of him. "We need to talk. Your office. Now."

Tillis peered over his shoulder, hesitated a moment, then jogged to catch up. He looked back at the front desk. "Hey, when those Quantico guys show up, send them to my office."

"You got it, Agent Tillis," the man replied.

He caught up to Stallard. "What wild hair crawled up your backside this morning?"

The two walked side-by-side and as they reached Tillis's office, Stallard continued. "I found something. A signature on the devices. Son of a bitch left us a calling card." He opened his brief case on the small table and laid out several pieces of the explosives that had been recovered from the three blast sites. "I just got the lab analysis back comparing the three vehicle-borne IEDs. This guy might be a genius hacker, but as I suspected, he's definitely a novice bombmaker."

"Looks like we arrived just in time," Surrey appeared in the doorway, capturing Tillis's attention.

"Morning. I don't think your timing could've been any better. Come in. Stallard was just getting ready to explain to us how our bombmaker is building his bombs."

Kate headed toward the table. "Is that what's left of the explosive devices?"

"Not all of it, but the main parts," Stallard added. "As I was about to tell Tillis, our guy left us some clues." He pulled out the report. "Labs came back and concluded the use of smokeless powder."

"Easily obtained just about anywhere firearms are sold," Surrey replied.

Stallard aimed gun-shaped fingers at him and winked. "Yep. Enthusiasts use it to load their own cartridges. And they're low explosive. So, if the intent was to avoid harming a lot of people, that's the way to do it. However, even that moderately low charge is all it would take to make a car go boom with the aid of the fuel as a propellant."

"All three of the devices used this powder?" Duncan asked.

"That's what we've found, yes. But that's not all." Stallard grabbed a pen from his shirt pocket and used it to shift a burnt can of Pepsi that lay on the table. "That right there, that Pepsi can is the casing. And again, all three used the same casings. And finally, we've concluded that the devices were remotely detonated. No timers found. That was a given since I didn't see timers anywhere on the remnants."

"Then he had to have been in the area watching his victims," Kate replied.

"That's a big fat affirmative. There's no other way around that. It would require a clear line of sight to his targets."

Tillis pressed his hands against his waist. "Look, nothing against your theory, Stallard, but we scoured the CCTV footage and found nothing out of the ordinary. Bushes, behind columns, down a narrow pathway. No one was seen near the bomb who was just hanging out—lingering."

Kate considered the question for a moment. "It was possible, at the first two blast sites, that the bomber could've been inside another building and watching from there. He was close enough to initiate the livestream. Could he have been inside somewhere?"

Tillis nodded. "That could easily be confirmed."

"But that last two locations, the strip mall and the park, there aren't any buildings in the immediate area to hide in." Kate glanced up. "Let me rephrase that. He could've been hiding in one of the businesses in the strip mall, but..."

"None of them were open at the time," Tillis cut in.

"Right. So where was he?" Kate asked.

Tillis glanced up as if considering the question. "He might've found a dead spot in the camera coverage if he'd scoped it out ahead of time."

"But you didn't see anything unusual in the days leading up to the bombs on the CCTV, right?" Duncan asked.

"No," Tillis replied.

"He's there, but we can't see him. That's some magic trick," Surrey added.

"Not magic. He's a hacker. We're overlooking the obvious." Kate moved in to view the remnants. "If he can clone phones, hack into people's social media...how hard do you think it would be for him to hack into closed circuit television cameras?"

"If they're cloud-based, probably not that hard," Duncan replied.

Kate peered at Tillis. "Then we need to look again at the footage from the surrounding areas right before the blasts."

"What are you hoping to see, Agent Reid?" Tillis's tone grew sharp.

"A glitch. A signal interruption. I'll bet if we look closely at the timestamps, we'll see it doesn't match up."

"He erased the footage before we got to it?" Stallard asked.

"No. I'm saying it never recorded the moments he was there. I'm saying, he hacked into it to make sure he wasn't captured on camera."

Tillis started into the hall and turned back. "Well, you guys coming or not?" He waited while they caught up. "Let's go back and talk to Forensics and see if your theory pans out, Reid."

They arrived at the lab and Tillis pushed inside. "Hey, Colangelo, do me a favor?"

"Yeah?" the agent pulled away from his computer screen.

"Cue up the footage we've been scrubbing for the past few days. We need to confirm something." Tillis stood near him. "Specifically, the minutes leading up to when the bombs went off. All three locations."

"On it." He quickly typed in the commands and pulled up the first incident on Fourth Avenue. "Okay, this is the Delaney case." He pressed the button and leaned back in his chair with his arms folded. "We didn't see anything but don't take my word for it."

"Stop!" Tillis leaned closer. "Roll it back." He stared at the timestamp in the upper right-hand corner. "Play it again. Slow down the frames."

"Whatever you say." Colangelo played the footage again.

Kate's mouth opened, but she didn't speak and only looked at her teammates. They appeared to have noticed it too.

"Son of a bitch." Tillis glanced at Kate. "You see that?"

She nodded.

"Everyone saw that," Stallard said. "How the hell did that get overlooked?"

"I—we must've assumed it was a signal interruption caused by the blast," Colangelo replied.

"For almost a minute?" Tillis asked. "Jesus. Show me the rest of it."

"We still don't see a vehicle or anyone nearby," Kate said, almost apologetically.

Tillis eyed her. "You were right, Reid. We may not see him, but he was there."

9

The detail could have been missed by anyone. It was a reasonable error in light of who they were dealing with. That was what Kate told Tillis while he looked on in disappointment.

In her former life, Kate worked in Evidence for the San Diego Police Department. Oversights were common. However, this one set back their case exponentially. Had it been discovered earlier, Tillis and his people could've canvassed the surrounding buildings; talked to people to learn if they'd noticed anyone unusual. Now, days and weeks had passed and none of those people would remember even if they had seen anyone suspicious. So while Kate had picked up on the mistake, it did nothing but confirm what Stallard already knew and that was the bomber had been on the scene because he had used a remote detonator.

Now, they had returned to Tillis's office, wiser, but no closer to identifying a suspect. Stallard eyed the remnants of the bomb materials. "Going back to what we've got here. Smokeless powder can't be made, only bought. So, I'll get my team running on purchases made at gun shops around the city."

"It can be purchased online too," Surrey added.

"Yes it can, but that would mean the bomber left a money trail," Stallard replied. "If he's smart enough to screw with a CCTV signal, clone cell phones, and God knows what else, I don't see his downfall being in the online purchase of items used to make his bombs. No. He'll use cash and we already believe he's from around the area, so that's where I'll start." He packed up his things. "At least we know what we're up against. I only hope this guy doesn't wise up and learn how to make a device that can do a lot more damage." He turned to Tillis. "Let me know if something turns up on your end. I'll do the same. Good work today, Reid. I guess there's a reason you're with Quantico."

As Stallard left, Duncan appeared hesitant to speak. She moved toward Tillis who sat at his desk. "The first two victims, the bomber took his time with. But based on the details we received about when the phones were cloned, it looks like Sienna Page's phone had only been cloned about a week prior. Why the rush?"

"He altered his pattern with her, not only in speeding up his timeframe, but she's the first female victim as well," Tillis replied.

Kate approached them. "She was some kind of social media star, right? So let's see what she was up to in the past several days."

"You think she might have come across her killer?" Tillis nodded. "I don't know his criteria for how he chooses his victims, but we have to start somewhere."

"Duncan, your buddy in Unit 2 said the phone was cloned about a week ago?" Surrey asked.

"That's right. We should start in the days before and leading up to her death," she replied.

"I've got her account pulled up," Tillis said. "Let me scroll back to around the 8th and see what we can find. She kept herself busy. Lots of information on her comings and goings."

Kate peered at the monitor. "She fits the part. Based on these posts, luxury cars, exotic locations. She seems to be everything this bomber doesn't like. But how did he find her?"

"This girl has almost one million followers. If he's one of them, how the hell would we know?" Surrey pressed on. "There has to be a way to tighten these parameters. We'll be here for days following up on every location Sienna Page posted about."

A knowing smile played on Kate's lips. "Hang on. That's not necessarily true."

Tillis shot her a glance. "I see where you're going with this. Look only at the posts here in the city. She traveled, clearly, but we agree the bomber is from the area. That should be our focus." He scanned through the posts again. "I want to stick closer to around the timeframe of her death. Okay, this dates back to the 10th. Two nights ago. Looks like she visited two local bars with a couple of friends."

"Then let's track down the friends who were with her and see if they were sober enough to remember any details from that night," Kate replied.

Surrey shoved his hands in his pockets. "We should consider splitting up on this. If everyone's on board, Tillis and I can talk to the bar owners in these posts. Take a look at their security footage, assuming this guy didn't screw with the cameras. Reid and Duncan can have a sit down with the friends and see if Sienna might've had a run in with anyone recently, especially on the night of the 10th. Between the friends and bar owners, we might be able to put two and two together. He found Sienna Page. Now we need to find him."

As it approached midday, Kate drove to the home of Gina Morenci. Based on Sienna's Instagram, she seemed to be a close friend. "It's just over the David McCullough Bridge, right?"

"Yep. Not a bad part of town, is it?" Duncan asked. "Look at the views of the river."

"Not bad. And not far from Downtown either. There could still be something to the idea he's finding his victims in the downtown area."

"I agree. We can't rule out anything yet." Duncan turned away for a moment. "Hey, about earlier at the hotel..."

Kate eyed her. "Yeah?"

"Does that happen a lot?"

She creased her brow. "What?"

"Kate, I heard you making noise in your sleep. Then you shot up out of bed and nearly scared the shit out of me. If you don't want to talk about it..."

"No. It's fine. I'm sorry I woke you up. Hazards of the job. You must get that way sometimes."

Duncan regarded her. "Not usually. Don't get me wrong, I take my work home like the rest of us, but I've never been through what you have. And you've been through it more than once. Kate, it's okay to admit that you're having a tough time getting over the Lehmann case. I think the worst thing you can do is to ignore your feelings."

Kate sighed. "I'll be fine. I just need time to get over it. Once we figure out..." she stopped cold.

"Figure out what?" Duncan continued.

"I mean, once George Lehmann is sentenced, I'll be able to move on. His trial isn't over, and I feel like it's been dragging out."

"I get that. Murder trials are never speedy. It still wouldn't be a bad idea for you to sit down and talk to someone. Don't keep it in, Kate. It'll only eat you up."

She turned down the street. "I think this is it."

Duncan eyed the address on the file and peered up again. "Yep. That red brick building right there."

Kate pulled alongside the curb. "This girl is only 23 and she lives here?"

"Social media pays well." Duncan stepped out and peered at the high-rise condo.

Kate joined her and the two walked to the entrance where a doorman waited outside. "We're here to see Gina Morenci. FBI."

"Of course." He cleared his throat as if nerves took hold. "Just let the front desk know and they'll let you onto the elevators."

The foyer revealed a grand entrance with high ceilings, black iron fixtures, and a concrete floor. The lobby desk was just ahead as Kate approached. "Afternoon. We're here to see Ms. Gina Morenci. Agents Reid and Duncan, FBI."

The man behind the desk appeared concerned as he glanced at Kate's ID. "Is there a problem?"

"Not at all. We're just here to ask her a few questions about a friend of hers."

"Yes, of course. Please follow me." He led them to the elevators and inserted a key. "Please, step in. Sorry, but guests of our residents are usually shown up by the residents themselves. And you're sure Ms. Morenci is expecting you?" He stepped inside following the agents and pressed the button

"She is," Kate replied.

"Well then, here we are. She's in unit 891 near the end of the corridor. Please let me know if you have any problems. You'll be able to come down the elevator unaccompanied."

"Thank you." Kate started into the hall and turned to Duncan. "Yeah, we're in the wrong line of work. I couldn't afford a place like this on my salary."

"Me neither. Although maybe if we were roommates." Duncan laughed.

"If only..." Kate knocked on the door and held her badge. When there was no answer, she looked at Duncan. "Again?"

"She said she'd be here."

Kate prepared to knock again when the door opened. "Oh, Ms. Gina Morenci?"

"That's me." The young woman with light brown hair that hung straight down the length of her back peered at them. "You're the FBI, right?"

"Yes, ma'am. I'm Agent Reid. This is Agent Duncan. We're here to talk to you about your friend, Sienna Page."

"Come in." She closed the door after they entered. "Do you want something to drink? I have water and Diet Coke. White Claw, too, if you're interested"

"No, thanks. None for me," Kate replied.

"I'm good. Thank you, though," Duncan added. "I'm very sorry for your loss, Ms. Morenci."

"You can call me Gina." She walked to the living room and sat down. "Have as seat. So, have you found the asshole who killed my best friend?"

"That's what we're working on," Duncan replied.

"And we're hoping you can help," Kate added. "First of all, can you just confirm for me that you and Sienna were at Alloy's Bar with another one of your friends, Sarah, on the night of June 10th?"

"That was the night before last, right?" Gina asked. "Sorry, I've lost track of time since all this."

"Yes. We do have access to Sienna's social media, and we know she posted on Instagram that you three were there," Kate said.

"Then you already know we were there," Gina replied.

"Right. Then I'd like to ask whether you recall anything

unusual from that night, or frankly, from the previous couple of days before that."

"What Agent Reid and I want to know is if Sienna had a run in with anyone recently. Either while you all were out or at another time," Duncan added. "Someone who gave her the creeps."

"I mean, I don't know. We get a lot of attention if you know what I mean."

"I can imagine," Kate replied. "But this is really important. We need you to think hard about this. Did anyone run into you guys, buy you drinks, anything like that."

"It's not weird for dudes to buy us drinks, but I do remember..." Gina turned up her gaze for a moment. "I remember this guy running into us outside Alloy's. We were getting ready to leave. It was late. I know we'd had a few, but we weren't like drunk or anything. We were outside taking pictures. That's kind of what we get paid to do."

"Sure, go on," Kate replied.

"Some guy, who I guess wasn't paying attention, he just ran right into us, Sienna specifically. Almost knocked her over."

"Did anyone get hurt?" Duncan asked.

"No. We stumbled back, but luckily we weren't drunk enough to lose our balance. And he looked like he wanted to apologize, but just kind of froze. I don't know. He was weird."

"Weird in what way?" Kate asked.

"Just the way he looked at Sienna. Like she had horns growing out of her head or something. Just weird, I don't know."

"Okay, can you tell us what this guy looked like?" Duncan pressed on. "Think about it. Please be as specific as you can."

Gina peered at them. "Do you think he was the one who blew her up? Seriously?"

"Right now, we're following every possible lead," Kate said. "Everything and everyone are important to us."

"Um, okay. So, I guess he was young. Maybe my age, or just a little younger. Um, not super tall, but not short either. Skinny. I remember that. Okay looking, not like hot or anything. I think he had light hair. Maybe blonde. I don't really remember anything else about him."

Kate jotted down her description. "Did you notice him inside the bar?"

"No, I didn't. I don't know if anyone else did. Of course, we can't ask Sienna anymore."

"No, we can't," Kate replied. "Is there anything else you can remember? Had Sienna mentioned anything after that night about that guy or anyone else?"

"What do you mean?" Gina asked.

"Anyone who she thought was creeping her out lately. Or anyone she might have met and liked," Kate added.

"No. She had just broken up with someone. Sienna wasn't looking for any new relationships. She just wanted to focus on her work."

"Sure. I understand that." Kate looked at Duncan. "Can you think of anything else?"

"No." Duncan pulled out her card and handed it to Gina. "If you do remember something, would you mind reaching out? Even if you don't think it's important. Just call."

"I will. Thank you, Agent Duncan. Agent Reid." She stood to show them out. "By the way, I think it's pretty cool that you're both women. Like female FBI agents. That's totally badass." She reached for her phone. "Could I take a selfie with you and put it on Insta?"

They traded glances before Kate spoke. "Actually, we kind of have to keep a low profile. I'm sure you understand with the job and all."

"Oh yeah, no, I totally get it." Gina opened the door. "Thank you for what you're doing." Her eyes welled. "I miss Sienna so much. She was my best friend and she'd be glad to know people are out there looking for the person who did this."

Duncan stepped out and Kate followed.

"Oh, you know what?" Gina leaned against the door. "There was something. It didn't occur to me until just now."

"What's that?" Kate asked.

"I remember the other day. I think it must've been earlier this past week. Sienna said she thought someone had been following her. It was kind of in passing, like no big deal, so I guess I hadn't thought about that until you said something."

"Following her on social media?" Duncan asked.

"No, like IRL. I mean, in real life. She thought it might have been an Insta follower who found out where she lived or something. Said she saw this same car for like a couple of days but then —nothing."

Kate's pulse quickened. "Did she describe the car to you?"

"White. Just said a white car. That's all," Gina replied.

"Thank you, Gina. That helps us a lot. You have our contact information. Let us know if you remember anything else," Kate said. "Take care. Goodbye."

"Bye." Gina closed the door.

Duncan eyed her. "I see that look in your eye, Reid. Calm down. We don't know anything yet. Could be nothing."

"It isn't nothing," Kate replied as she hurried down the hall. "You know it isn't nothing."

"Yeah." Duncan smiled. "I do."

10

In the dining hall of the care home, Melanie sat at the linen-covered table across from her brother. The state-run facility offered the bare-minimum, but the dining tables always had fresh linen cloths. Danny watched her pick at her breakfast. Misery masked her face. He closed his eyes and took in a long deep breath. "I'm trying to get you out of here, Mel. You have to believe me."

"It's been days already. They said I won't get to go back home, and I'll have to stay here forever." She peered at him. "What did I do, Danny? Please tell me what I did."

He reached for her hand. "Nothing. You didn't do anything wrong. It's these government assholes. But I promise you, I filled out the paperwork and I'm just waiting for them to approve my guardianship. It shouldn't be much longer until I can get you out of here. Okay?"

"I miss watching movies together," she added. "They have movies here, but I have to go into the common room and watch them with a bunch of strangers. I don't know these people, Danny. I don't want to know them. I just want to go home."

He grew enraged at her despair, though he was helpless to do anything more than what he had done. "I'll keep coming to see you every day until I get this fixed, okay? Every. Day. But I need you to keep taking care of yourself in the meantime. You have to eat. You have to do what they say." He peered at the nurses and workers milling around. "Listen, I have to go and turn in the paperwork." He pushed up from the chair and walked around the table, kissing Melanie on top of her head. "I promise I'll fix this, Mel. I love you." His eyes stung with tears as he slung his backpack over his shoulder and walked away.

Danny hated leaving her there and the guilt bore down on him. He stepped into his car and keyed the ignition.

Within minutes, he was on his way to the state office to file the paperwork. It was all bullshit. He was saving the taxpayers' money by taking care of Mel, the only person he cared about. And the state pissed on him for it. Claiming she wasn't being cared for properly was bullshit too. One fall. One damn fall and they said he was negligent. He took better care of Mel than he did himself. None of that mattered to the bureaucratic assholes.

He arrived at the office and walked inside to a waiting area full of people. It was almost 10am and the good news was that he would probably get seen before they closed. Whether his boss would understand why he had to take off another day remained to be seen. Danny needed this job. No way would the state let him bring home Mel without a steady job. With the ticket in hand, Danny sat down and waited.

～

AGENT TILLIS STEPPED out of his car and started toward the row of bars in the trendy night spot. Surrey opened his passenger door and joined him. He was still getting used to his role on this team, considering it had changed since he was brought on. Nevertheless, his relinquishing of the role he'd been hired for to Kate Reid had been the right move. She was the better person for the job. It would've only been a matter of time before the rest of the team saw that, assuming they hadn't already.

It felt different here from his field office in Denver. The work was different, and the way investigations were conducted was different too. Here, they had to coordinate with the local offices. Investigations were never theirs to run with alone. It was a change that took some getting used to. Playing second fiddle was never Surrey's strong point. However, the feather in his cap for the new job title as BAU agent would propel him through the ranks if that was what he wanted. It was a desire he wasn't sure of just yet. Time would tell.

"The manager agreed to open earlier to talk to us." Tillis opened the door to the empty bar with few windows that let in scant sunshine on this still gray morning. Hi-top tables scattered throughout along with a bar that displayed microbrew taps. Bottles lined the wall from house liquors to top-shelf booze.

"Good morning, I'm Agent Tillis." He held out his badge. "You must be Simon."

"That's me." Simon offered a handshake before turning to Surrey. "You're also FBI?"

"I am. Agent Surrey. Nice to meet you."

"Back at you." He eyed them. "What can I do for you both this morning? I hear this has something to do with a suspect you're after."

"That's right," Tillis replied. "We'd like to take a look at your security footage from two nights ago. A woman was here who was murdered, and we need to know if anyone was harassing her or stalking her."

"Holy shit. Well, yeah, of course I can help. Come on back and I'll show you what I have." Simon led the way to a storage room at the back where kegs and boxes on pallets lined the walls. "It's not real sophisticated, but it does the trick." He sat down at a desk with a laptop. "This is hardwired to our cameras. The footage is dumped every 14 days, so it's a good thing you're here now. I sure would hate to have had this purged and then you show up."

"Does any of your surveillance cover the outside of the bar?" Surrey asked.

"Sure does. The frontage and a little bit of the street," he replied.

"We'll want to see that too," Surrey added.

"You got it." Simon keyed in the commands and retrieved the data. "Here you go."

Tillis leaned closer with his hands pressed against the folding table. "This is from the other night?"

"Yes, sir," Simon replied. "Just like you asked. "It was a week-night. Ladies' night, actually."

Surrey stood behind him and with arms folded, he gazed at the screen. "That's her, right there."

"Yep. I see her," Tillis replied.

"Who?" Simon asked.

"The woman who was murdered. She's with a couple of friends," Tillis added.

"Oh, her? Her and her friends come in a lot. Holy shit, I can't believe she's dead."

Tillis glanced at Surrey. "Hey, can you reach out to Reid and Duncan and see if they've talked to the friends yet?"

"On it." Surrey picked up his phone and made the call. "Reid, it's Surrey. Have you and Duncan interviewed the friends yet?"

"We're on our way to see Sarah. We did get a description from Gina of a man who ran into the girls outside Alloy's bar. Could be something to it."

"Then you did good. We're at Alloy's now," Surrey replied. "What's he look like? We're viewing the interior surveillance footage now."

"Light hair. Blonde, she thought. Thin. Average height."

"Shit. That describes half the guys in the bar," Surrey replied.

"It's the best we could get. Do they have exterior footage? You might have luck seeing him outside. Apparently, he ran into them, literally. My guess was he did it to gain access to her phone."

"Sounds about right. We'll keep looking and let you know if we get a hit," Surrey added.

"Okay. We're arriving at the other friend's house now. I'll keep you posted, but Surrey?"

"Yeah?" he replied.

"Sienna was being followed by a white car a few days before she was killed. Driver could be the same guy she saw at the bar. Blonde hair, skinny build," Kate began. "If you see anyone who matches that, we stand a good chance he's our bomber."

"Fingers crossed. Talk soon." Surrey ended the call. "Blonde or light hair. Skinny build. Could be driving a white car."

"How are we going to see what he drives?" Tillis asked.

"I'm not sure, but Reid says this blonde guy ran into Sienna Page and her friends outside. If it's our guy, we might see him reaching for her phone. That could have been how he got to her."

"Excuse me, but what about this guy?" Simon pointed to the screen. "He's got light hair and looks kind of skinny."

Tillis returned his gaze to the monitor. "Do you recognize him? Is he a regular?"

Simon shook his head. "Not that I'm aware of. But I don't know, just based on what you guys just said, he looks suspicious to me."

"Freeze that video, would you?" Surrey asked. "Then pull up your exterior footage. I want to see if this was the same guy who ran into our victim."

"Whatever you need." Simon went to work retrieving the footage in question. "Like I said, it's just the outside frontage and a little bit of the street. But I know my neighbors on both sides also use CCTV. You might have some luck there too."

"That guy right there." Surrey pointed to the screen. "He's just standing there."

"He's not the same one from inside," Tillis replied.

"No, but he's lurking. Just hang on. We might see him make a move. There's the victim and her friends," Surrey continued. "Come on. Come on, asshole. Show yourself." His pulse quickened. "That's it! That's him. He nearly mowed them down before he grabbed her. Right there. You see how he's taking her by the arm and helping her up? I can't see it clearly, but he could be doing something with the phones. I don't know enough about it, but he matches the friend's description."

Tillis narrowed his brow as he gazed at the screen. "We can't jump the gun yet. If we can find this guy anywhere around the other crime scenes, we might have a break here."

WHY HAD it seemed that government workers were never happy in their jobs? Was it that they dealt with the public who generally despised visiting government offices? Probably. Was it that the public always saw them as lazy and unwilling to put in any effort? Yeah. So, when Adelaide Johnson called the next number, she expected the customer to already be angry at having waited for God knew how long. "Number 219D, Number 219D," she called out.

Danny King confirmed that was his number and approached her. "Here you go."

Adelaide viewed the ticket. "Take a seat, sir. How may I help you?"

Danny sat down. "I'm here to file a petition for adult guardianship of my sister, Melanie King."

She held out her hand in a silent request for his paperwork. "Thank you." Adelaide flipped through the pages, scanning each one to ensure they'd been filled out properly. "Your paystubs?"

"Oh, right." Danny handed over his proof of employment. "I've worked for them for two years."

She grunted and continued reviewing the paperwork. "Mr. King, it appears that you have everything filled out correctly."

A smile appeared on his lips as he watched her key in something on her computer. "Great."

"However, based on what I'm seeing in the system, it appears a court date won't be available for 12 weeks." She looked at him and watched his face turn sour.

"12 weeks. I'm supposed to let my sister rot in some shitty state facility for 12 weeks because you don't have a court date sooner than that."

"I'm very sorry, Mr. King. Family courts are always backed up. But you should know this looks to be a fairly cut and dry case. I don't foresee any issues," she added.

"You don't see any issues?" Danny's face reddened. "Well, I do. No way in hell I'm letting them keep my sister there for 3 months. Are you shitting me right now?"

"Mr. King, please don't use that kind of language." This was what Adelaide had come to expect. It was hardly her fault the courts were backlogged, but people didn't care. She was the punching bag and was about to get walloped.

Danny stood up hard, knocking over his chair. "You need to expedite this shit. No way am I waiting that long. I'll pay whatever. Just do it."

"I'm sorry, that's not an option. I wish I could do more for you..."

"No you don't. You don't give a shit." Danny's voice raised as people set their eyes on him. "None of you give a shit."

"Sir, I'm going to have to call security." Adelaide picked up the phone.

"Don't bother." He stormed toward the exit but stopped and turned back. "This is your fault. Bitch." He shoved open the doors and marched outside. "This isn't happening. No way. I won't let you sit there for three months. Not a chance in hell."

KATE SLIPPED BEHIND the wheel and pressed the ignition. "They both have the same story. That's a good sign."

Duncan buckled her seatbelt. "It's still a long way from bumping into someone to blowing up their car and killing them."

"I know, but it's a starting point. Surrey said they were heading back to the field office with a copy of the surveillance footage. We have a face, now we need to find a name."

"All we can do is push it through the facial recognition program and hope the guy's in the system somewhere," Duncan replied.

Kate continued toward Downtown Pittsburgh where they would meet with the rest of the team. "Have you talked to Fisher today?"

"Talked to him last night. We should probably update him now that we have a possible lead on the unsub."

"Do you think Surrey should run with that?" Kate asked.

"Why? You're the lead profiler, Kate. And you're senior to him."

"You're senior to me," she added. "I guess I'm still trying to figure out the chain of command here."

"We all work for Cam. If you want to update him, I have no problem with that. I doubt Surrey will either. Besides, he's starting to grow on me."

"Me too. The other day he actually asked my advice on something personal. Could've knocked me over with a feather I was so surprised," Kate said.

"He's a tough nut to crack, but after the way he stepped aside, insisting that the job should've been yours. Well, he earned my respect," Duncan added.

"He also thought I should've been taken off the Lehmann case after being held hostage." Kate glanced at her, waiting for a reply that never came. "Eva? Did you agree with him?"

"It was months ago, Kate. We were right in the thick of it and you were almost killed. While I didn't agree with his approach, it was probably the right call."

"Fisher didn't think so," Kate replied.

"I know. And I don't always agree with him either. Look, it's over now and you're in the role that should've been yours a long time ago. But I still think it would be worth your time to get it all off your chest. I didn't know you when the Hendrickson thing went down, but from what Scarborough said in the past, after he came over to Unit 4, it sounded pretty damn horrifying. Sometimes I look at you and I wonder how you keep your shit together at all."

"I push it down so deep; it can never see the light of day

again." Kate chuckled and noticed the look on Duncan's face. "Yeah, I know. I know you're right. If I feel as though my head isn't in the game, that I can't back up my team, I'll do something about it. I won't risk anyone's safety because of my own stubbornness."

The car was silent for a moment longer as Kate spotted the field office in the distance. "By the way, how are things with Cam? Did you two cut the cord?"

Eva eyed her.

"Didn't think so. Hey, it doesn't bother me. I won't say a damn word. Just watch your back."

"What do you mean?" Duncan asked.

Kate pulled into the parking lot and cut the engine. "I mean, it'll be you who suffers, not Cam, if things go south. He's the senior unit agent now. And Eva, you're the toughest agent I've had the pleasure to work with, I know you won't let your personal life get in the way. It's just, well, consider Scarborough and me a cautionary tale."

Duncan opened her car door. "I know we have some decisions to make. I'm just not sure I'm ready to make them."

They headed toward the entrance and Duncan placed a hand on Kate's back. "I'm glad I have you as a partner, Reid."

"Same goes for me." Kate pushed through the entrance and started toward Tillis's office when they noticed Surrey in the hall. "Any luck with facial recognition?"

"Good timing. Follow me. Tillis just teed it up for us." He turned on his heel and started toward the office again. "Been a busy morning for everyone. I think it was worth the legwork." Surrey walked into the office. "Look who I found."

"Perfect," Tillis replied. "I have forensics running facial recognition now. That'll take some time, but if you want to take a look at the security footage, you can see who it is we're aiming our sights on."

Tillis played the video. "We'll cross-reference this video with the footage from the crime scenes and look for a match. Fingers crossed, he'll be in the system."

Kate peered at the video. "That is the man Gina described." She looked at Duncan. "What do you think?"

"Oh, it's him. Whether he's our bomber, I have no idea."

11

During Nick Scarborough's tenure at the Bureau, his caseload ran the gamut. He considered himself a seasoned agent and had the confidence to accept the position inside BAU-2 when Unit Chief Cole suggested it. However, it was clear not all on his team had that same confidence. He'd heard the rumors. He was one of Cole's favorites. He'd run high-profile cases that brought positive media attention to the Bureau and that was why he had been chosen. What they hadn't known was that this was Nick's last-ditch effort at redemption. Cole knew it. Everyone inside Unit 4 knew it, even his wife. So when he assessed the latest case file with his new team, not only was Nick's job on the line, but so was his legacy.

His team was asked to assist the New York Field Office in their investigation after a widespread server outage left a major bank exposed to theft. The last time Nick had worked with that field office was when they tracked down a celebrity killer who liked to travel. That was long before his move to Unit 2, and before Noah

Quinn was placed there. The good news was that Quinn wasn't running this investigation.

"Organized crime is our primary target." Nick eyed his team as they reviewed the case file. "The bank is already working to close the security flaw and track down the origins of the hack. We'll be working alongside Interpol to look at the usual suspects. Ukraine, Russia, possibly Chinese syndicates. As we know, there's been a major shift in targets from individuals to large corporations and government infrastructure. Reach out to your people. Find someone who's willing to talk. Let's also give the field office everything we have on rising hacker groups looking to stand out." Nick's phone buzzed and he quickly peered at the message. "That's all for now. Thanks."

He gathered his files and looked again at the message. This was what he'd been waiting for. An old friend pulled strings to get Nick an appointment with the undersecretary at the Director of National Intelligence office. The NSA fell under their charge and it was someone inside that organization who helped Theo Bishop flee to Mexico.

Nick started toward his office with his phone at his ear. "Walsh, it's me. I just got the okay to meet with him." He nodded. "This afternoon. He's giving me 15 minutes. I'm heading out now and I'll let you know how it goes. If we can find out who scrubbed those logs..." He smiled. "That's right. We'll find the agent who told him to do it." He paused a moment. "Sounds good. I'll be in touch the moment I leave his office." Nick ended the call.

A quick drive into D.C. to the DNI office and then he had 15 minutes to plead his case. The plan had been for Nick to stay above the fray in order to keep his hands clean. But he was never good at delegation, nor was Levi Walsh. As both ventured deeper into the rabbit hole, there was no telling how much farther they would have to go to hit bottom.

Nick pulled his Lexus SUV into the parking garage at the DNI offices and headed toward the building. He caught the elevator up to see the man who was twice removed from the top. It was the equivalent of going to see Unit Chief Cole's boss's boss. Nick had done plenty of elbow-rubbing during his tenure but never with high-ranking officials in a presidential administration.

"Afternoon." Nick arrived at the security desk. "I have an appointment with Undersecretary Grisham. Senior Unit Agent Nicolas Scarborough, BAU Quantico."

The security officer viewed his credentials. "Put everything in the bin and walk through the metal detector, please."

Nick walked through and waited on the other side.

"Thank you, Agent Scarborough. The admin desk is straight ahead."

Nick returned a nod and headed to the desk. "Agent Scarborough here to see Undersecretary Grisham."

The man peered at a monitor. "I see your name here. I'll have someone take you up." He waved over another security officer. "Agent Scarborough has an appointment with the undersecretary."

"I'll take him up." He turned to Nick. "Right this way, sir."

Nick followed as he felt the red tape begin to wrap around him until they arrived at the third-floor office.

With a knock, the officer opened the door. "Mr. Undersecretary, FBI Agent Scarborough is here to see you."

"Show him in. Thank you." Grisham stood and adjusted his suit jacket. "Agent Scarborough. Thanks for coming over."

"Thank you, sir."

A tall, reedy man, Grisham looked younger than Nick would've expected for someone who held such a senior position. "Have a seat, Agent Scarborough. You're here regarding a situation at the NSA."

"Yes, sir. As I mentioned to one of your staff, this is regarding an old investigation that we're trying to close out."

"Of course. Unit Chief Cole sent you, is that right?"

This was the sticky part. Cole hadn't sent him. No one had. However, if this got out and Cole learned just exactly how Nick got his intel, he might not see the well-placed reasoning behind the decision. It would be made worse were Nick to make no progress on this and for Grisham to call Cole himself. The ice had thinned considerably, and Nick had to decide just how far to walk out on it. "He's aware of what I'm working on and I have his blessing." The lie hung in the air while Grisham appeared to consider the request.

"As the senior unit agent at BAU-2, I know you have the highest level of security clearance. However, the people under your charge..."

"I'll be the only one viewing the records, sir," Nick cut in.

Grisham pulled up closer to his desk and his face turned serious. "I do need you to understand one very important item, Agent Scarborough. What I'm doing here, I'm doing as a favor to someone who I've been looking to return said favor for a while. Frankly, I couldn't care less who at the Bureau you're after. And don't insult me by insisting I've misread your intent. If anyone at the NSA or the DNI is exposed for helping you or becomes involved in any way, understand that you will be the one who I point the finger at. Am I making myself clear?"

"Crystal, sir."

Grisham nodded. "Then I'll grant your request. And I expect you and I will have no further dealings."

"None at all, sir," Nick replied.

"Then I'll make the call and get you the files you need delivered via secure server."

"Thank you, sir. I appreciate your cooperation." Nick stood. "When might I expect the files?"

"Within the hour, Agent Scarborough. Is that soon enough?"

"It is, sir. Thank you."

THIS WASN'T how a 22-year-old was supposed to live his life. Scraping by while the system worked for everyone else. But not him. Not Danny King. He tried to level the playing field. Going after those who the system paid off in spades. And not one of them appreciated what they had. Not one of them did anything to help people like him.

Now, as he sat in front of the government building, reeling from the news that he would have to wait 12 weeks for a court date, he knew an example must be made. What he was doing wasn't working. It was like using a scalpel when he needed a hunting knife. But caution was in order because if he changed up his method dramatically, he might slip up and get caught. And then he would never get Mel back. She would live out her days in some shitty government-run home. But maybe he could make a bigger splash without the added risks. Go after higher-value targets. Still accomplishing his objective but making them all stand up and take notice.

Danny had seen the news stories. He'd done exactly the right things. Never taking too many risks but reaping the rewards. Hell, they even called him Robinhood. "Take from the rich and give to the poor." He laughed.

That wasn't exactly what was happening but what did Danny care? The public loved what he was doing, even if they wouldn't admit it. They hated the rich, the arrogant, the ones who looked down their noses at the rest of them just as much as he did.

He keyed the ignition of his car and pulled away from the building. It was time to up his game. Make his case so the people could see the targets for who they were. Just more in a long line of takers.

A small gun shop was located several miles away on the other side of town. If he was going to up his game, then he needed more supplies. He parked his car and pulled on his baseball hat and sunglasses because gun shops had cameras, and lots of them.

Danny opened the door and the little bell on top jingled as he walked inside. A couple of customers shuffled around looking at the sporting guns on display. The handguns were near the cashier inside a locked glass case. Each one had its own security tag.

"Afternoon," the cashier said. "Can I help you find something?"

Danny pushed his hands into his jeans' pockets and let his gaze roam around the store, finally pulling off his sunglasses, but keeping his head low. "You have any smokeless powder in stock?"

"Of course I do. Whatcha looking for? I got three different kinds. All available in multiple canister sizes. They're right over here if you want to follow me."

Danny had only purchased this once before since the job hadn't required much, and that had been based on the recommendation from like-minded people. "Yeah, sure."

"So, you looking for shotgun use or handgun?" The man said as he walked toward the aisle.

Danny knew precious little about the subject, so he was going to have to answer on the fly and not sound like an idiot, or a person with ulterior motives. "Uh, handgun, actually."

"Great. Right here." He picked up a canister. "This is the best one for handguns, in my humble opinion. It'll maximize velocities. Great for 9 mil, 38 super and 40 S&W's pistol loads."

He was talking over Danny's head, and this needed to come to a conclusion, so he went with it. "That should do the job. I'll take that one."

"You want the small canister or the larger one?" he asked.

"I'll take the large one. Should get me by." Danny smiled as if he knew what the hell he was talking about.

"Oh, it'll get you by just fine." The man turned on his heel and returned to the cashier station. "I'll just ring that up for you, sir." He scanned in the cannister. "How long have you been reloading?"

"Sorry?" Danny replied.

"Your cartridges. You're buying the powder to load your own cartridges, right?"

"Right. Not long, actually. I'm just starting to see the benefit of it, and it's been something that's interested me for a while."

"Uh-huh."

Danny noticed the man's eyes change. Maybe he was being paranoid, but he was sure the look was now one of suspicion and not one of a gun enthusiast, much as he must've been. "My dad was big on all this and I wanted to follow in his footsteps. He died when I was a teenager."

"Oh, I am sorry to hear that. I'm sure he'd be happy to know you've taken up one of his hobbies. That'll be $126.97, then. Debit or credit?"

"Cash if that's okay." There was the look again. "A buddy of mine just paid me back for something and I figured there was no point in depositing this into the bank. I mean, people still use cash, or so I hear."

"Cash is always accepted here," the man replied.

"Great." Danny handed over the money. "Thank you for your help."

"No problem. I'll just need you to sign the bill of sale and I need to see your driver's license. Rules and all that."

"Oh, sure." Danny's nerves shot on end. He reached into his back pocket and retrieved his license. "Here you go."

The man eyed it. "Thank you. And just the signature please."

"Sure thing." Danny took the pen while his hand hovered over the receipt.

"Everything all right?"

"Yeah, sorry. Just reading the charge." Danny scribbled a signature and handed back the receipt.

"Great. You be safe now. Takes a real steady hand, what you're doing."

"I hear you." Danny walked out and felt the man's stare on the back of his head. He shoved the copy of the receipt in his pocket and tugged down on his hat as he started toward the car. His trembling hand fumbled with the key and it took a moment before it slipped into the lock. When he finally opened the door, Danny slipped behind the wheel and threw his hat onto the passenger seat. "Jesus Christ."

The other components had been easily procured, but it was the powder that was the main charge and the only element that was more easily traced. While he had to show an ID at the last store he visited, no signature had been required. So either the other place didn't care, or this guy cared too much.

Danny was back on the road to his side of town. The cannister he'd purchased wouldn't run out anytime soon so he could avoid another risk like that. And it was clear the cashier hadn't bothered to view his signature because he would've seen that it was illegible and incomplete. Nevertheless, it was the closest he'd been to exposing himself and it scared the hell out of him. Danny was an expert at computers, cyber tech, and smart phones. But when it came to this, he knew just enough to get him by. And he knew that weaknesses were how people got caught.

~

TILLIS RETURNED to his office where Stallard and the BAU team waited. His expression told them everything they needed to know.

Stallard cast down his gaze. "No hits?"

"No. The kid's not in the database. Not that I'm surprised, but I guess I had my fingers crossed that we'd end this thing before he had a chance to kill someone else."

"What about cross-checking his identity with bystanders around the crime scenes?" Kate appeared to hold out hope.

"Still working on it. That's going to take some time."

Surrey shrugged as if looking on the bright side. "Then we still have something to go on."

"You're assuming the blonde kid is our bomber," Stallard continued. "I'm not convinced of that and we have zero evidence to suggest it. Is it a coincidence he ran into one of the victims? Sure. But we all know that's not enough."

"I understand where you're coming from, Agent Stallard," Kate began. "But that timing is critical. Two days before Sienna Page's death and she's practically knocked over by a kid who fits the profile."

"How exactly does he fit your profile, Agent Reid?" Stallard pressed on. "Young, white male. That's all you have. And that's not nearly enough to convict that kid right there on the screen. Look, I'm just playing devil's advocate here. I want this son of a bitch as much as the rest of you. But damn if we don't need more than what we have."

"What about a search for the white car?" Kate asked.

"We're already on that too. Every damn frame is being scrutinized right now. The blonde kid, a white car. We won't overlook anything again." Tillis set his sights on Stallard. "It would be helpful for ATF to make some headway on their end."

"We're making some headway with the ammo shops. We just got a warrant to collect the data on people who purchased smokeless powder in the city."

"And if the buyer used cash?" Duncan asked.

"Won't change anything for us. These gun stores protect themselves. Cameras everywhere. Bills of sale. They have to track every purchase for this very reason. My guys will look at the corresponding video from each purchase, cash or credit, and see if any match the man on that video, or if we find someone else who we can track back to a white car. There are ways to find this person. It'll just take time, patience, and cooperation. I get that we all want the same thing." Stallard cast around his gaze. "And some of us are experts in getting into the minds of these folks while the rest of us do what we can to gather evidence. It's time we all come together to find this person before he takes things to a level we don't want to see."

The link to the intel arrived on Nick's computer while his team lead sat across from him. He glanced at Moskowitz. "Just keep me in the loop. I have a call with the New York ASAC this afternoon. Let's get as much as we can over to them beforehand."

Moskowitz nodded. "You got it, boss. If there's nothing else?"

"No. We're good." Nick waited for him to leave and opened the email that contained an encrypted key to log into the server. He ran the encryption through the reader and typed in the results. The verification process took a few more moments and then what appeared on his screen was what Nick needed to see. He pulled in closer to the monitor and narrowed his gaze. The log listed each entry from every event on the southern border that night. Nick was only interested in one. The entry that showed Theo Bishop's passport was checked and then removed only to be added back in later when it was too late for them to capture him before he crossed.

"This is the one." Nick re-read the entry multiple times, checking it against his notes, making sure the passport number matched. "Son of a bitch. This is it." With his index finger, Nick traced the line across the screen to the authorization name. "G. Coletta. Who the hell is G. Coletta?" An ID number was in the next column over and Nick jotted it down. He took a picture of the records with his phone, knowing he wasn't allowed to save the information or record it anywhere, meaning he'd just broken the law. With his phone in his hand, he made the call. "Walsh, it's me. I have a name."

12

_____

F resh out of new leads, the BAU team resigned to head
back to their hotel for the night. Tillis insisted his people
would continue on the hunt for a white car or the blonde-
haired kid at the crime scenes. It was hardly a secret he thought
Quantico's contribution to date was minimal, at best. This was
Kate's first lead investigation, and it currently rested on stagnant
ground. They had banked on the idea this blonde kid was their
guy despite a lack of proof. Assumptions were all well and good
until somebody died because Kate got it wrong.

The hotel was about a mile from the Pittsburgh Field Office.
The team walked inside the humble three-star accommodation
when Surrey noticed the restaurant near the lobby. "I could use a
bite to eat. Anyone else?"

"Sure. Why not?" Duncan replied. "Kate?"

"Probably should eat."

They slipped into a booth and a waiter took their order,
quickly returning with drinks. "Your food will be up shortly."

Kate waited until he was out of earshot. "Is it me, or does anyone else feel like we're just glorified field agents?"

Surrey tossed back a swig of beer as he sat opposite the women. "You have something against field agents?"

"Not at all. But Tillis doesn't need more of them. He needs experts. That's supposed to be us, and we aren't living up to our end of the bargain," she replied. "I should say, I haven't lived up to that. He was right about my profile. It was generic and offered little more than what he already knew."

"We aren't the cavalry, Kate." Duncan glanced at her. "We're all busting our backsides to do what we can. You know it's never that easy. If it was..."

"Everyone would be doing it." Surrey raised his glass with a smile. "Tillis doesn't think too highly of us. I think we can all agree we weren't his first choice. But we just have to keep doing what we came here to do."

"Fair enough." Kate paused while the waiter set down their plates. "Thank you." A moment later, she continued. "What are we missing, then? What about this guy makes him want to blow up people he thinks are either rich, or privileged in some way, to the disadvantage of others?"

"He's misguided. Young. Angry," Duncan began. "His first victim, Rob Delaney, wasn't wealthy."

Surrey raised his index finger. "Ah, but he appeared to be. What do they call those people? $30,000 millionaires? The ones who don't make a lot of money but make it look like they do by leasing fancy cars and renting apartments in nice areas. Meanwhile, they're in debt up to their eyeballs."

"I'm not sure that's what Delaney was about," Kate added. "But it's all about perception, isn't it? Perception is what drew the bomber to him."

"How is he finding them, though?" Duncan pressed on. "Is he following them on social media, or does he find them at random on the streets? They appear to fit his perceived profile, so he hacks into their lives and discovers he doesn't like what he sees."

"That's what we have to find out." Surrey finished his glass of beer. "None of the victims knew each other. They lived in different parts of town. Two were more outspoken on social media. Delaney was at odds with that impression, in my opinion. But the unsub still found something about him he didn't like."

Kate considered their points as she peered through the window into the hotel's parking lot. "What is driving his selections?" she said, almost in a whisper. "There has to be some commonality we aren't seeing."

"Why? Why can't it be random?" Surrey asked. "Crimes of opportunity. Nothing new there."

Kate turned her gaze to him. "He didn't like his victims for a reason. And right now, we think that reason could be socioeconomic."

"Sure, but what else? Dig deeper," Surrey replied.

Duncan looked on as the two seemed to feed off each other, prompting one another to get to the root cause of the killer's motivation.

"What if they're coming to him?" Kate asked.

Surrey returned an inquisitive gaze. "How so?"

"He earns a living somehow. What does he do for work? Does he come into contact with customers or clients?" she pressed on.

"You did initially think that he might work for a cell phone provider. With his knowledge of cyber tech, let's assume he's some kind of tech support guy." Surrey cast down his gaze, appearing to ponder his assumption. "Smartphone support? It would explain his knowledge of cloning."

Kate nodded. "That's possible. Apple store employee?"

"We can verify that," Duncan cut in. "We know what he looks like."

Surrey turned to Duncan. "If he's our guy. Again, we have no actual proof. But like you said, we can easily determine if the man in the security footage works at an Apple store in the city. It would explain how he came across people he perceived to be well-off."

"We're on the right track. We start checking computer shops, phone stores. Until we can get a hit on surveillance, it's our next best shot." Kate's attention was drawn to the waiter who approached.

"Is there anything else I can get you folks? We're about to close the kitchen."

Duncan peered at him. "I think we're ready for the check. Thanks." She returned her attention to Surrey and cast her gaze between her colleagues. "I'm not sure I've seen that before."

"Seen what?" Kate asked.

"The dynamic between you two. Don't you see it? You're like two halves of one mind."

Kate considered the comment and Duncan wasn't wrong. She'd felt it before during her time with Surrey working the Mercy Killer investigation. She recalled the moment clearly as they'd been in his hotel room, sitting at the tiny table, reviewing the case files. They bounced ideas off one another, traded probing questions. Kate had shared that sense of connection to Nick, but this was different.

Surrey smiled awkwardly as he looked at Kate. "Great minds think alike."

They returned to the elevator and as the doors parted on their floor, Duncan stepped into the hall. "Goodnight, Surrey."

"Night. Night, Reid." He started ahead in the opposite direction toward his room.

As Kate and Duncan reached their room, Kate touched her shoulder. "What's going on?"

Duncan opened the door and stepped inside. "What do you mean?"

"You know what I mean. The way you looked at me back there. At the table. Do you think there's something going on between Surrey and me?"

"No, of course not." She slipped off her shoes and pulled the elastic band from her thick caramel hair before dropping onto the bed near the window. "It was just weird the way you two were back there. You were never that way with Quinn."

"Gee, I wonder why?" Kate took off her shoes and sat down on the other bed. "Quinn tried to use me."

"I know. But what you and Surrey have is incredible. I get that it's not physical or emotional. I'm not trying to say that at all. What I am saying is that you two together? Call me crazy, but he brings out a side of you I think you've been keeping to yourself."

In the dark living room as midnight approached, Danny sat on his sofa with his laptop resting on his knees. The light of the screen turned his face a sickly blue. He punched at the keys and waited for a reply.

"Kingmaker, you want a deal? I told you what I need. Get that and we'll talk."

The tradeoffs he'd already made had gotten him this far. If Danny wanted to continue his crusade, he was going to have to pay up. *"I'll send it tomorrow."* He pressed "enter."

All kinds of commodities were bought and sold on the dark web. Danny was one of many who traded. People believed it was a dangerous place. They were right. It was an entire community of soulless criminals and when he'd first ventured into this murky world, he had been surprised by it. Not anymore. He'd become one of them. Groups existed inside that world in numbers that could bring about revolutions and plunge the world into chaos with a single command. Danny's part was insignificant by comparison. Nonetheless, he still had a part to play. And until he could bring home Mel, he wasn't finished.

Danny eyed the phone on the coffee table. It was a copy of the phone that had belonged to his new friend, Jeff. He had learned a few things about Jeff. Like the fact that he and a woman named Laura were sexting each other. He typed his reply to a message that arrived earlier. *"I'll just bend you over my desk. You'd like that, wouldn't you?"* Danny smiled but it quickly faded. "Whore."

He'd also learned that Jeff was a lawyer. Many of the messages were from what looked to be clients. Danny scrolled through the messages and opened another one. "Golfing? You like to golf, do you Jeff?" His tone was laced with sarcasm. When he prepared the reply, Danny laughed. *"Go fuck yourself, Dave."* He hit send. "That'll cost you, won't it, Jeff?"

While Jeff kept mostly to himself and didn't seem to post a lot about his life on social media, it became clear that he was nothing more than an ambulance chaser. And the man couldn't put down his phone long enough to have a decent conversation with another human being. So Jeff was rich. Strike one. And he was a douchbag. Strike two.

Danny walked to the front door and swiped his keys from the bowl on the table. Outside, the air was muggy even as darkness blanketed this part of the earth. It was no surprise to learn that Jeff lived in one of the Victorian-style mansions in Shadyside. In the city's East End, the wealthy neighborhood was a place Danny would never experience first-hand.

On arrival, he pulled to a stop along the curb beneath the large canopies of the tree-lined street. The compact community left no room for luxuries such as garages, so cars were parked along the roadway.

Danny was certain cameras would be mounted to every home in this neighborhood, so he parked several houses down and would walk under the cover of the trees. Dressed in a black hoodie and black pants, Danny was nothing more than a shadow.

Propped up against the headboard on the firm hotel bed with his legs outstretched, Surrey pressed the TV remote to change the channels. In socked feet, he rubbed them together like a cricket while his eyes stared at the screen. None of what passed before his gaze registered. Instead, he conjured scenarios as to how the bomber planted the devices and trailed his victims until just the right moment. A meticulous plan predicated on assumptions of security cameras, crowds of people, and blast radius. The more he considered it, the more he thought these were not crimes of opportunity. Far too much planning had taken place. The killer was careful to the point of obsession. Careful to avoid detection at all costs. Careful to avoid collateral damage. Kate had it right. His victims must've come to him in some manner. The killer didn't seek them out. And when they didn't meet his standards, to whatever degree that was, he placed them on his list of people who were against all that he stood for. The killer had been wronged on some level and sought revenge for it.

Surrey peered at the time, knowing he should close his eyes. And now he realized that Duncan had been right about Reid and him. The move to BAU-4 from Denver had been a risk. And he'd relinquished a truly coveted position for the good of the team, for the good of Reid. She was better than he in many ways, but they complimented each other. He felt it before, back when he shadowed her on an investigation.

His eyelids grew heavy, and he turned off the television. Surrounded by darkness, he lay flat on the bed, his gaze toward the ceiling. "Computer. Phones. Tech support. He works for someone in that field."

Surrey's phone lit up with an incoming call. The bright light of his screen forced him to squint when he answered it. "What is it? Is everything okay?"

"We need to search the victims' phone records again." Kate's voice sounded on the other end of the line.

"Tech support," Surrey replied.

"Yep. Rather than us searching for where he might work, I'll bet we'll find some kind of tech support company that the victims called in the weeks or days ahead of their phones getting hacked."

"They all called the same company," he continued.

"Has to be. I've been laying here in bed, searching for the connection."

"You and me, both," Surrey added.

"Good. Let's jump on it first thing."

"You got it. Get some rest. Night." Surrey ended the call while his lips drew up into a smile.

At 6 am, most people were either just getting out of bed, or if they were really ambitious, were just arriving at the gym. The BAU team was walking into the Pittsburgh Field Office. But Tillis had beaten them and awaited their arrival.

"I got your message. I have coffee ready. Come on back and let's get started." He headed to the ops room and glanced back. "You guys don't sleep much, do you?"

"BAU doesn't make allowances for sleep." Duncan laughed. "You're one to talk, huh?"

"Me?" Tillis placed his hand on his chest. "I'm just trying to keep up with you guys." He opened his office door. "I have the phone records printed out with copies for everyone. They go back three months. Based on what we know now, it looks as though our guy follows them for a few weeks after their phones are cloned before doing the deed, with the exception of our Instagram influencer. So, he must use a similar pattern when it comes to picking out his victims. We'll see if your theory pans out, but I like it."

Kate set down her carrier bag at the table. "What about the videos? How are you guys coming along?"

"I have to confess, the moment I got in, I pulled these records, so I haven't followed up with Forensics. I'll let you three settle in, grab some coffee, and I'll run down there now for an update. Fingers crossed."

After he left, Surrey sat down next to Kate and grabbed a highlighter from his bag. "Let's see if we're right."

Duncan peered at them, still standing at the table almost frozen in thought.

Kate looked at her. "You okay?"

"Just thinking. We shouldn't rule out that these people are connected in another way. I don't want to come between you two and your theory, but it is possible they knew each other."

"We can't afford to overlook anything. I'm always open to ideas." Kate kept her eyes on Duncan while she finally sat down. "Is there anything else you think we should consider?"

"Online groups, fan pages. These victims may have had common interests. Let's not forget that this guy chose to livestream their murders via their own accounts. Any of the groups they might have belonged to could've led him to find more victims. We should analyze their social media behaviors—their likes and follows." Duncan picked up her copy of the records. "But this is a step in the right direction."

As they started their search, Tillis returned. "We got a hit." He rushed to one of the laptops and inserted the flash drive. "A white car near the Financial District."

"Where Delaney was murdered?" Kate asked.

"Yes, ma'am." He cued the video. "See for yourselves."

Kate studied the screen while the others joined her. "Where was this in relation to the incident?"

"Across the street, down three buildings on the left." Tillis folded his arms and gazed at the screen. "There. Right there." He stopped the video. "You see that car?"

"I see a front bumper and a tire," Surrey replied.

"Yeah, well, our guy isn't stupid, but I think he missed a camera. Tried to stay out of the shot, but we got just enough. It's white. A small white car that appears to be an older model Ford Focus."

"How can you tell that from what's shown?" Duncan asked.

"Ran the image and cross-referenced it with compact and sub-compact vehicles from every manufacturer. My guys were up for hours running this just to be certain it was a white Ford Focus. I'm going with it. They're working on pinning down a model year and right now, it's between a 2008 to 2013. We get that pinpointed; we got ourselves a solid lead. And a car to search for at the other scenes."

A knowing smile played momentarily on Kate's lips. "How much longer before they finish scouring the other sites?"

"Hours," Tillis replied. "We're getting down to the wire now. And if your theory pans out, we are well on our way to identifying this son of a bitch." His phone rang with an incoming call and he stepped out of the room. In the hallway, he answered. "Yeah, what's up?" Tillis's face drained of color. His shoulders dropped and he rubbed his hand on his forehead. "When? Where? I'm on my way. No, I'll call Stallard." Tillis returned to the room.

Kate noticed the look on his face. They all had. "No."

"Near Shadyside. Call came into Pittsburgh Police. That was Lieutenant Crenshaw. We need to hustle and get down there. Now."

13

The FBI's Baltimore Field Office was where Nick Scarborough tracked down G. Coletta. No obvious connection to the Boston Field Office where Richard Lehmann's belongings had been in holding, which left Nick with more questions than answers.

He waited for Walsh to meet him for a coffee this morning off the Quantico compound. Now he needed to find where the Coletta piece of the puzzle fit.

"Morning." Walsh approached the table and sat down. "I wouldn't mind one of those."

Nick garnered the attention of the barista. "Another coffee, please."

"Sure thing," she replied.

He returned his attention to Walsh. "He's in Baltimore. That's all I could find. What about you?" His eye caught movement beyond Walsh's shoulder. "Fisher."

Walsh pulled out a chair. "He needs to be here for this. I was going to tell you, but I thought you might object."

Fisher joined them. "What kind of trouble have we gotten ourselves in now, eh, Scarborough?"

"I know you get how serious this is," Nick began. "Walsh filled you in?"

"He did. She's a member of my team. I do understand how serious this is and I should've been brought in at the beginning," Fisher replied.

"Walsh and I are handling things. Bringing you onboard would've exposed you to details you might not want to know. Walsh knows what's involved and has accepted the risk. So have I."

"Maybe if you'd given me a chance, huh? This isn't the old days, Scarborough. You can't run this show alone." Fisher turned to the barista. "Coffee, black, please." He shifted in the chair and eyed them. "So, who's G. Coletta and what does he have to do with the message that Reid got from a dead man's phone?"

"That's what Walsh is here to explain. I got the name, he's been working on the details." With his eyes on Walsh, he added. "So?"

"Gordon Coletta is a 15-year Bureau veteran, currently the SSA at the Baltimore Field Office," Walsh began. "He has ties to top brass at Headquarters and worked there for a short time."

"Doing what?" Nick sipped on his coffee.

"Corruption." Walsh eyed them. "Antitrust, bribery. Interesting, right? Same as Gustafson."

"So we have Gordon Coletta, who authorized the request to alter Theo Bishop's passport data," Nick began. "But what's more important is who asked him to do it?"

"Have we ruled out Coletta, himself?" Fisher asked.

"I wasn't able to track back any direct links to Carol Whitman. I have no idea if he's ever been in contact with her on his own,"

Walsh added. "My hunch is that Coletta was operating on someone else's instructions. We still don't know who that was."

"How long has it been since Reid received a message?" Fisher took the coffee from the woman. "Thank you."

"Just the initial text," Nick replied. "It's been quiet since then."

"That's been almost 4 months. If he wanted to go after Reid, what's he waiting for?" Fisher poured in a pack of sugar.

"The right time," Walsh said. "He's waiting for something. We just don't know what yet. Scarborough and I have worked since the beginning on this and as you can see, we haven't gotten far. Fortunately, the DNI undersecretary sent Scarborough the Coletta information."

"For a price," Nick added. "Let's just say I'm going to owe him now."

Walsh eyed him. "So, we know Coletta is involved. We just don't know why or who he's working for."

"What's our play, here, guys?" Fisher pressed on. "I've got half my team hunting down a serial bomber in Pittsburgh. And I got a call from Duncan a little while ago telling me they were headed out to another bombing. Reid is exposed. What are we going to do about that?"

Nick stared at his coffee before turning up his gaze. "We think they've been gathering evidence to use against Kate. This involves Richard Lehmann or else why use his phone? That was no accident. Everyone's playing a waiting game. Us and them. They're waiting to see how deep we'll dig, how close we'll get. We're waiting for them to come at us, to tell us what they want. One of us is going to have to blink."

"Reid is their leverage," Walsh said. "I've been looking into this since the security footage from the train station showed Theo Bishop purchasing the tickets. Someone figured that out too. And because Reid has a checkered history in and out of the Bureau, that's what they'll use to put a stop to us getting any closer."

The black Cadillac Escalade smoldered. Smoke still billowed. Firefighters stood on the flooded street while the hydrant still dripped and began to put away their equipment. The two cars parked near the Escalade suffered extensive damage.

Tillis rolled up behind Agent Stallard. He turned around and spotted their arrival.

The agents stepped out of the car and approached the scene when Tillis began, "I don't know why I'm asking, but is this the work of our guy?"

Stallard peered beyond him while the BAU agents quickly caught up. "I see you're all still here." He turned on his heel and headed toward the Pittsburgh police lieutenant. "Tell them what you told me."

Tillis creased his brow. "What's going on?"

"The victim has been transported to the hospital," Crenshaw replied.

"He's alive?" Kate cut in.

"For now," the lieutenant added. "He's in critical condition, but he's alive."

Stallard rubbed his chin with his thumb and forefinger. "The bomber didn't finish the job. And it was him. Not a copycat. No one knew the bomber was using a soda can as a casing. He chose Sprite this time."

"Holy shit." Tillis paced as though ready to sprint out of there. "We need to talk to the victim right now. Which hospital?"

"AGH," the lieutenant replied.

"Allegheny. Okay." Tillis spun around and headed back to his car. He stopped short and turned back. "Am I going alone or is anyone else interested in learning whether this man knows the bomber?"

"I'll go." Kate turned to Surrey and Duncan. "Gather whatever you can here, and I'll meet you guys back at the field office. We can pick up where we left off, hopefully, with more information." She hurried to catch up with Tillis. "How far is it to the hospital?"

"Twenty minutes." He slipped behind the wheel. "Get in, Reid. We're wasting time." He waited until Kate climbed onto the passenger seat and turned the engine. "We'll need to get an image of our blonde guy in front of the victim."

"Who can I call at your office to get it sent to me?"

"I'll do it." He pressed his Bluetooth, and the line rang. "It's Tillis. Get me Hernandez." He waited while the line was transferred. "Hey, buddy. I need you to shoot over a screenshot of blonde boy ASAP. Our victim is still alive."

"Right. Yeah, okay. I'll get on it. Are you with him now?"

"Not yet. You got ten minutes. Send it to my phone. Thanks, man. I gotta bail." Tillis ended the call. "And that's how you get things done around here."

Kate regarded him. "You don't think much of us over at BAU, do you, Agent Tillis?"

He glanced at her with a smirk that revealed his true feelings. "That's not the case. Look, I just think that you guys are the big brains and us field agents are the muscle. Thing is, sometimes it takes more muscle than brains. No offense."

"None taken," Kate replied.

"Take your profile, for example," he pressed on. "Nothing wrong with it. Straight forward, concise. But frankly, it didn't help us one bit. Sometimes it's the legwork that makes the difference. That's all I'm saying."

"Respectfully, I disagree. If the person who had run into Sienna Page that night hadn't fit my profile, was a woman, or anyone other than what I suggested, we wouldn't have assumed he was our guy. You might not put a lot of faith into what we do, but that's okay because I do." Kate stared through the windshield at the road ahead. "And if you want to make things interesting, how about a small wager on the theory that the bomber works at a tech company, in support, most likely, and that the victims had been in contact with him for those purposes, which was the reason I asked for the phone records again." She turned to him. "Sometimes, big brains are necessary."

Tillis cast her a sideways glance. "Like I said earlier, I'm not dismissing your theory. It could well be the case." He paused a moment. "Look, Reid, I understand you don't get to be at BAU because you don't know what you're doing. I'm sorry. I was out of line. But I know a thing or two as well. Right now, we have a victim who's still breathing. If, like Sienna Page, he ran into the bomber at some point before this, all we'll need to do is show him the picture."

"I guess we're about to find out."

Tillis offered a half-smile. "This is the hospital here."

They hurried inside and Tillis had his ID in hand as they approached the administration desk. "FBI Agent Tillis. We need to see the car bombing victim who was just brought in."

The nurse peered at his computer and pressed a few keys. "Mr. Hardy is currently in surgery."

Tillis sighed and glanced at Kate before turning back to the nurse. "We have to talk to the doctor. Please. This man has a chance to save other lives. We have to see him."

A woman in a white coat approached from beyond the corridor. "I'm sorry, did I hear you correctly? You need to see the man who came in with third-degree burns over half of his body and is currently in surgery?"

Tillis turned to her. "Are you his doctor?"

"One of them. I performed triage before he went in for surgery."

"Did he say anything to you?" Kate asked.

"He was unconscious."

"When do you expect him to come out of surgery?" Kate pressed on.

"Assuming he survives, it could be hours. The extent of his injuries is, well, horrific," the doctor replied.

Kate turned to Tillis. "Then we need to get back to the field office. There's nothing more we can do here until he comes out."

"*If* he comes out," the doctor added.

Tillis grew distraught, thrusting his hands on his hips and eyeing the doctor. "We don't have time. The more time that goes by, the bigger lead our bomber has on us. Doctor, please, is there anything you can do? Lives are at stake. You have to understand."

"I can't wake him, if that's what you're asking. First of all, I don't know if he would wake up, secondly, the amount of pain that man would be in..." she sighed. "He'd have to be so drugged up that I doubt he'd be able to answer any of your questions. I'm sorry. I really am. I can have the surgeon make contact with you just as soon as the surgery is over. But like I said, it could be hours."

Tillis nodded. "Yeah, okay." He handed over one of his cards. "Please. Just as soon as someone knows something..."

"I understand, Agent Tillis. I'll do my best."

He turned on his heel and started toward the exit again, leaving Kate to catch up. The spark of hope that this might come to an end vanished from his eyes as they returned to his car.

"He's still alive. That's the takeaway here." Kate stepped into the car.

Tillis closed his driver's side door and slammed the steering wheel. "Fuck. Fuck. Fuck. We had him. We had him and he's slipping through our fingers again."

"No. Not yet," Kate replied. "We have no idea if the victim ever saw the man we assume is the bomber. And we won't know that until he wakes up. What we do have is a promising link between the victims and the bomber. It's time we explore that until we know otherwise. I asked Duncan and Surrey to meet us back at the field office." Kate studied him for a moment. "I get it, okay? I know exactly how you're feeling right now. Believe me. I've been close enough to taste the blood and still I couldn't grab hold."

Tillis studied her a moment. "Maybe I was wrong about you, Agent Reid."

"I've been in the field, same as you. There's no difference between us. It takes thinking like them to find them. And I'll tell you one thing, I've learned to do that exceedingly well."

DANNY PULLED onto his driveway and stepped out, carrying a bag of fast food. He glanced up at the early morning sun, still wearing his baseball hat as he walked through the front door.

He dropped onto the sofa and thrust his hand into the bag, retrieving an egg and cheese breakfast sandwich. Work waited for him and if he was late for his shift again, they might actually fire him this time. Danny still needed money. And if he lost his job, the court would never grant him guardianship over Mel. After his shift, he would go to see her. If he didn't get her out of there soon, she might never get back to her old self.

It was easy for him to compartmentalize his acts of violence. While he sat in front of his TV eating a breakfast sandwich, it was as though this morning had been just like every other morning.

Mostly because he thought he was acting for the greater good. Partly because he hadn't seen his victims as human beings.

He shoved the last bite of the sandwich into his mouth and chugged back the cooled, bitter coffee. Danny walked into the kitchen and sat at the folding table where his computer lay. He put on his headset and logged onto the system.

The company who had hired him was a chain store that operated three locations in the Pittsburgh area. Calls were directed to Danny from those in the area because he knew the local internet providers, the network's capabilities as well as the cell phone carriers. It was easier for him to deal with local residents because he could direct them to the nearest store to buy new equipment when that was the end result of the calls. About 60% of the support calls he received required the customers to purchase some sort of upgraded equipment or service. It was all a big scam, but the customers never cottoned onto it. Or if they had, never said anything. The usual response was, "okay, thanks anyway." Or "Where should I go to buy that?"

After he started his shift, Danny opened a new window to check the news. Surely, the story had already broken, and he wanted to see how cleverly phrased the headlines might be.

Danny got his news like everyone else—online, although he avoided social media sites except for his work. The version of truth available there was only what they wanted their users to see. Still, there was no guarantee any news site offered more than their version of the truth. Danny just played the odds.

The site loaded and he figured it would be in the local story section, so he scrolled down until spotting it. *"The So-called 'Robinhood' Strikes Fear in Quiet Community."* His face lost all expression as he read on. "What? No. No." He swallowed hard. "No way he could've survived that." He devoured the rest of the article, but that was it. The victim was in the hospital in critical condition. Nothing more. "He's still alive." Danny's hands trembled. "That's not possible. No one's survived before. No one. How the hell?" He took in a long deep breath. "He won't make it."

There was no way to be sure. And if Jeff didn't make it, would he have had time to talk to the cops? "He wouldn't remember me." Jeff knew Danny's name. A mistake he only now seemed to regret.

14

The phone records remained scattered atop the table inside the operations room that had been set up for the BAU team. Some pages had been marked with yellow highlights. Others waited to be scrutinized. More than an hour had passed since Duncan and Surrey returned while Kate had gone to the hospital with Tillis.

Duncan checked her phone and read the text from Kate. "They're on their way back. No chance to talk to the victim. He's in surgery."

Surrey shook his head. "Damn. Then all we can do is continue sifting through these records." He regarded her a moment. "You know, I haven't known Reid or any of you for that long, but is it me, or have you noticed a change in her since the Lehmann situation."

She returned a chary gaze. "How so?"

"You know her better than I do. You don't see it?" he pressed on.

Duncan glanced away. "I see that she's taken the lead here and that's never really happened before. She's never been given the opportunity until now."

"Because of her husband, Senior Unit Agent Scarborough?"

"Partly, but also because of Noah Quinn."

"Right. The man who attempted to blackmail Reid and Scarborough."

"I'd known Quinn for a long time and while I knew his ego was delicate, Reid's abilities shattered it. He never could recover and now he's not here anymore."

Surrey stopped what he was doing and held Duncan's gaze. "But you've noticed Reid change since Lehmann?"

Duncan pulled back in her chair. "We're all aware of what you thought about her continuing with that investigation. Kate's been through more shit than any of us. More than any agent I've ever known. I understand that's not an excuse, and she would never use it as such, but she's going through something right now and I don't know if she'll come through it whole. If she was ever whole to begin with. Frankly, who among us are?"

"Do you think she's compromised in some way?" Surrey asked.

"No. Kate will always put the job first and that's the real problem." The door opened and captured her attention. Kate and Tillis walked inside. "Is he still alive?"

"Last we heard." Kate walked toward the table where they sat. "We just have to keep our fingers crossed. How are things going with this? Any luck?"

"Maybe. There's still a lot to look at, though," Surrey replied.

Kate pulled out a chair to sit. "Then we should keep going, unless you think differently, Tillis? This is still your investigation."

He dropped onto a chair. "Is it? I wasn't sure." He shook his head. "Hell, I'm sorry. I didn't mean that. I appreciate the work you all have put into this. We asked you to help and that's what you're doing. I'm just feeling the strain right now. We need this guy to live, damn it."

"It's okay," Surrey replied. "Reid's right. We'll follow your lead."

"There's a lot of information here." Tillis held out his hand. "I'll take a share of it." His phone rang in his pocket and he held it to his ear. "Tillis here. Okay. Did they recognize him?" He shot a look at the team. "Just the one-time purchase, though. No, that's great news and we needed it. Keep me posted. We're closing in on him. Thanks, man." He ended the call. "That was Stallard. His team got a hit on a small gun shop where a large canister of powder was purchased, with cash, about a week ago. ATF talked to the guy who rang him up and showed him a picture of blondie, he believed it was a match."

IT WAS rare when Levi Walsh could put to use the skills he'd developed as an Army Intelligence officer. After having served in the Gulf, Walsh could easily have transitioned to the CIA. Instead, he'd chosen the FBI because he preferred to catch the bad guys, not just gather intel and hand it over for others to bring them in. He was always more of a hands-on type, and he also happened to be an expert at getting people to talk. It was time to call upon those slightly rusty skills to uncover who was behind Gordon Coletta's illegal authorization to have the NSA partake in the aiding and abetting of a known killer.

While the rest of his team hunted down a serial bomber, it was Walsh's job to ensure his team remained whole. Never leaving any of them exposed.

With a confident smile, Walsh approached the security desk at the J. Edgar Hoover building in D.C. FBI Headquarters. "Afternoon. SSA Levi Walsh, Quantico. I'm here to see SSA Jason Long."

"Of course." The security guard viewed Walsh's creds. "I'll let him know you're here."

Walsh stepped away from the desk. He'd met Agent Long a few years ago during an investigation. It had been a while, but the two had clicked and Walsh was going to use his talents to learn what Long remembered of Coletta, who had once worked here at this office.

"Levi Walsh." Long appeared with a smile and an outstretched hand. "Good to see you, brother. It's been a while."

"Good to see you, too, man." Walsh accepted his hand. "Hey, I appreciate you setting aside some time to talk."

"Yeah, absolutely. Let's head over to my office and you can catch me up." Long started ahead. "Still with BAU-4, huh?"

"Yes, sir," Walsh replied.

"I'll tell you, it takes a special kind of person to do what you all do there. I'm only dealing with corrupt public officials and companies. You're dealing with a whole scary kind of crazy."

Walsh chuckled. "You could argue that public officials display the same kind of narcissism as some of the folks I chase after. It's a thin line, brother. A very thin line."

Long opened the door to his office. "You have a point. Come on in. Can I get you anything to drink? A coffee or something?"

"Nah, man. I'm good. I just wanted to talk about something that, well, I wouldn't mind if you kept to yourself."

Long creased his brow as he returned to his desk. "Oh, sure. Hey, you know me. I got your back."

Walsh sat down across from him. "This is a somewhat delicate situation and like I said, I need to know it won't make the rounds at the water cooler."

Long held his gaze wearing concern. "Do we need to take this outside?"

"No. Listen, this situation; let's just say that I'm dealing with some powerful forces possibly looking to keep something quiet. Something that almost cost us a case."

Long pulled back and cocked his head. His black hair was gelled neatly into place and his white button-down shirt and blue tie were pressed. "What do you need to know, man? I'll do what I can to help."

Walsh pulled up in his chair and leaned in. "What do you know about SSA Gordon Coletta? Works in the Baltimore field office, used to be here in your department."

Long's expression turned cold. "I know him."

"The look on your face suggests you know him pretty well."

Long shrugged but kept a cool mien. "In simplest terms, Coletta is the quintessential 'yes' man. I knew him when he was here. I was still green, learning the ropes, but what I saw in him changed my perspective of the Bureau to some degree."

"Was there a reason he made the move to Baltimore?" Walsh asked. "Agents don't typically jump from HQ to a field office. It's usually the other way around."

"Let's just say that I don't think it was voluntary. Coletta has friends in high places. His ass was covered pretty damn well. I think he was sent there to keep him from getting into more trouble."

"Who was his ASAC at the time?"

Long glanced around as if he might be overheard. "Chansing. ASAC Leon Chansing. Retired now, but he ruled the roost in those days."

"You know who else worked under Chansing who might've been a similar thinker as Coletta? You know, looking to get ahead by doing whatever it took?"

"I can get you some names of guys who, uh, well, let's just say they hung around in the same circles. Needless to say, I wasn't part of their circle. Levi, those guys—they're not like us. They're more like political operatives than agents."

"That's what I figured. I just need names. I'm looking for a connection to an influential former head honcho, Gustafson, who's long since retired and passed about 10 years ago. I have a feeling he still has a few disciples on the payroll."

Long folded his arms and held Walsh's gaze. "Gustafson? He was a heavy hitter back in the day. What's this really about, Levi? Is there a storm coming?"

He shook his head. "This one's not directed at me. But it is directed at an agent who doesn't deserve it. I won't let that happen."

"Then you'd better protect yourself and this agent, man. Because once you poke that bear, you might find that he's awful hungry."

KATE STOOD outside the ops room on a call with Nick. "We're still waiting on word from the hospital. The team is combing through the victims' phone records. Nick, I'm sure this bomber is some kind of tech support guy. It just makes sense."

"Do Surrey and Duncan agree?" Nick asked.

"Everyone agrees that it's a possibility. And possibilities are all we have at the moment. Anyway, between us and the ATF, we're narrowing in on our unsub. So, how's things going on your end?"

"Nothing new here."

"Nothing?" Kate asked.

"Nothing I'm prepared to mention yet. Not until I know more. But that's not something you should be thinking about right now.

Your head needs to be in the game. You've got a serial bomber out there and it's going to get ugly if his victim survives."

Kate grinned at the agent who brushed by her in the hall. "That's what I thought. It'll push him to the extreme because he'll feel like the walls are closing in on him."

"Exactly. He'll become erratic and unpredictable and when that happens..."

"We will lose him. Yeah, I know." She turned back when Tillis appeared before her.

"The hospital called. He's awake," Tillis said.

Kate returned to the phone call. "Hey, I gotta run. The victim just woke up. I'll keep you posted." She ended the call and looked at Tillis. "Can he talk?"

"We're about to find out. Let's roll."

Kate walked back into the ops room and looked at Surrey and Duncan. "The victim's awake. We're heading down there now."

"Before you go, you might want to see this." Surrey pulled aside two of the sheets in front of him. "This is our Instagram influencer, Sienna Page, and Tom Messena from the gym. Both contacted customer service for PivoTech Electronics in the recent past."

"The big box electronics retailer," Kate replied. "And the other victims?"

"I was still going through Delaney's records when the call came in from the hospital," Tillis said.

"I hadn't finished up my review of Hardy's records either." Kate appeared to mull over the results. "I say we reach out to the company and find out who in the Pittsburgh area works their tech support line. Specifically, male, mid-twenties. Let's keep it as narrow as possible. They're a huge organization and we don't have the kind of time it'll take them to hunt him down."

"We'll get on it," Duncan replied. "And if the victim can ID our unsub?"

Kate eyed her. "Then we get out the information ASAP. If we get corroboration from the owner of the gun shop, we might just stand a chance at finding him."

ALLEGHENY GENERAL HOSPITAL came into view, and Tillis pulled into the parking lot. Without a word, he jumped out of his car and headed to the entrance, leaving Kate trailing behind. She hurried to catch up to him once again. "Hey, Tillis, you ever work with a partner before?"

He marched on, reaching the entrance. "Not if I can help it."

She reached for the door to stop him. "Listen, we don't know the kind of condition he's in. We can't push this man."

"We'll do what we have to do, Reid, to ID the bomber." Tillis headed inside with his badge in hand. "FBI. We need to talk to Jeff Hardy. Now."

The nurse behind the desk made the call. "The doctor is coming up to speak to you. If you'll just wait a moment."

Tillis appeared agitated and Kate noticed. "I know we want this guy to point to our unsub and say, 'yeah, that's him,' but we have no idea if he knew him. We need to be prepared for what's ahead."

"I appreciate your advice, Reid, but I didn't ask for it. This is my city and now four bombs have gone off, killing three. ATF is busting their humps to track down our guy and so are we. So, let's just see what he knows before you shut it down, yeah?"

Kate held up her hands. "You got it. This is all yours."

Tillis was smart but desperation radiated from him like bad cologne. He had more years at the Bureau than Kate, and it was a fine line she'd learned not to cross. But she knew how fragile the victim would be and pushing him wasn't the answer. Maybe she'd misread Tillis's intentions, but it appeared that he was going in full-bore and that was exactly the wrong way to approach the situation. She spun around with wide eyes and flinched when someone touched her shoulder.

"Whoa, sorry Reid. Didn't mean to startle you." Stallard appeared behind her. "Tillis called me."

The doctor approached before she had a chance to respond.

"You all are with the FBI?"

"Those two are. I'm ATF. What's the good word, Doc? Our victim in good enough shape to talk?" Stallard asked.

The surgeon pressed together his lips until they formed a thin white line. "If I had my way, I'd say absolutely not. That man has third degree burns over most of his body. He's pumped up with all kinds of pain meds. Frankly, I should put my foot down."

"But then we have a bomber still at large," Tillis added. "And your patient might be able to identify him. I appreciate where you're coming from, Doctor, I really do. But more lives are at stake."

The doctor appeared resigned. "Fine. But only one of you goes in. I'm sorry, but that's how it has to be."

"I'll do it." Tillis didn't let anyone reply and started ahead. "Show me the way, Doc."

Kate stood in the middle of the lobby and dipped her head.

Stallard noticed. "He just wants to get to the bottom of this. We all do."

"I understand that. I just don't know how reliable the victim is going to be and if Tillis pushes him..."

"All we can do is wait, Reid. I hear your team got a lead on a company called PivoTech."

"That's right. They're working on it now. And your guys found a gun shop employee who ID'd the unsub," she added.

"It's shaky and I have an aversion to unreliable witnesses. But an employee thought he recognized the man in our video as the man who bought the powder. We're looking for more shops and if we can get another hit, then I'll feel more confident we're dealing with the same man. It's still a lot of circumstantial evidence right now. Not unless or until that man in the hospital bed tells us otherwise."

15

The words uttered in Danny's ears hardly registered. His mind obsessed about the consequences of Jeff surviving the blast. But as he sat in front of his computer, listening to a woman with no idea how to work a laptop, let alone the internet, she repeated her question.

"Hello? Hello? Are you still there?" she asked.

Danny blinked. "Yes. I'm here. You'll have to turn off your laptop and restart it. If that doesn't work, I'll need remote access to it so I can see what's going on." He could hear her mumbling and keys being punched, but all he wanted to do was to drive to that hospital and find out if Jeff had talked to the police. "Just calm down. He won't remember you."

"I'm sorry?" the woman asked. "I am calm, thank you very much and I'd appreciate you not taking that tone with me."

Danny closed his eyes and took in a deep breath. "I can't do this shit." He cut the call and ripped off his headset. With a quick search, he found the story online, but it still read that it was a developing situation. Meaning they didn't know if Jeff was alive or dead. "Son of a bitch." He jumped from his chair and paced the kitchen. Sweat formed at his hairline and his pulse quickened. "Don't panic." Somehow, as smart as he was, he hadn't planned for this to happen. There were to be no survivors. "No one knows who you are. You jammed the cameras. You did everything right." He spun around as if arguing with himself. "Then why is he still alive!" A purple vein on Danny's forehead raised and his face reddened. With his fists clenched, Danny roared. The primal broadcast echoed throughout the empty house.

He couldn't just wait for the cops to bust down his door. Something had to be done. He had to leave. It wasn't safe for him here anymore. Danny took wide strides up the stairs and ran into his bedroom. A duffle bag lay in his closet and he snatched it from the floor, tossing it onto his bed. He grabbed whatever clothes were in his dresser and threw them inside it. The room spun and there wasn't enough air to breathe. Danny's hands trembled as he filled the bag with whatever he could find.

Inside the bathroom, he yanked open the medicine cabinet and took everything. And on closing the cabinet again, he stared at his reflection. Sweaty, his curly blonde hair that hung in one length to his chin, clung to his cheeks. The whites of his eyes were lined with red veins. Panic set in. Danny reached the edge of the cliff, but would he jump?

Agent Tillis remerged from the hospital corridor, capturing Stallard's attention. He nudged Kate. "Here he comes. Fingers crossed."

Kate watched him approach but he had the most unreadable face she'd ever seen on anyone. No hints revealed as to how the interview went. As he neared, she swallowed hard and waited for him to speak.

Tillis kept his head low and his hands in his pockets. He tilted up his gaze as he stopped in front of them, and the corner of his mouth raised slightly. "He recognized him."

Stallard licked his lips as if anticipating a juicy steak dinner. "And? Did he give us a name?"

"Danny. He said the man's name was Danny. I tried to get more out of him, but he went into cardiac arrest. They couldn't bring him back. He's gone."

Kate put her hand over her mouth and closed her eyes for a moment. She took in a deep breath and with her shoulders back, she continued. "Under no circumstances can we let this get out to the media. This is our chance. Danny, you said?" She eyed Tillis for a moment. "He's on edge. He doesn't know what condition his victim is in or whether he talked to the authorities. The moment he learns Jeff Hardy is dead, we lose our advantage. He'll think he got lucky and redouble his efforts, making zero mistakes in the future."

"I agree," Stallard replied. "We're coming at this from three different angles, and now we have a name. If he thinks we're as close as we are..."

"He'll go dark," Tillis replied. "Let me take care of the media. I'll get with my ASAC and make sure this doesn't get leaked." He peered outside. "Which might be tougher than we think."

Kate spotted the media van through the glass doors. "Shit. Is there a back exit? We have to get out of here."

Stallard walked to the front desk. "Hey, uh, we can't talk to those guys out there right now. Any chance someone can show us a way out through the back?"

The nurse peered through the entrance doors and picked up the phone. "Yes, of course. I'll take care of that for you." When the line answered, she continued. "Hank, you mind coming up to the lobby? I have some federal agents who need to slip away before the media hounds them to death. Thanks." She returned her attention to Stallard. "Hank is our head of security. He'll get you guys out."

"Appreciate you." He offered her a sincere smile and headed back to the others. "We're about to be escorted out of here."

The lobby doors opened and a man with a microphone hurried inside, followed by a camera man. He spotted the agents, whose appearance did little to deny their roles. "Excuse me? Stuart Ramon, Action News Four, are you the FBI? What do you know about the latest Robinhood victim?" He thrust a microphone in Kate's face while motioning for his camera man to move in.

She wanted to shove the microphone right back at him and tell him how he was glorifying a murderer. But Kate had learned better. For years she'd faced off with the press who were never kind, with the exception of Marc Aguilar, though their relationship had been strained in the beginning. Now Marc was a big-time reporter in New York City. "I can't comment on an ongoing investigation."

The security guard approached and waved them over. "Right this way."

As they hurried alongside the guard, the unabashed reporter continued to trail them. "Wait. I just want to ask how he's doing. Is the victim still alive? Can you give us a name? Was it the so-called Robinhood bomber?"

Another guard quickly cut him off as the agents entered the hall. "That's enough. Get your story somewhere else."

Kate glanced back over her shoulder and noticed the guard had stopped him. "We're clear."

"Right through here, folks." Hank pushed open the door. "You'd better hurry. They can smell you from a mile away."

Tillis smiled. "You're a good man, Hank." He looked at Stallard as they made their way outside. "Any chance you're parked back here?"

"I didn't think that far in advance. We'll have to slip by while the reporter is in the lobby."

They hurried to their respective cars and Kate slipped onto the passenger seat, waiting for Tillis.

"Christ, I can't stand those people." Tillis closed his door and keyed the ignition. "I know they have a job to do, but sons of bitches don't know when to keep their mouths shut."

"I have some experience with them on that front," Kate replied.

Tillis pulled away. "It was a good call to keep this from them—the media. It's like you know what you're doing."

"What can I say? I get lucky sometimes." She smiled.

He cast her a sheepish glance. "I know I can be a little intense at times. Don't take it personally. I'm like that with everyone. You and your team know what you're doing. I'm sorry for coming off so strong."

"Don't worry about it." She paused for a moment. "Hey, do we know if the Hardy explosion was livestreamed like the others?"

"If it was, he didn't seem aware of it. Made no mention." He took in a long breath. "He couldn't say a lot anyway. Not the way he looked." Tillis cleared his throat as if to shake the image from his mind. "But when I showed him the picture, he whispered to me the name, Danny. He also asked me to tell his wife he loved her."

"He was married? Another first for Danny. None of the other victims were. Have the police contacted her yet?" Kate asked.

"I don't know. We'll get on that when we get back to the office."

"She'd be the first one to come forward if it was livestreamed. Makes me think he didn't do that this time." Kate gazed through the passenger window. "Why would he have chosen someone who was married?"

"I don't think anything about this guy is taking me by surprise anymore. There seems to be no rhyme or reason for how he chooses his victims. Male, female, rich. Shadyside is a pretty upscale area, so I'm thinking Hardy had some cash."

Kate nodded. "Maybe it won't matter soon enough, depending on what ATF uncovers."

Tillis pulled into the field office parking lot. "Until he's in our custody, everything about the bomber matters."

They returned inside to find Duncan and Surrey still poring over the records in the operations room.

"Danny," Tillis said. "His first name is Danny and that's all I got from the victim because he died moments later."

"Oh, no," Duncan whispered. "He didn't tell you anything else?"

"He did, but it's something reserved for his wife," Tillis added.

"He was married?" Surrey asked. "That's a first."

"And I doubt it will be the last." Tillis walked toward them.

Duncan reached for a piece of paper on the table. "We found the same calls were made to PivoTech with all three victims. I'm not sure we need to wait to see if Jeff Hardy's records show the same. Frankly, this is enough for me. Surrey and I have been working our way through the ranks at PivoTech to try to get someone who has the authority to give us employee information."

"And?" Kate asked.

"We're getting the runaround. It might be time to hit them with a subpoena. Especially now." Duncan looked at Tillis. "Can you make that happen quickly?"

"I'll get it done." Tillis turned on his heel and walked out.

Kate waited until he left to continue. "The media is out in full force on this one. Tillis agreed to get his boss to keep the status of the victim quiet. We need the bomber to think the victim is still alive."

"He'll squirm. He'll get desperate," Surrey replied. "I agree. Once that happens, he'll start getting sloppy."

"What concerns me more is that he might go bigger thinking he has nothing left to lose," Duncan added. "We should take that into consideration as well."

Kate eyed her. "I'd like to see where Fisher stands on the matter."

"Then let's make the call." Duncan dialed the number and put the call on speaker. The line rang and a moment later, he answered. "Fisher, it's Duncan. I'm here with Reid and Surrey. You're on speaker."

"How's things going up there?" he asked.

"We're closing in on our unsub," Kate began. "The latest victim lived long enough to give us a first name. But I made the call to ask the field office to keep quiet about the victim's death. Duncan brought up a good point." Kate nodded for her to continue.

"I'm afraid if we do keep this quiet before we have a chance to move in, he might decide the victim talked and realize he's out of time, making his actions even more unpredictable," Duncan said. "We'd like to get your thoughts."

"Surrey, you there?" Fisher asked.

He leaned in. "I'm here."

"Reid wants to keep the unsub in the dark. Keep him questioning whether he's about to be found. Duncan thinks that could backfire. What do you think?"

Surrey traded glances with his team. "Well, I'm not sure either would happen. He could be scared. Scared enough to pull the plug and take off. This kid, he sees what he wants to see about his victims. I think if we're going to try to keep him on the hook, we might need to play up to that."

"How so?" Fisher asked.

"We keep the media on their current narrative. He's watching the news. Until we learn more from the wife, we can have them play up the fact that the man lived in a wealthy part of town. Drove an expensive car. These are the things he wants to hear, that he killed someone who was everything he isn't. It may be the only way we keep him on an even keel."

"ATF is working on linking the purchase of the components to the unsub," Duncan cut in. "That's crucial right now and could be the nail in his coffin. Point is, do we keep quiet the fact that Jeff Hardy is dead until we can pursue these other leads?"

"Keep it quiet," Fisher began. "While it does present a risk, to Duncan's point, it could keep him in one spot long enough to work on an exit strategy. Might buy you all enough time that it'll work in your favor. I think word gets out that the victim died, there's a chance he'll go after someone else believing he got away with it again."

Surrey nodded. "You're the boss."

"Thanks, Fisher. We'll keep you posted." Duncan ended the call. "There you go."

Tillis returned to them. "Okay, we're getting a subpoena now. Should be within the hour and we'll be able to get the names of the customer service staff at PivoTech." His phone rang again. "Oh, hang on. We might have something here." He answered the call. "Tillis here. Yeah. You did? Great, what is it?" He nodded. "Okay. 2010. Got it. Hey, man, thanks for this." He ended the call and peered at the team. "Now that we have a positive ID on Danny, we can run the name against the owners of a 2010 white Ford Focus. This whole thing might be over by tonight."

FROM HIS CAR, Danny peered at the doors of the hospital where Jeff Hardy had been taken. Some reporter stood outside the hospital earlier when they went to him live for an update. It was pretty easy to figure out where Jeff was after that.

It had been four hours and Danny still had no idea if Jeff was dead or alive. Did it even matter at this point? The police hadn't come pounding on his door. If Jeff talked, they would've by now, or at least put his face out there for all to see. Maybe he was in the clear, or maybe it was time to cut bait. He'd risked a lot going after Jeff. He recognized now that he'd lost control of his impulses and was now paying the price for it. The thing was, he couldn't leave without Mel. He had to protect himself and he had to protect her. There was no job to go back to at PivoTech. They would've fired him after what he'd done today. No job meant no money. "Think." He pounded his palm against the side of his head and looked up when an idea struck.

Danny picked up the phone in the center console. Jeff Hardy's life was copied onto that phone. "Someone had to have posted something on his page." He scrolled through the social media posts and stopped. "His wife." He'd learned about Jeff's wife after he hacked into his Facebook account. Not that it mattered much to him. It wasn't like he had kids. But there it was, a post from his wife. His face wore relief. "He's dead. Okay. This is good. This was how it was supposed to go." He looked again at the post.

"Jeff was a victim of the so-called Robinhood bomber, but whoever it is, murdered my husband. Please keep our family in your prayers." her post read.

"Whoever it is," Danny began. "They don't know. They don't know it's me."

16

When ATF Agent Chris Stallard reached the entrance, he smirked at the sign posted on the glass door. *"Guns allowed."* He walked inside the gun shop located near the north end of town after learning that his team had picked up on a possible sighting of the bomber. Stallard took it upon himself to find out if the man they now suspected to be named Danny had been there. Having a second witness to the same man buying the same materials made for a strong correlation.

With his badge in hand, he approached the cashier's station. "ATF. Is the owner available to speak to?"

"Uh, yes, sir. I'll go get him." The young man hurried into the back.

Stallard surveyed the shop. Rifles, ammunition, hunting gear. He was a gun enthusiast himself, and an expert in explosives. No surprise, then, his choice of career.

An older stocky gentleman approached with his hand extended. "Hello. I'm Roger Hayes, the owner. You must be Agent Stallard."

"That's me." Stallard accepted the greeting. "As discussed, I'm here to talk about the young man who came into your store recently."

"Of course. As I told one of your agents, a man in his early 20s came in looking for powder. I didn't think much of it at the time. Lots of people buy powder. But there was something different about him." Hayes pushed up his eyeglasses.

Stallard retrieved the photo. "Is this the man you saw?"

Hayes took the image and studied it. "Oh, that's him all right. It was maybe 3 or 4 days ago. A week, tops. And of course, the attacks have been all over the news."

"You said he was different," Stallard began. "How so?"

"Well, he just didn't seem to be all that familiar with reloading. I mean, people who come in here to buy the cannisters of powder generally know what they're doing. If you don't know, chances are good you'll lose a hand, or worse. Fact of the matter is, this kid seemed like a greenhorn."

"And that was why he stuck out in your mind?" Stallard pressed on.

"I suppose so. Course, with all that's been going on, it tends to put you on your guard if you know what I mean. People like me, gun shop owners, we're pretty big targets of all that goes wrong somehow."

"I understand. Do you have a bill of sale? Did he sign a receipt?"

Hayes keyed in commands on his computer and turned the screen. "This is the receipt. He paid cash."

Stallard eyed the screen. "Did you look at this signature?"

"No, sir. Not really," Hayes replied.

"What about his ID?"

"Well, sure. I have to check ID, but this wasn't an ammo or

gun purchase. No background check required. Signature was only needed because it's classified as a hazardous material."

Stallard pulled his gaze from the monitor and peered at Hayes again. "The name on this receipt is illegible. I have no idea who signed this."

"I'm very sorry, sir. Some people have chicken scratch for handwriting." He peered at Stallard. "That doesn't help you much, does it?"

Stallard sighed. "It helps that you recognized his photo. Listen, you give me a call if you see him again." He handed over a card. "I don't want you to confront him. Just give me a heads up. Although, given what we do know about this man, I doubt he'll make another appearance here."

"Will do, Agent Stallard."

"Appreciate your time." He turned on his heel and walked out the door. With his phone in hand, he made the call. "Tillis, it's Stallard. I confirmed a positive ID on Danny. The owner recognized him and said he purchased a cannister of smokeless powder. A large one." He nodded. "Paid cash. Goddam signature was illegible. Visual of the ID only, so we still don't have confirmation of a name. But I feel like this kid is our bomber."

❀

TILLIS RETURNED his phone to his pocket and perched on the edge of the table inside the ops room. The BAU team looked to him for an update. "Stallard got a positive ID from the gun shop owner. Couldn't read the name on the receipt, though. Says our guy stocked up on powder. Lots of it."

"Which makes it all the more critical to get that information back from PivoTech," Surrey replied. "They should've responded to the subpoena by now."

"Not if they're in cover-your-ass mode right now," he added. "Imagine, a tech support employee using a customer's personal information to hack into their accounts, clone their phones. These guys are exposed, and they know it."

"While they're scrambling, the bomber could be planning something else," Duncan cut in. "What about the motor vehicle search? Your team narrowed down the model year."

"They're on it." Tillis stood and paced the room. "I'm not an expert in serial killers, so I'm looking to you all. If we get a location on our guy and we go there, what are the odds we'll be running into a booby trap?"

Kate shrugged. "That depends on how desperate he feels. And it depends on how quickly we can put together an operation. Because if he catches wind that we're close, all bets are off. He's already someone with a grudge. Someone who believes he's been slighted and overlooked his whole life. If we get a name, I want to locate any family members because they may be our only hope at bringing him in."

"Let's just hope we get that far. I'll go see how we're looking on the car registrations." Tillis started toward the door. "You guys need to get on top of PivoTech. Maybe you can put some of your D.C. muscle on them to speed them along."

"I can get down there now and back up your agent who's waiting," Kate replied.

"Good. Then we'll keep in close contact until one of us gets a break." Tillis headed out.

After he left, Surrey appeared to consider an idea. "Here's what I'd like to do if you two are good with it. Reid can head down to visit with the lawyers at PivoTech, like you said. When you get the details, assuming we're all right about this guy working there, then send me Danny's address. I'll make a run to the house and take a look at what we're going to come up against."

"You don't know what you'll be walking into," Kate replied.

"My goal isn't to make contact. If I see the kid, I'll call Tillis and get a squad car there. And if luck is on our side, I might catch a glimpse of the car. We're still operating on assumptions. It's time to end that and work to bring in this killer."

THE PIVOTECH corporate office was located less than two miles from where the first explosion happened. While Kate hadn't believed there was a connection, it tickled the back of her mind and she kept note of it.

She walked into the lobby with her credentials and the subpoena in hand. It was late afternoon and the company had failed to respond. They were buying time the FBI didn't have to sell.

"FBI Agent Reid. I need to speak with Anya Gilstrom. This is urgent."

The woman behind the desk scrutinized her. "Do you have an appointment? I believe she's in a meeting at the moment."

Kate unfolded the document. "I have a subpoena. As I said, this is an urgent matter."

"Then you must be with her." The woman pointed to the waiting area.

Kate spotted the agent. "I'm with her."

"Fine. I'll have Ms. Gilstrom's secretary interrupt her. Just a moment please." Wearing a concerned look, she made the call.

Kate walked over to the agent at the seating area. "You must be on Tillis's team? I'm Kate Reid."

"Andrea Taylor. Pleasure. I've been sitting here for a while. Good to have some backup."

"Agent Reid?" the woman behind the desk returned her attention. "Ms. Gilstrom is on her way down. It'll be just a moment."

"You must have some pull, Agent Reid." Taylor smiled.

"Not as much as you might think." Kate spotted a lean figure step out from the hall. Wearing a pencil skirt and stiletto heels, she assumed it was Anya Gilstrom. Her harsh expression lent to an overall attempt at intimidation. Maybe that was needed for a woman in her position, however, if she'd hoped to employ such a strategy toward Kate, it wouldn't get her far.

"Agent Reid?" Gilstrom approached. "I am so sorry for the delay. I've been informed as to the information you're looking for."

"You mean the subpoena your office has had in its possession for the past few hours? Here's a copy for your records if you need it," Kate replied.

"Of course." She eyed Taylor. "And you are?"

"The agent who's been sitting here for three hours," Taylor replied.

Gilstrom scrutinized her. "Follow me and we'll have our lawyers take a look." She started on.

"This information was sent to you from the FBI's Pittsburgh office more than three hours ago, and you've wasted Agent Taylor's time as well," Kate began. "I'm not sure if you're aware, but we are on the hunt for a bomber, Ms. Gilstrom. Every second counts."

"You're assuming the person you seek works for PivoTech. I'm not entirely sure that's true, however, we will get to the bottom of it."

Kate shook her head in disbelief. "Four people are dead. I'm sure you can understand our need for expediency and cooperation."

"Right through here." Gilstrom opened the door to a large conference room where four people in suits let their eyes rake over the new arrivals. "This is our inhouse team of attorneys. Please, Agent Reid, Agent Taylor, take a seat and we'll see what we can do."

Heat rose under Kate's collar. "As I said, I have a subpoena. This is non-negotiable so my sitting down with your lawyers is a waste of time I don't have." She tossed the paperwork onto the table. "I know you've seen this already."

"As a matter of fact, we have, Agent Reid." One of the lawyers picked up the document. "And we do have a list of current employees at PivoTech in the Pittsburgh area."

"May I see the list?" Kate asked.

"Of course." He pushed the file toward her.

Kate opened it to find three pages of names. "This is everyone or just tech support?"

"Everyone, Agent Reid, per the subpoena," another lawyer replied.

She scanned through the list of names, which were in alphabetical order by last name. "And you're sure this is conclusive?"

"Yes, ma'am. Everyone currently on our payroll in the area," the man replied.

Kate was wrong. Could it really have been just a coincidence that the victims called the same tech support line? She was sure that was how he found them, though she had to admit, Jeff Hardy had no such connection that they knew of yet. Her shoulders sank. Kate had just squandered precious time on a hunch. "Is this my copy?"

"Yes, it is," the man added.

"Thank you."

"Does it help you, Agent Reid?" he pressed on.

"Not as much as I had hoped. We would've appreciated it more had you offered this earlier to Agent Taylor. We'll show ourselves out."

As they walked through the hall, Agent Taylor began. "What are you going to do now?"

"I don't know. Hope for a miracle, I guess." Kate turned to her. "Thanks for your help."

She hurried ahead, making her way back to the lobby and then outside into the late afternoon heat and humidity. "Damn it. God damn it."

Stepping into the car, Kate turned the ignition and made the call she hadn't wanted to make. "It's me." She peered through the windshield. "No luck."

"What do you mean, no luck?" Surrey asked.

"I mean, they gave me a list of staff. Everyone in the Pittsburgh area. Danny, Daniel, Dan. No one with that name is on the list. So either he gave a fake name to Jeff Hardy, in which case, we're screwed, or I was wrong about the whole thing."

With Jeff Hardy dead, Danny grew more at ease. Unfortunately, in panic-mode, he'd cost himself his job. The emailed Notice of Termination had been sent shortly after he hung up on a customer. Add that to the growing list of missteps and getting fired sounded about right.

It was time for a breather. Danny had risked more than he bargained for in the Hardy debacle. But now that he was gone, it was time to resolve Mel's situation. And maybe it was a good thing to take a step back for a minute. He'd lost control and it could have cost him everything.

Danny pulled back the curtain on his front window and spied the quiet street. Rays from the setting sun blinded him for a moment. He could almost hear the sirens as he expected a SWAT team to roll up right about now. But for the moment, Danny believed he just might be in the clear. The victim was dead, and he was still free. No one was coming for him. Not yet.

When he checked the time, he knew he had to see Mel. His promise to visit her daily already broken, it was time to make amends. He walked outside and took in a deep breath of stagnant air. With his hand in his pocket, Danny rummaged around until he retrieved his keys.

"Hey, Danny."

He shot around and noticed Janie walk outside her house. "Janie. Hi."

She started toward him. "Are you leaving? Where's Mel?"

He peered at his front door for a moment. "Oh, she's at a physical therapy appointment. I was actually headed there now to pick her up."

"Great. I hadn't seen her in a while. Wanted to make sure she was all right. And you?" Janie eyed him. "Are you all right?"

"Me? Yeah, of course. Busy as usual," he replied.

"Good. Glad to hear it. Well, listen, I was just leaving myself, but I saw you and..."

"Yeah, no. Thanks. We're good here." He thumbed to his car. "Well, I gotta go..."

"Sure. See you later. Tell Mel I said hey."

"Will do." Danny stepped into his car and watched Janie get inside her Toyota Rav4. He wondered why there were so few people like Janie in this world. She was kind, caring—pretty. He lowered his gaze and gripped the steering wheel before turning the ignition and heading out into this world in which he never really belonged.

For a moment, there was regret. A fleeting sense that he could've been somebody else. That he could've meant something to someone like Janie. But the fire had grown too big and burned too hot. Danny would never know normalcy again. Perhaps that was just the price he needed to pay to make things right. Danny was a martyr now, and they would all thank him at the end of this.

He arrived at the facility and took in the sight of the plain beige building with windows dotted around. A few trees out front and a circular driveway for the ambulances to come and take away the sick and the dead. Danny stepped out of his car and walked inside.

The older woman dressed in scrubs smiled as he approached the desk. "Hi, Danny. We missed you yesterday."

"How's she doing today, Sue?" he asked.

"Been pretty unhappy, as you know, but I think she'll come around in time. She's in the common room. They just finished dinner. Go on in."

"Thanks." Danny walked into the long corridor toward the dining area and the adjacent common room. Inside, he spotted two televisions on either end, a few tables and chairs, and then he saw her.

Mel sat expressionless, her eyes staring off into the distance.

"Hey, Mel."

"Danny." She cocked her head. "Where were you yesterday? You left me here. You said you would visit every day."

He pulled out a chair to sit down. "I know, Mel, and I'm so sorry. It was work and I couldn't get out of it, but I'm here now." He reached for her hand. She pulled it away. "Don't be mad. It won't happen again."

"When do I get to leave this place, Danny? You promised I could leave soon," she pleaded.

"I know, and I will keep that promise. It's just going to take some time. You know what it's like. A bunch of red tape crap. But you'll be coming home soon," he replied.

She turned her gaze to the television and sighed.

Danny couldn't stand it when Mel was mad at him. Even

when they were children, he looked to her for approval. She was his big sister. "What did you have for dinner tonight?"

"Hamburger and French fries." She refused to look at him.

"You love burgers."

"Not these. They were awful," Mel replied.

"That sucks. I'm sorry about that." Danny turned his sights to the television as the news broadcast started.

The so-called Robinhood bomber claimed his fourth victim today as yet another in a terrifying string of car bombings took place in the city. In a statement issued by the Pittsburgh Bureau of Police, the victim, 33-year-old Jeff Hardy, is still in the hospital in critical condition. Police are asking citizens to stay vigilant and if anyone has any information, they ask that you call the hotline on our screen. I'm Stuart Damon Action News Four.

"Are you afraid?" Mel asked, finally setting her sights on him.

Danny realized the report mentioned Jeff was still alive. Why were they lying? He returned his attention to her. "Afraid of what?"

"The bomber. He scares me."

"You don't need to worry about anything, Mel. I won't let anyone hurt you," Danny replied. "You're here and you're safe."

"Are you just saying that or are you lying like when you said you'd come visit me every day?"

He closed his eyes while guilt bore down on him. "No one will hurt you, Mel. Not as long as I'm alive." He stood up again. "I have to go now. I'm sorry."

As Danny started to leave, Mel called out. "You have to take me with you, Danny."

He stopped for a moment and choked back his emotions. There was nothing more he could say, and so he continued on without looking back.

"Leaving already, Danny?" Sue asked. "That was a quick visit."

He whipped around to her; his eyes darkened while anger heated his face. "What the hell do you care?" Danny hurried out of the building and returned to his car. "Fuck this shit." He stepped inside and pressed hard on the gas. His tires squealed on the asphalt. "They think they can screw over me and my family? Not if I get to them first."

17

Few things burrowed under Kate's skin as deeply as being wrong had. She rarely faulted others for it, but she was always harder on herself than anyone else ever could be. And this one stung. This was supposed to lead to the capture of the serial bomber. While there was still a shot at the motor vehicle records, the one theory she had pushed hard for had fallen flat.

"It's not over yet," Tillis replied. "All we need to do now is tie this kid, whatever the hell his name is, to the white car and we have enough to bring him in. Once we track down registration details for owners in the Pittsburgh area, I promise you, one of them will match the blonde kid." He tossed photos onto the table where the team sat. "My team finished scouring CCTV from a 1000 foot radius of the bombing sites. Take a look there and you tell me we're screwed."

Surrey pulled the photos closer and peered at the images. A hint of a smile flashed on his lips. "It's the white car."

"Damn straight it is. And now we know it's a 2010 model year. We aren't pulling this plug yet."

"With the car information, the positive ID from two gun shops, and the video of the unsub running into a victim, we have enough to bring him in if we can find him." Duncan peered at Kate. "So that's the question. What's our next move?"

"The car, obviously...."

"Oh, shit." Tillis cut in as he stared at his phone. "I can't believe this."

"What is it?" Kate asked.

"The lieutenant just informed me that Jeff Hardy's wife posted on her social media that her husband was dead." Tillis eyed the team. "The kid knows. He has to."

"We have to live with it now," Kate replied.

"What do you mean? You were adamant about keeping it quiet," Surrey jumped in.

"You're right. I had hoped his uncertainty about whether Jeff Hardy told the cops anything would force him to take a step back, wait things out. But there's nothing we can do about that now. If the victim is dead and the cops haven't shown up at his place, then he assumes we know nothing. We know a lot more than nothing. This wasn't the ideal scenario, but here we are." Kate looked at Tillis. "We're still ahead of the game as far as I'm concerned. All we can do is pursue the car registration lead."

"I'll push my guys. There's going to be a ton of them registered, but we'll just have to work our way through it no matter how long it takes." Tillis left the room.

Duncan walked to the credenza and poured a glass of water. She turned on her heel and crossed her arms over her chest. "Something's still off about PivoTech. It can't be a coincidence that three of the victims called their support line. Can we get them to provide more details on those particular calls? They know who was working the lines on those days. We might not know his name, but they sure as hell do."

"Hang on." Kate grabbed the list of names from PivoTech and scanned the pages. "Oh my God. Why didn't I see this before? PivoTech gave me a current list of employees."

"That's what the subpoena called for," Surrey replied.

"Current employees, yes." Kate scoffed. "Those assholes. They must've fired him. They took him off the payroll. It's the only explanation."

"They complied with the subpoena but didn't tell us the whole story to save their own asses," Surrey added.

"Sure as hell looks like that's what happened. They were willing to risk another attack, another murder just to save their reputation."

"So we get another subpoena for anyone who had been employed there dating back six months," Duncan replied. "Reid, you may not have been wrong after all."

WHEN THE KNOCK CAME, Nick already knew who waited on the other side of his door. He pushed off his sofa and walked in socked feet, still dressed in suit pants and a button-down shirt. Nick opened the door. "Hey, come in."

"I'm not interrupting anything, am I?" Walsh asked. "I know it's getting kind of late."

"No. I just got back from an AA meeting though, so I'm glad for the company of someone who isn't an alcoholic." He laughed. "You want something to drink?"

"Wouldn't mind a glass of water." Walsh continued inside, his dress shirt sleeves were rolled up to his elbows and he wore black trousers.

Nick returned with a glass of water. "Sit down. It must be

important for you to drive all the way over here from your place." He noted Walsh's expression. "Really important."

Walsh sat down on the sofa and Nick on the side chair. He took a long drink of water while Nick looked on.

"Okay, now you're starting to worry me," Nick said. "You might as well spit it out. You obviously learned something you didn't like."

Walsh cleared his throat and set down the glass on the coffee table. "You remember me saying my buddy at HQ was going to give me some names?"

Nick didn't reply and only waited for Walsh to continue.

"I got those names earlier this evening, just before leaving the office. I had a chance to take a look at them. Had Fisher glance at them too."

"And?" Nick rubbed together his hands with growing impatience.

Walsh reached into his carrier bag to retrieve the list and handed it to Nick. "This is what he sent me."

Nick eyed him and then turned his sights to the list. "These are guys who are in Coletta's circle?"

"Affirmative. And it turns out Coletta did have a direct line to Gustafson, Carol Whitman's father, before he passed."

"Who else is in that same line?" Nick swallowed hard.

"Man, I know you know at least one of those names."

Nick tossed down the paper onto his coffee table and scoffed. "I know three of them. And there isn't a chance in hell it's the one you're thinking of. It's not Quinn. First of all, he was never at Headquarters. He came from..."

"Boston," Walsh cut in. "So he probably still has buddies there. Buddies who could get access to Richard Lehmann's personal belongings, including his cell phone. And he would've had Kate's number."

"But he didn't know Gustafson. It was long before his time at the Bureau," Nick pressed on.

"That's true, but this guy does." Walsh pointed to another name. "And he was at Boston with Quinn for a year before he moved to Headquarters in Public Corruption."

"Gene Goodman. I know him," Nick added. "Crossed paths a few times at various conferences back in the days when I was at the Washington Field Office."

"We know Coletta worked at Headquarters in Public Corruption. So did Goodman. They both knew Carol Whitman's father," Walsh replied.

"And you're telling me Quinn pulled strings at Boston to access Richard Lehmann's phone because Goodman told him to." Nick shook his head. "Why the hell wait until Lehmann was dead to come at Kate?"

"Because they knew we were looking. They knew we figured out someone scrubbed the passport logs and let Theo Bishop into Mexico. They waited because they had nothing to use against us. Nothing that would prevent us from exposing them for helping a killer escape because the grandfather was a heavyweight at the Bureau."

Nick peered at him. "And they do now?"

"They must. It has to have something to do with what happened on the plane when Kate and Surrey were bringing Richard Lehmann into the Boston field office. Because why else use Richard Lehmann? George Lehmann was alive and in custody. So what did they know about what happened?"

"Nothing happened. Kate defended herself and saved Surrey. He said as much."

"What if there's more to it than that, Nick? What if Surrey was covering for Kate?" Walsh took in a deep breath. "They'd have nothing on Kate otherwise."

Nick pulled upright on the chair. "So, you're saying if we keep going with this, expose whoever is behind altering government records which aided in the escape of a killer, these guys will use whatever it is they think they have to get to Kate?"

"With Quinn's help, I wouldn't doubt it." He paused for a moment. "And if we're being honest, I'm not sure it's Kate they're after."

"But you just said..."

"They're going to use her, Nick. We come out with all this, they'll use Kate to get to you. You're the one they want. Kate doesn't have the clout you do. You have Cole's ear. You know enough that it scares them. And they know she's your wife."

Nick pushed off the chair in a huff. "Son of a bitch. Are you kidding me with this shit? Quinn is still turning the knife in my back?"

"Not just yours, Kate's too." Walsh got to his feet. "What do you want to do with this?"

Nick turned to face him. "What did Fisher say?"

"He says he can push for Quinn to get fired. I don't think he has that kind of pull, but maybe he does."

"No way will he be able to do that, even if he had every reason to. He's pissed about all this, same as me, I imagine. Except that it isn't his wife whose career is on the line. I don't give a shit about mine, but I won't let her suffer the consequences of top brass getting exposed."

"So we drop it?" Walsh asked. "And don't tell me you'll go after Quinn. He's untouchable now."

Nick paced the living room, pushing his hand through his thick salt and pepper hair. "What the hell do they have that could destroy her career? She did nothing wrong. That killing was justified."

Walsh shoved his hands in his pockets. "Maybe we need to talk to Surrey about that. He was there."

"You think he's hiding something to protect her?" Nick asked.

"I don't know, man. But if something else went down on that flight that we don't know about, then we need to talk to Surrey and find out. Then we can figure out just what those guys have."

AGENT TILLIS RETURNED to the operations room where the BAU team waited. "Judge says he'll get us the subpoena as quickly as possible."

"It's after 9 o'clock already. Can we get into PivoTech after hours?" Duncan asked.

"I don't know that they'll allow it. They still have rights to ensure we don't access more than what the subpoena grants us," Tillis replied.

"I don't want to sit on this until morning," Kate said. "What if we push for a warrant to pull their personnel records inside their building tonight? Forget waiting until morning for them to shuffle us around again."

"On what grounds do we have to get a warrant?" Tillis asked. "They complied with the subpoena and figured out a work around to cover their butts. That's on me. I didn't specify former employees because we assumed the bomber was still employed. I don't see probable cause for the judge to issue a warrant when we can't prove to him we know anything other than the fact our victims called PivoTech's help line. If we had more..."

"Then we make one up," Kate replied.

Surrey cast her a sideways glance. "I'm all for catching this guy, but there's a fine line, Reid. I don't need to tell you that."

"I'm sorry, but I don't see another way. What happens if he

kills tonight? First thing in the morning? I don't want blood on my hands because we were hamstrung by the system." Kate pushed off the chair. "We push for this, and there's a damn good chance we get this man tonight." Kate started toward the door. "I need some water." She made her way into the hall and walked toward the breakroom. Footsteps sounded behind her.

"Reid? Reid, wait up." Surrey hurried to catch up to her. "Hang on." He grabbed her arm.

Kate glanced at his hand until he quickly pulled it away.

"Sorry. Look, I understand your frustration. We should've made the subpoena happen. Not knocking Tillis, but I'm not sure we would've made the same mistake. Maybe, but it doesn't matter now. Point is, I know you don't have a problem walking that line. I've seen you do it before."

Her expression revealed what they both already knew. "You want someone else to die?"

"Of course not. But going to a judge and making up something to show probable cause will get you fired. Do you understand what I'm saying? That is a step too far over the line." He sighed. "I know your work in the past. Your work with your husband. Things were done that were probably not entirely by the book. I'm not saying I've never danced in the gray, but you can't follow down Scarborough's path. Look at where it got him."

She wanted to be pissed he'd said anything about Nick, but deep down, she knew he was right. Nick had done things to get what he needed, and she overlooked them. She learned how to do it and maybe Surrey was right. She'd crossed the line before, and it changed her.

He held her gaze. "I don't think I can follow you down this path, Reid." Surrey turned on his heel and walked away.

Kate continued into the breakroom and grabbed a bottle of water from the fridge. As she drank, Duncan appeared out of the corner of her eye. "You come here to tell me I'm out of line too?"

"Kate, you know me. You know I stand by you. Hey, we're the only women on this team and we have to back each other up."

"But?" Kate pressed on.

"But I think this is a bad call. You're the lead profiler now. Fisher made you the lead. I respect that. But you're also my friend and I care what happens to you. I saw what happened after Richard Lehmann. The look I saw in your eyes that day is the same look I'm seeing right now."

"Why do I always feel like you guys are trying to talk me down from a ledge? I just want what we all want and that is to get our guy."

"Yeah, I want that too." Duncan regarded her. "Not like this. Obviously, we can't pull employment records on a man whose name we don't actually know. Whose address we don't know. I get your frustration. I understand the desire for a warrant on Pivo-Tech's records, but we simply have no proof to offer a judge. A couple of phone calls isn't nearly enough."

"The last victim ID'd him. Doesn't that carry any water?" Kate pleaded.

"Without proof he was actually employed by PivoTech? Without proof that was his real name? Kate, the judge would reject it almost immediately. Look, I feel like I know you pretty well now. You're a good person and a hell of an agent, but we don't get to make up our own rules because we think it'll save lives."

Kate turned down her gaze. "I still have nightmares about it. When George Lehmann took me hostage." She looked up again. "I thought I was going to die that day. I almost did. And then something in me snapped. I'd been the victim too many times before and I was tired of it. That was the whole reason I decided to join the Bureau. I was sick and tired of being the victim."

Duncan reached out for her. "You're not that person anymore, Kate. You're anything but a victim."

"Do you know what happened to me when I was a kid?"

Duncan shrugged. "Some of it."

"Yeah." Kate took in a breath. "It was Nick who showed me that I could stop them. That I had the power to track them down and stop them. And yet, I failed to stop George Lehmann."

"We all screwed up that day, Kate. You didn't fail. We saw our guy and went after him the wrong way."

"But it was me who he came for," Kate added. "I get what you're saying. Maybe it is crossing the line, but damn it, Eva, we can't let this guy kill again. If we don't stop him just as soon as we possibly can, then it's on us. His next victim will be our fault."

"There might be something we can still do to move forward tonight," Duncan began.

Kate's ears perked up. "I'm listening."

She peered around as if looking for eavesdroppers. "We communicate with him."

"Draw him out? How?"

"I don't know how he'll react, or if he'll react. It could blow up in our faces, literally, but he could still have the cloned phones of our victims," Duncan replied. "So we send him a message from Jeff Hardy's phone, assuming his wife hasn't disconnected his service yet."

Kate considered the option. "What do we say to him?"

Duncan shook her head. "You're the profiler. You know him best. You tell me."

18

What was left of Jeff Hardy's phone lay in a Ziploc bag on the table inside the operations room. The screen was shattered, the plastic components melted, it was toast.

Agent Tillis peered at the evidence. "I contacted Mrs. Hardy to request that she keep on the service while we run with the investigation. She agreed and changed his social media settings to private in the event the bomber attempted to post anything under his name."

"The only way we'll know that he's received the messages will be if he responds," Kate said.

"We'll have to check the usage reports from the carrier. It can take a while for it to register, but obviously that phone there won't do us any good. But the question is, how do we do this so as to avoid scaring him off?" Surrey asked. "Do we want to risk him realizing that we do know who he is, but that we just can't find him?"

"What if we pose as a reporter?" Kate asked. "Claim that he got an anonymous tip suggesting the police know he's cloning the phones. He got hold of Jeff Hardy's number and is testing the theory. The media has already dubbed him Robinhood. A reporter could imply he was willing to get out Danny's message for him."

"After today, they're starting to turn on him, though," Tillis added. "He killed a guy with a wife."

"Then let's spin that around," Duncan cut in. "Posing as a reporter to get his side of the story, to let him tell that story. It could work."

Tillis appeared to consider the idea and glanced at the time. "We have 8 hours before we'll get into PivoTech."

"Whatever we can do to keep him occupied is what's safest for the community," Kate began. "There is a risk, but I think Danny wants to say more than he's been able to say. Posing as a reporter suggests that we can give him that vehicle, and, in the process, we might just learn more about his intentions. Isn't it worth the risk?"

Tillis raised a brow as he appeared to consider the proposal. "I have a friend. An ally who will back us up with cover. I don't want to mistake our Robinhood for being obtuse. If we pose as a reporter, we'd better be ready for him to check it out. She'll help us with that."

Kate took in a breath. "Then we'll wait until you can give us cover."

Tillis grabbed his phone and walked into the hall. Surrey waited for the door to close before he began. "The reporter angle could work, Reid. At the very least, it'll buy us time to learn more about who he is. This is a good way to get into his head."

"You can thank Duncan. It was her idea," Kate replied.

"Sure, make me the fall guy," Duncan snickered. "I don't know if he'll engage us, but what do we have to lose?"

Tillis returned to the office. "She's agreed but wants to be part of it."

"That's not possible," Surrey added. "I appreciate her willingness to back us up but letting her communicate directly with the bomber is reckless. She can't be the one running the unsub. This has to be in our hands."

He raised his hands. "That's what I told her, but she says she's the only one who can sound authentic. I gave her the okay so long as she keeps the story quiet until we capture him. Then she gets the exclusive."

Kate wore uncertainty as she appeared to consider the demand. "I'm the last one to side with the media, but we need her. As long as we get the final say on what gets relayed, then I don't have a problem with it. When can she be here?"

"She's on her way now."

THE APARTMENT DOOR opened to a face Nick hadn't seen in a long while. He peered at the beefy agent who was ten years older but was in damn good shape. "Hugo Bryce. Good to see you, man."

"Scarborough." The Boston native offered his hand. "I gotta be honest with you, I didn't think I'd see your pretty-boy face again." He laughed. "Come on in."

"Appreciate it. I know it's late. I got the last flight out because I had to do this in person." Nick walked inside. "First of all, I have to say how sorry I am about what happened to Agent Murphy during the Charles River case. I know that hit you guys hard back in Boston. I didn't get a chance to say that to you at the time."

"Yeah, he's been missed, I can promise you. Damn Southie son of a bitch was just a kid, you know?" Bryce walked toward the kitchen. "Hey, you want a beer or something?"

"No, thanks. I'm good."

"Suit yourself." Bryce pulled open the tab of a Pabst Blue Ribbon and tossed it back. "Sounds like you got some serious shit to discuss, what with you coming all this way. Take a load off. Sorry I wasn't expecting company. Place is a mess."

"Don't worry about that." Nick cleared a spot on the sofa. "I have a situation and I need to know if I can trust you to take a look at something for me."

"Hell yeah, you know you can. What's going on?" He sat down on the nearby recliner, resting his arms on the side of the chair. They were as big as Nick's leg.

"About 3 months ago, we worked on a case that spanned most of the New England area. Boston field office got involved with it at the end. The son of a bitch was killing couples who were out hiking in the woods."

"Yeah, yeah, man, I remember it. Holy shit, you guys were in on that?" Bryce asked. "You should've called me. I would've been all over that."

"To be honest, we had a lot of agents and local cops in on that one. It was chaotic. The thing is, the reason I'm here is that I wanted to know if you could look into something for me."

"You name it."

"Your office handled some aspects of the case, particularly, it handled evidence relating to and the body of one of the killers."

"Okay," Bryce replied. "I can find out who was running that if that's what you need."

"It'll give me a leg up for sure, but this has to stay quiet." Nick leaned in with his elbows on his thighs. "I need to know who had access to the deceased man's belongings. I made a couple calls in the last week or so, just checking around and at the time, records showed no one in your office signed in to view anything. But I know more now, and I think I came up empty-handed earlier because the people involved in this made sure of it."

"I see. You want me to get into the weeds a little bit. I can handle that."

"But like I said, no one can know. I mean, no one," Nick added.

Bryce regarded him. "I hear you, but you gotta tell me why. What's going on? Why the covert ops?"

Nick took in a long deep breath. "You remember Agent Kate Reid?"

"Yeah, course I do."

"She's my wife now and…"

"Wow, congrats, man. I didn't know. That's friggin' awesome."

"Appreciate that. This last case we worked… this is going back several months now…some things happened, and I think there are operatives inside the Bureau looking to bring her down."

"What?" Bryce pulled back. "What did she do?"

"Defended herself, but I'm not sure everyone sees it that way or they know something I don't. Look, Bryce, this is serious. Deadly serious. You know I wouldn't be here otherwise. Word gets out that I came to see you…"

"It won't. Like I said, you can count on me. You want me to see who was snooping around that case, fine, I can do that. I can keep it on the down low. Wouldn't be the first time, you know what I'm saying?"

"Just a name. That's all I need," Nick replied.

"You got it."

Jennifer Allen from Action News Four appeared from behind Agent Tillis as he showed her to the ops room. At 5 feet 9, and wearing 3-inch heels, she looked like she'd just stepped off the catwalk. A stunning woman with bronzed skin and black hair, she looked every bit the news anchor. However, she wasn't one yet and Kate suspected that was her reason for wanting to be involved in the ploy they were about to carry out against a serial bomber. She'd done her own research into the woman while they waited for her arrival.

"Everyone, this is Ms. Jennifer Allen. She'll be working with us." Tillis turned to her. "Jennifer, these guys are FBI Quantico. Serial killers are what they specialize in."

"Nice to meet you all. Sounds like you've got an interesting take on the person responsible for these car bombs."

"We appear to be on the right track." Kate stood and offered her hand. "I'm Agent Reid. These two here are with me. Agents Surrey and Duncan."

"We should get started." Tillis continued inside. "I brought Jennifer up to speed and it's getting late. We need to make this happen now." He showed her to the table. "Take a seat."

"We'll feed you the questions and see if he bites," Kate said. "Are you ready?"

"I think so," Jennifer replied. "And you're sure this is the guy you're after?"

"That's what you're here to find out." Kate moved in next to her. "Let's start by putting him at ease. As soon as he sees a message from that number, he'll turn suspicious. So, you'll tell him that an anonymous source fed you information about the cloned phones and that you got the number from your own detective work."

"I can do that." Jennifer retrieved her cell phone. "What's the number?"

Tillis relayed it to her. "Fingers crossed he's desperate to get out his message."

"I think he has a lot to say," Surrey replied.

Kate nodded. "Go head, Jennifer. Whenever you're ready."

"Got it." She typed in the message, going back and forth a few times on the precise wording, eventually settling on short and to the point. "How does this look?"

Kate peered at it and turned to Surrey and Duncan. "What do you guys think?"

Duncan nodded. "Good start. I say go for it."

"Same here," Surrey replied.

"Tillis?" Kate turned to him. "You good with this?"

He nodded. "I'm good. Let's do some fishing."

Kate looked at Jennifer again. "Press send."

Jennifer, who had walked in appearing confident, looked much less so now. She appeared to swallow down her nerves and pressed the button. "Now we just wait, I guess."

"Now we wait," Tillis replied.

Kate felt the tension rise in the room. Everyone seemed to fear that whoever Danny was might see through the ploy. What would happen if he had was obvious; he would simply vanish. The risk was Kate's to shoulder, and she accepted that. Danny was a man who already straddled the line between right and wrong and probably had for some time. He perceived that society had kept him down and there was only one way to level the playing field. Danny was desperate to be seen and desperation made people dangerous.

THE LATE SHOW was on TV and the screen was the only source of light inside the living room. Danny propped up his feet on the coffee table and slouched down on the sofa. A beer in his hand and a bag of chips lying next to him, he stared at the TV, but his head swam with thoughts of how to get Mel home. Without a job, he'd just screwed himself. And having killed four people might put a damper on the judge's review.

One of the phones on the kitchen table sounded and drew his attention. He only had three active clones at the moment, and one was from a dead man. Danny walked into the kitchen to see what had been sent and his expression dropped. "What the hell?" He picked up Jeff's cloned phone. As he read the message, his heart jumped into his throat. "What the..." He shot around as if someone had entered his home. His pulse quickened and his throat turned dry. Someone had found him, but that was impossible. He'd taken every precaution.

"A goddam reporter? Seriously?" Sweat formed on his brow and his hands turned clammy. "They know. How do they know?" It seemed that Danny King hadn't realized that law enforcement could figure out that he'd cloned the phones. He hadn't given them enough credit and now cursed himself for it.

He held the phone in his hands, staring at the message. How could he trust some reporter he didn't even know? No way, this was some kind of trap. It had to be. He brought the phone with him into the living room and returned to the sofa.

Several minutes passed as he stared at the television, then the phone, and then back to the television. "If they knew where I was, they'd be here already." Danny jumped up again and peeked through his front room window out onto the darkened streets of his neighborhood. No suspicious cars. No one walking by. It was almost midnight and the streets were deadly quiet.

The phone buzzed again in his hand and he jumped. "Shit. What do I do?" He looked at the message, re-reading it several times. With the back of his hand, he wiped the sweat from his forehead.

"You don't have to give me your name. I just want you to tell me your side of the story," the message read.

"She doesn't know my name. Okay. Okay, so maybe she's not lying. Maybe the cops said something to her." He'd seen Jennifer Allen on the news before, but how could he be sure this wasn't a trap? That the cops weren't with her right now waiting for him to reveal his location? That's what this was, he knew it. They'd figured out he had cloned the phones, but how? "How the hell did you know that?" He had to ignore the message. There was no other choice. He didn't know if it really was the reporter, but that didn't matter. Revealing anything would lead to the cops pounding down his door.

"But she doesn't know my name," he insisted as if trying to convince himself. Maybe this was his chance to tell his side of the story. Why weren't the cops busting down his door? "Because they don't know it's me. No way this phone will track back to me. It can't." Danny was good at a lot of things, but he'd become especially proficient at hiding his location. "Do they think I'm an idiot?" He considered the message again, vacillating on a response. "Okay, bitch. You want to hear my side? I'll tell you."

THE REPORTER's phone rested on the table and it finally lit up with a reply. Jennifer shot a glance to Kate. "That's him. He responded."

"Let's see if he feels like talking." Kate took the phone and pressed the screen. "You mind entering your passcode?"

"Oh, right." Jennifer used her thumbprint to open the phone and was the first to view the message. Her face fell.

Kate noticed her expression and took the phone. She eyed the message and smirked before handing the phone to Surrey. "It's safe to say he's our guy."

Surrey nodded. "No denial of that."

Tillis leaned in toward him. "What's it say? Oh." He placed his hands on his hips and dipped his head. "I was hoping for more than 'go fuck yourself'."

"Weren't we all," Surrey replied. "Do we have a response to that, Reid?"

"You can't argue that we got to him," Kate began. "I can only imagine what's running through his head right now."

"But the question now is, what will he do? Stay put or figure we're too close and take off?" Tillis's attention was drawn to the phone again.

All eyes were on the reporter as she swiped open the screen. Her eyes darted among them. "It's him." She turned the screen to them after reading it. He says, "You have no idea what I'm capable of."

19

It had been Kate's call as to whether to follow up on the bomber's final comment. It hadn't gone exactly to plan, and she had underestimated him. This kid might've wanted to make a statement, but he made it clear it would be on his own terms.

Kate gazed through the passenger window while Surrey drove them back to the hotel. In the black of the night, she had no idea whether the plan had worked or whether they'd only prompted the bomber to take further action. She suspected the latter, given his response. "I'm not sure I stand by my risk/reward assessment."

Duncan placed her hand on Kate's shoulder from the backseat. "We were working with limited options. We had to take the shot."

"It was a good move." Surrey glanced at her from behind the wheel. "I think it was the only move, like Duncan said." He pulled into the parking lot. "We should get some rest. We'll have the new subpoena first thing in the morning. And who knows? Maybe Tillis's guys will have pinned down a match on the car registration.

That's probably our best shot at tying this whole thing together now."

Kate opened her door and started ahead. The night was hazy and warm. Peaceful. The glow of the city lights in the distance looked haunting in the heavy air. She opened the door to the hotel and waited for the others to catch up. Maybe she hadn't been ready for this. She'd been so reliant on others. Quinn, Nick, Fisher. And Fisher was the one to give her the shot she thought she'd always wanted. Now she stood in the shoes of someone whose job it was to stop killers. It seemed those shoes were feeling pretty big right about now.

When they stepped off the elevator, Surrey started down the hall. "Good night, ladies. See you in a few hours."

Kate secured the hotel room door after Duncan followed her inside. "Now that we're alone. You want to tell me what you really think about how things went tonight?"

Duncan slipped off her shoes and dropped to the bed. "It was my idea, Kate. You backed me up, so whatever happens, it's on me."

"Did we provoke him?" Kate sat down next to her.

"I don't know. I can't say if he believed he was talking to a reporter or not. We all assume this young blonde kid is our suspect. I agree with that. There's too much evidence that points to him. Even if we may not know his real name. Thing is, he's young, he's desperate. We might've made him feel as though his time was up and that he was running out of options. Honestly, Kate, I can't get a clear read on this."

"We'll know more in the morning, whether we want to or not." Kate climbed into her bed and switched off the lamp between them. She stared at the ceiling in the pitch black. The curtains in the room shut out the light, except for a sliver that seeped under the door into the hall.

Everyone was concerned about whether PivoTech would hold the answers they sought. Now that the name of the unsub was in question, the end of this felt miles away. Kate's nerves were impossible to hide, and she knew the team saw that. If only she could talk to Nick. He would comfort her; reassure her. Insecurity had a death grip around her neck. To fail at this, her first lead assignment, would shake her confidence, which was already in tatters as she dealt with the aftermath of George and Richard Lehmann. It would undermine the confidence the team had placed in her. Surrey gave up this job so that she could take her supposed rightful place.

Her phone lit up on the nightstand and Kate peered at the incoming message. She glanced at Eva, who appeared to be asleep, so Kate slipped out of bed and pulled on her shorts. Quietly, she opened the door and padded into the bright hallway toward Surrey's room.

A quiet knock and he opened the door. "Hey. You weren't asleep, were you?"

"Not yet. Eva's asleep, though. I saw your message. What's going on?"

"Come in." He stepped aside. "I couldn't sleep. There's been something nagging at me about this guy." Surrey wore a pair of gym shorts and a t-shirt. He pushed his hand through his black hair and paced the small room. "His last words to us."

Kate sat down on one of the beds. "About us not knowing what he was capable of."

"Right. So, I'm starting to think that the closer we get, the more dangerous he'll become."

Kate sighed. "That was on the table when I made the decision to reach out to him. Look, all we can do is work to find him through PivoTech. They'll be able to tell us who exactly the victims called. We have the dates and times. It was one of their employees, and that person is the only connection we have to three of the victims."

"I agree that should be the break we've been waiting for." He sat down next to her. "There's something we don't know about him. Something important that could change our tactics."

Kate furrowed her brow. "I think I know what you mean, which was why I was so hot to get to PivoTech tonight."

"I know. And I'm sorry I didn't back you up on that. I really am." Surrey took in a breath. "I just can't operate that way. I can't. It's too slippery a slope."

"I understand and I'm glad I have you and Eva to stop me from taking leaps like that with no safety net beneath me. I've done that too many times and I've gotten lucky. But my luck will run out." She considered him a moment. "I think I know what you're getting at with Danny's intentions. Why the crusade? Who wronged him to such a degree to livestream his attacks? Who does it..." Kate shot up onto her feet. "Hang on. We need to see that surveillance footage again."

"Which one?" Surrey asked.

"Outside the bar. He was wearing something. It was on his shirt."

"Well, what was it?" Surrey insisted.

"I don't know. But that's what we're missing. Something's been tickling the back of my mind." She turned to him. "I think this is it. Do you have the video on your laptop?"

Surrey reached for his bag. "I don't know, but I have the temporary log in Tillis gave us to view the files." He opened his laptop. "Okay. Let me see if I can find the footage."

"Should be under the Sienna Page file," Kate said.

"Right. Yeah. Hang on." Surrey typed quickly until he pulled up the file. "Here it is. Let me see if..."

"There. Right there." Kate pointed to the file name. "Open it."

"Okay, okay. Give me a second here." Surrey opened the file and pressed play. "What are we looking for?"

"The moment he comes across them outside." She peered at the screen as the video played. "It's coming. Hold on." She thrust a finger at the screen. "Stop it there."

"I hate to break it to you, Reid, but I don't see anything."

She sat down beside him. "Trust me on this. Zoom in. Look at his shirt. It's small and I don't know if we'll be able to see it clearly enough."

"Holy shit." He shot her a glance. "How the hell did we miss this?"

"It was a fleeting moment and then he's out of the shot again. "It's a name tag, isn't it?" she asked.

He peered at it closer this time. "It says 'Visitor.'"

"Where? Come on, you gotta get us a better look. There's a name on that tag."

Surrey zoomed it in again. "That's as close as I..." While he squinted at the screen, he pulled back. "Oh my God."

"You see it?" Kate slapped his shoulder. "It's a visitor badge from ManorCare. He visited someone."

"Family?" Surrey's lips upturned as it appeared to dawn on him what she'd found.

"Probably. Can you see if they have a website?"

Surrey typed again on his laptop. "ManorCare senior and assisted living facility." He scrolled down the screen. "Opens at 7am."

"It's 4am now. Gives us 3 hours. We could get a warrant."

"It would be open by the time we got one, and we have no idea who we're looking for. I think you and I should head there as soon as they open and let Duncan and Tillis serve PivoTech for the files. One of us has to get a hit.

Kate smiled. "That's what we were missing. Someone he loves is in that home. And we're going to find out who it is."

~

THE SUN HAD BARELY RISEN when Kate's eyes flew open. She turned to see Duncan rouse as well. "Eva, we found something last night, uh—this morning, whenever it was."

"We?" She sat up and turned to Kate.

"Surrey and me. He texted me shortly after we went to bed. I went to see him, and we found something."

"Why didn't you wake me?"

"There was no point because we couldn't do anything about it until now. I remembered seeing something on Danny's shirt when he ran into Sienna Page at the bar. I don't know how or why I recalled it when I did, but the point is, it was a visitor's tag from a place called ManorCare. We checked it out online and learned that it's a senior and long-term care facility. Eva, he'd been visiting someone there that day."

"Family. It has to be." Duncan shook off the sleep in an instant. "Holy shit. Do you know what this means?"

"It means we're going to find him—today. Between this care facility and PivoTech, there's no escaping it. We're bringing him in today." Kate hurried to dress and brush her teeth. She stepped out of the bathroom with the brush still in her mouth. "I think you might've been right about Surrey and me. It's like we're one mind. This is what I needed, Eva. Someone who thinks like I do."

"I wouldn't go that far. God knows there's only one Kate Reid." She pulled on her pants. "This is good news, Kate. Very good news."

A knock sounded on the door.

"I'll bet that's Surrey." Eva smoothed down her hair and

tucked in her dress shirt. On opening the door, she noticed the grin on his face. "I hear you and Reid conspired without me last night. Come in. We're almost ready."

"Reid told you what we found, huh?" Surrey walked inside.

"Yeah, after I woke up this morning. I thought we were a team?" Eva eyed him. "Don't worry, I gave Reid the same speech."

"There was nothing we could do until this morning anyway. Might as well have let you sleep a little," he replied.

"How very thoughtful." Eva slipped on her shoes and cast her gaze to the bathroom. "Time to go, Reid."

Kate stepped out of the bathroom with her long brunette hair pulled back in a ponytail. "Has anyone called Tillis yet?"

"I'm on it. I'll wait for you two in the hall." Surrey picked up his phone and walked out of the room.

"The sooner we get answers, the sooner we can get to him," Kate began. "Regardless, I don't want to take anything for granted."

"Agreed." Duncan reached for her bag. "We can't afford to underestimate him. You ready?"

"Ready." Kate followed her into the hall where Surrey ended the call. "What did he say?" The look on his face sent a chill down her spine. "What happened?"

Surrey cleared his throat. "Uh, there was an explosion about half an hour ago. Tillis got the call just a few minutes ago and was about to contact us."

Kate swallowed the lump in her throat. "He warned us we didn't know what he was capable of. How many? How many are dead because I risked provoking him?"

"Reid, this has nothing...."

"Surrey, how many, goddammit?"

"No one, Reid. The blast happened near the train station

where commuters were just arriving. People are hurt, but no one has died."

"Oh, thank God." Duncan lowered her head and turned away.

"He didn't livestream it either. In fact, this went against his M.O. No one person was targeted that Tillis is aware of yet, but that might still be revealed."

Kate's stomach turned, but when an idea struck, she set her eyes on Surrey. "No livestreaming. No target. It wasn't him. This has to be the work of a copycat. What does Stallard say?"

"I don't know. Right now, what I've told you is everything Tillis told me. Maybe you're right and because the details of the IEDs were kept out of the press, that could be a good indicator of a copycat," Surrey replied. "But we have two possible leads that will point us to the bomber. We have to pursue them asap. Tillis and Stallard are going to be forced to shift their focus onto this new situation. We can't afford to lose any more time."

Kate raised her eyes to the ceiling and took in a breath. "Okay. The three of us need to split up and make it happen. I'll go to the care facility. That will only require one person. Searching the personnel records at PivoTech will take both of you to get through."

"I agree," Duncan replied. "We'll hit the field office to grab the subpoena and Surrey and I will head down there now. We touch base when one of us finds something."

KATE SPLINTERED off from the team after the three arrived at the Pittsburgh field office. She borrowed a car and drove toward the ManorCare facility where she was sure the bomber had visited a family member. Her head spun at the thought that a copycat was out there, but the possibility existed that it could still be their guy.

Only Stallard could make that determination. If the bomber had gone that far off the rails, there was no telling what he might do next.

The facility came into view as Kate double checked the name and address. Leaving the visitor tag on his shirt seemed like a benign mistake. And had the surveillance footage captured him from another perspective, they might not have seen it at all. This man had been so careful in his approach to the killings. But as Kate recalled Marshall Avery's words from what seemed like a lifetime ago, "*it's the little things that bring down the worst criminals,*" she knew he was right.

Kate walked into the lobby where three staff members in scrubs sat behind a long counter. "Good morning." She held out her ID. "I'd like to ask a few questions about one of your visitors who I believe has a family member here."

"Of course. I can try to help." The older woman eyed her credentials. "You're with the FBI?"

"Yes, ma'am. I'm working on an investigation with the local police and your facility came up. I realize this might sound like a strange question, but have you ever seen this man?" She held up a photo of Danny from the surveillance footage. "And more specifically, who does he come here to visit?"

20

The early morning flight back from Boston left Nick exhausted and without answers. No doubt Agent Bryce would learn the name of whoever had access to Richard Lehmann's effects, but this waiting game had gotten to him. Kate's career hung in the balance and she hadn't yet known the extent of the threat. Regardless that there was too little to say on the matter, more importantly, she had to keep her head in the game. He wouldn't chance the distraction.

With a quick shower and a fresh change of clothes from home, Nick headed straight for the office. The Quantico compound was just ahead and as he parked, a call rang in on his cell phone. "Yeah, Walsh. What's up?"

"Are you at the office?"

"Just about to walk into the building now."

"Something hit early this morning on that deal we're working on. It'd be a good idea to sit down and talk if you have a few minutes," Walsh replied.

"My office?"

"I was thinking maybe the café in building 2. Say 10 minutes?"

"Okay. See you there." Nick ended the call and walked out of his car. While Bryce worked to learn who accessed Lehmann's belongings, Walsh might just have real proof that Quinn and Gene Goodman conspired to cover for Coletta, Gustafson's protégé. He could only hope.

Nick dropped off his things at his office and hustled toward the café. Within a few minutes, he'd arrived and spotted Walsh at one of the tables. "Morning."

"Morning." Walsh waited for him to take a seat. "Don't you want to get a coffee or something?"

"No. I'm good. I flew to Boston late last night and just got back. I must've tossed back three cups of coffee on the flight."

"Who'd you talk to?" Walsh asked.

"I met Hugo Bryce at his place. I figure if anyone could help us out, it'd be him."

"Bryce? Oh, hell. I hope you told him how sorry we were about what happened to Murphy."

"I did," Nick replied.

"You have to know that the more people we bring in on this..."

"He can be trusted," Nick cut in. "You must have some news for me."

"As a matter of fact, I do. Goodman is the lynchpin. Coletta was instructed by him to alter the records to show the Mercy Killer didn't cross over into Mexico until hours later than we thought."

"How'd you figure out that one?" Nick pressed on.

"A few well-placed friends who know all too well the group we're dealing with. Once I learned there had been a direct link between Goodman and Gustafson, it got easier to piece together. I also learned that Goodman instructed one of his cronies to look into Richard Lehmann. I don't know who that someone is yet or what he may have uncovered."

Nick regarded him. "Probably the same someone who checked out the phone. Bryce may get that answer for us soon."

"My first thought was that something happened on the plane that resulted in Richard Lehmann's death. Something that maybe Goodman and his buddies knew about and decided to hang onto until just the right moment to use against us, or Kate." Walsh lowered his gaze to the coffee cup before him. "Well, it looks like what they're doing is looking into whether Richard Lehmann, in fact, had anything to do with the murders his brother was accused of."

"We already know of at least one because George Lehmann admitted to it," Nick replied.

"Right, but Nick, based on what my buddy said, evidence exists that Richard Lehmann was nowhere near his brother when his brother killed McKowan. That party he was at? The one that made him late to report for duty?"

"Yeah," Nick replied.

"They tracked down a woman who claimed Richard Lehmann had been with her during the time the McKowan girl was killed."

Nick slowly nodded in recognition of the implication. "Tracked down, or dug up? They dug around until they found someone to give Richard Lehmann an alibi. And that's what they're going to use against Kate and me, maybe even you, to shut this down."

"That's it, man. If they lock in this witness, they'll be looking to throw the book at Kate for murder because Lehmann was, according to their witness, innocent of those charges. Which means they never should've brought him in. They never should've put him on that plane."

"Even if this bullshit story was true, that doesn't change the fact that Richard Lehmann tried to kill both Surrey and Kate. All Kate did was defend herself. Case closed. If he was truly innocent, why the hell did he go after them?"

"I don't know and he's dead, so we can't ask him," Walsh replied. "But you're missing my point. It doesn't matter if it was self-defense. What they're looking to do is tarnish her reputation. Kate made a bad call, things went south, and someone died. It would be all too easy to destroy her career with that alone, even setting aside possible murder charges."

"Son of a bitch." Nick looked away. "All this just to protect a killer?"

"Not to protect the killer, but to protect a legacy at the Bureau. No one can know that Gustafson's grandson was the Mercy Killer. Coletta, Goodman, Quinn, they're all making sure of that. And I have no doubt they'll destroy Kate, you, and me, if we reveal what we know. Kate's just the tip of the iceberg, man."

THE PIVOTECH BUILDING loomed large in the distance. Surrey pulled into the parking lot and stopped the car. "Listen, about this morning..."

Duncan held up a preemptive hand. "Don't worry about it. I see how well you two connect. Frankly, after what happened with Noah Quinn, it's a welcome sight. And without Scarborough here, she needs that back and forth. Profiling isn't my thing. It isn't Walsh's or Fisher's. It's Reid's and now you, so I do understand. But just know that there are things about Reid that make her more vulnerable than the rest of us."

He regarded her. "I don't understand."

"What I mean to say is her gift, for lack of a better word, can be dangerous. Not only to Reid, but to the rest of us. She's the best,

Surrey. I know you see that. That was why you stepped down. An admirable thing to do that I doubt any one of us would've considered."

"That's not true," he began.

"It is. We're all competitive here and well, it doesn't matter. My point is, if she's looking to you, it'll be up to you to keep her from going too far. I think you know what I mean."

Surrey looked away for a moment. "She doesn't see risk in the same way as we do."

"That she does not," Duncan replied. "Reid doesn't see risk, period. That makes her dangerous. We've all learned that about her but without Scarborough keeping her on an even keel, that job falls squarely on your shoulders."

"I understand." He peered at the building. "We should go in." Surrey pushed through the double glass doors and approached the front desk with his ID. "Agent Jonathan Surrey. We have a subpoena for your personnel files."

The man behind the desk peered at the badge, glanced to Duncan, and eyed the document. "I'm going to have to get the director. I'm afraid I can't let you in without an escort."

"Then I suggest you make it fast. As you can see by the paperwork, we don't need your permission. You have two minutes." Surrey turned away and started toward Duncan.

"What if they start hiding things?" Duncan asked.

"They'd be crazy to and what would be the point? It would only make it look like they were obstructing an investigation."

She tossed a glance over his shoulder. "Whoever that is looks pretty important."

"Can I help you?" Gilstrom asked. Her eyes were sharp, and her thin frame appeared stiff inside the fitted blouse and pencil skirt.

"FBI. We have a subpoena for your personnel records." Surrey held up the document.

"We already complied with that subpoena. I don't understand what this is about," she pressed on.

"It's about your lawyers playing lawyer tricks." Duncan stepped up. "This is the result. Now you can show us, or we'll go in search of the records ourselves and hope nothing else catches our eye." Duncan knew that wasn't going to happen. Still, it sounded good.

"Fine." She turned on her stiletto heel. "Follow me. It's unfortunate you didn't alert us to your arrival. We could've had everything ready to go for you."

"Appreciate the concern, but we'll manage and then we'll be out of your hair," Surrey replied. "It's just a shame you all didn't do whatever you could to help us out. We do what we do because lives are at stake."

"I'm not oblivious to that fact, Agent Surrey. This is our personnel department." She opened the door to a front desk. "Lisa, we'll need to show these agents our records."

"All current and former staff for the past six months. If you'd show us the way, we can get started," Surrey added.

"Yes, sir." The young woman stepped out from behind the counter and appeared nervous. "Um, we keep everything on the server, but we can print out whatever you need. I'm happy to help."

"Thank you, Lisa," Duncan replied. "We'd like to ask that you run a report that includes the names of any former employees from the past sixty days."

"Of course."

~

THE OLDER WOMAN behind the counter put on her glasses and studied the image Kate held in her hands. "Well, I'm not entirely sure, but that does look like Danny to me."

Kate's heart jumped into her throat. "Danny?"

"Yes, ma'am." She eyed Kate with some suspicion. "Has he done something wrong?"

"We're interested in talking to him, but I can't be more specific with you right now. Can you tell me who he comes here to see?"

"Well, I don't think I can. Patient privacy and all that," she replied.

"Sure, I understand. It's just that, well, Danny could be in trouble and it's possible that he might not get a chance to come back here and visit. I'm sure he wouldn't want those closest to him to worry."

"I'm sorry, ma'am, but I simply can't give out the names of our patients. I'm sure you must understand. Now, I've told you what I know. That man in the photo is Danny King. He stops by almost daily. I don't know what more I can do to help you."

"I completely understand and I'm so sorry to have bothered you. I'll go through the proper channels should I need any further information. Have a good day." Kate turned on her heel as a smile spread on her lips. She pushed outside and picked up her phone. "Surrey, I have a name. King. His name is Danny King. He comes here almost every day."

Surrey pulled the phone away from his ear and turned to Duncan. "Danny King."

Duncan's eyes widened and she looked at Lisa. "Can I ask you to pull the file of Danny King, or Daniel King."

"Sure. Just let me key that in."

Surrey returned the phone to his ear. "Hang on Reid, we're looking for his file now. Where are you?"

"Just leaving ManorCare. I couldn't get the name of who he

was visiting, but the woman at the front desk recognized Danny and gave me his last name. She says he comes there to visit almost daily."

"Holy shit. We got him," Surrey replied.

"Here it is," Lisa peered over her shoulder at Duncan. "Do you want me to print this up?"

"Yes, please." She eyed Surrey and both glanced at the employee photo. "That's our guy."

Surrey nodded and returned to the call. "That's him, Reid."

"What's his address?" Kate asked.

He lowered the phone away from his ear. "Address?"

"We'll need his address as well, Lisa. Thank you," Duncan said.

Lisa returned with the printed papers. "This is what we have in the file. He worked here up until." She double checked the dates. "Well, up until just the other day, by the look of it."

"We have an address." Duncan held up the paper for Surrey. "We have to get in contact with Tillis and Stallard."

"Agreed." Surrey returned to the call. "Reid, meet us back at the field office. We'll head there now."

AGENT STALLARD SQUATTED in front of the charred vehicle. "Have all the injured victims been ID'd yet?"

Tillis stood over him. "I sent one of my team to the hospital to find out. This doesn't look like the work of the serial bomber."

Stallard pulled upright. "No, and that's what scares me. He either did a 180, or we have ourselves a copycat. I don't like either of those scenarios."

Tillis spotted a bystander on the opposite side of the street. "Where's PBP? They need to keep this area clear."

"They have."

"Then who the hell is that guy?" Tillis tossed a nod at the man.

Stallard peered at him. "Hell if I know, but he looks like one of us."

"Yeah, well, everyone needs to steer clear." He started across the street with his hands in the air. "Hey, man. You can't be here. It's time to move along. Nothing to see here."

The man surrendered and stepped into his car.

Tillis watched him drive off and returned to Stallard. "So how soon before you can identify the components used?"

"Well, I can tell you right now based on what I'm seeing here, this is easily twice as large as his previous attacks."

"Hey, Boss?"

Stallard turned on his heel as one of his agents approached. "Yeah?"

"You might want to come see this." He started ahead.

Stallard waved for Tillis to follow and caught up to his agent. "What'd you find?"

"Maybe we should rethink the idea that this is a copycat." The agent pulled back a blue tarp from near the blast site.

"Is that a soda can?" Stallard's face hardened.

"Two, actually," the agent replied.

Stallard shot a glance at Tillis. "No f'ing way. This blast? Not a chance this was done with the same materials. Not that radius and not the blast wave." He pointed to the sidewalk. "Look at that. The debris field reaches way the hell over there."

"What else could explain the cans?" Tillis asked. "Could he have used two devices?"

"Sir, it's possible the bomber upped his game and learned how to make a larger vehicle-borne IED," the agent replied.

Tillis placed his hands on his hips. "I gotta know, man. Is this our guy or not?"

21

The choice had been made abundantly clear. But letting this go, letting Quinn and those he answered to get away with threatening to destroy Kate was a decision Nick railed against.

On his return, he sat at his desk and held his phone in his hands, preparing to make the call to Agent Bryce. In the end, it was really no decision at all. He would always protect his wife, no matter what.

"Scarborough, you're back." Moskowitz appeared in the doorway. "We still on for that follow up on the Hughes Corp case?"

"Yeah. Yeah, of course. Give me ten, would you?"

"Sure, you got it." He started out but stopped short. "Hey, you doing all right?"

"Yeah. Didn't get much sleep last night. I'll see you in a minute." Nick waited until Moskowitz disappeared into the corridor.

He couldn't tell her. He couldn't say one word about who was partly behind all this because he knew she would never give up until she made Quinn pay. Only it would be Kate who suffered the consequences because it seemed she had been wrong about Richard Lehmann. That fact alone would send her reeling. No one was harder on Kate than she was. Noah Quinn might not have been the driver on this team, but he was part of the pit crew and if she discovered that, Kate would bring about the end of her career all on her own.

Nick prepared to make the call when a text message arrived along with a photo. He opened the image. "What the hell is this?" The caller ID revealed only a number, no name. He read the message.

"Another bomb goes off in Pittsburgh. Didn't see your girl there."

Nick's face reddened and the vein in his neck bulged. He hadn't spoken to Kate yet this morning and had no idea there had been another attack. "Are you watching her? Are you watching my wife?"

Somehow, they knew she was working the case in Pittsburgh. "Son of a bitch." Nick jumped to his feet and swiped the keys from his desk. With his phone in his hand, he called the one person who could tell him what the hell was happening. "Fisher, it's me. Hey, man, we got a problem. I need to see you. Now."

THE COPS SCREWED UP. The first rule of engagement; don't give away your position. That was exactly what they'd done last night. Using a reporter was a nice touch, but Danny wasn't a fool. If they'd figured out that he cloned his victims' phones, it was only a matter of time before they figured out how he knew his victims. Then it was over. However, Danny was prepared with an exit strategy. Now it was time to implement that plan.

As midday approached, he arrived at the ManorCare facility and walked into the lobby. "Hey, Sue, how's she doing today?"

The older woman behind the desk stared at him.

"What's wrong?" Danny slowed his stride. He glanced to either side and peered over his shoulder. "Is Mel okay? Is she hurt?"

"Uh, Danny. I'm sorry." She shook off the stare and smiled awkwardly. "I wasn't expecting you. Mel's fine. She's just having lunch right now, I think."

Danny found his footing again and moved ahead, his face void of emotion. "What's wrong, Sue? You look upset." His curly blonde strands fell into his eyes and he brush them away.

"I—I don't know what to say, exactly."

He could see the fear in her eyes. "It's okay, Sue. Just tell me what's going on. You're starting to scare me. Are you sure Mel's doing all right?"

"Yes. Yes, she's just fine, like I said." Her voice faltered. "Danny, a woman came around this morning asking about you."

A wave of panic shot up his spine. Danny feared his face would betray him as he tried to steady his nerves. "Oh? Who was she? What did she want?"

"I don't really know if I'm supposed to say..."

"Sue, it's me. You know me. I take care of Mel. I try to visit her every day. What did this woman want? Who did she work for?"

"Danny, she worked for the FBI."

Her words lingered in the air. He could hear the pounding of his heart in his ears. "Did she say what she wanted?"

"No. She just asked if I'd seen you recently. And well, I didn't know anything about anything, so I told her you come here to visit someone. Mind you, I didn't say who it was. That's against the rules."

Danny nodded. "I see."

"Son, are you in some kind of trouble?"

"No. Nothing at all like that. I think it's part of the background check. See, since I'm trying to get Mel back, I started looking for a better job. And I might have a shot at this government gig, but you know, they gotta look into me and stuff." He thumbed back toward the hall. "Hey, can I go see Mel? I was thinking I'd take her out on the grounds for a walk."

"Sure, Danny. I'll bet she'd like that very much. You go on ahead."

"Thanks, Sue. And hey, don't worry about anything. The FBI can be scary, but it's nothing. I promise you." His smile faded as he made his way into the hall.

Sue waited until he disappeared into the corridor and peered at the FBI agent's card. With the card between her fingers, she picked up the phone.

KATE'S PHONE buzzed in her pocket and she answered the line. "Reid, here."

"Agent Reid, this is Sue down at ManorCare. I thought I should tell you. And you know, everything is fine, but I thought you might want to know that Danny is here. He's come for a visit. I'm sure you could straighten out all this job nonsense."

Kate wore mild confusion. "You know, that's a good idea. I'll run down there now. I'll be there in just a few minutes. Thanks so much, Sue."

"He's there?" Surrey asked.

"He's there. He must've given her some BS story about a job, I don't know. She sounded afraid."

"If you picked up on that over the phone, I have no doubt he did when he walked in. We won't have much time." Surrey made the call. "Tillis, Danny King is our guy and he's at a place called ManorCare assisted living. This is your show, man. What do you want to do?" Surrey nodded. "Yeah, no I get it. We'll wait for you here." He ended the call. "He's going to the facility with two of his agents. They're going to bring him in."

Duncan turned to Kate. "If they see he has a white Ford Focus, that'll make it even easier to bring him in for questioning. It's a direct link to the bombs, but where does that leave us?"

Kate considered an idea. "It seems strange that he would waltz into the facility hours after blowing up a car in front of a train station. Is he so arrogant to think we wouldn't step up efforts to hunt him down?"

"He did text that we didn't know what he was capable of," Duncan replied. "Maybe he was proving it to us."

"I don't know. Something doesn't fit about this last attack. He's single-minded," Kate pressed on.

"What are you saying?" Surrey asked. "According to Tillis, Stallard found matching evidence to what Danny had used in his other attacks. They don't think it's a copycat."

"It just goes against everything we've learned about him so far." Kate paced the makeshift operations room. She stopped and turned back to the team. "Unless it was a test run."

"A test run for something bigger," Duncan said.

"He's on the edge right now. Maybe because we pushed him there, I don't know, but if that was a test run, we need to know why. What's his reason for wanting to go bigger?" Kate sat down at the computer. "Daniel King. So we have his full name now and an address. "Okay, looks like the house belongs to Ellen King. The mother?" She typed in more commands. "Oh, I see."

"What is it?" Duncan moved in.

"Ellen King's died two years ago. Vital Records show cancer." She continued her search. "Ellen also had a daughter, Melanie."

Surrey sat down next to Kate. "What can you find out about her?"

Kate typed again and when the screen populated, she turned to Surrey. "Remanded to state care."

"The ManorCare facility," Surrey replied.

"Probably, but why?" Kate scanned through the information. "Doesn't say why she's there."

Duncan leaned over her shoulder. "It does say that there's a pending court date to determine adult guardianship of Melanie King. She must not be able to care for herself."

"Which is why she's in a state facility," Kate added. "Danny doesn't like this. He's fighting it. If the mother died two years ago, he must've been taking care of the sister up until recently. Something had to have happened for the state to place her in a home."

"Do you think he hurt her?" Duncan asked.

"No, I don't think so. I think he's fighting for her." Kate peered at them. "If Stallard can confirm the train station bombing ties to Danny King, then I think it's safe to say it was a trial run. I think Danny King is going to punish whoever he deems responsible for taking his sister from him."

"Who the hell could that be?" Surrey asked. "The state?"

Kate peered at them. "Who else?"

FISHER PULLED the toothpick from his mouth and returned the phone to Nick. He leaned back in his desk chair and stared through the window. "You're telling me these guys, including Quinn, are there in Pittsburgh and are trying to find Kate." He shook his head. "No way. It's a scare tactic."

"A scare tactic?" Nick rubbed his forehead. "They're in Pittsburgh. The photo shows the train station where a car bomb went off. They know she's working that investigation. I don't know how they know, but they do. If they wanted to scare me into silence, asserting a threat against my wife isn't the way to do it." He took in a breath. "Quinn knows what I'd do to protect Kate."

"They won't hurt her, Nick. Come on."

"It's time to take off the blinders, Cam. We're dealing with powerful people. We both know what the higher-ups at the Bureau are capable of. They can destroy any one of us at any time. They don't care who gets in their way."

Fisher regarded him. "You sound paranoid."

"If it was Eva, you'd feel the same way," Nick added. "I want you to get her out of there. She's not safe."

Fisher chewed on another toothpick with unrelenting force. "You really believe they, whoever 'they' are, would hurt Kate? Would kill her? Why would they do that when they have the evidence to prove she was wrong about Richard Lehmann?"

"That's what they want me to believe," Nick replied. "I'm not so sure. If they did have real proof, why go through the trouble of going to Pittsburgh and lingering around the latest crime scene? They're threatening her because they don't have the proof. They know we're calling their bluff, and this is the result. They want me to know they're watching her. I'm telling you, Cam, we don't know how far they'll go with this, and I'm not willing to gamble with Kate's life."

"Look, man, you need to take a step back. I get that the forces at play here are dangerous. But you're going out on a ledge with this theory, and I can't follow you, Nick. You already know what I think. We have no choice but to end this. That's how this goes away without collateral damage."

"You sound like Walsh," Nick replied.

"If you truly want what's best for Kate, then let it go, man. What does it really matter anyway? The Mercy Killer is dead, so whatever they did to help him failed anyway. We got our man in the end."

"Because what they did goes against the very reason for our existence," Nick insisted.

"I'm not pulling her off the Robinhood case. They know who they're after and it's almost over anyway. Last I heard, the local field agent was about to bring in the unsub for questioning. It'll all fall into place after that. Reid is doing the job she was hired to do. You can't control her, man. Not only will she hate you for it, but it'll wreck her confidence. I can't have that in a lead profiler. You know I wouldn't put any of my agents at risk. You gotta let it go. Look at that message again. They won, man. I'm sorry, but they did."

DANNY WALKED into Mel's room wearing a smile. "Good afternoon, sunshine."

"Danny!" Mel pulled up in her bed. "Why are you here so early? You don't usually come until dinnertime."

"Can't a brother want to surprise his sister?" He walked inside and removed his hand from behind his back. "Look what I brought for you."

Her eyes lit up. "Reese's. My favorite. But I just ate lunch."

"Save it for later then." Danny peered over his shoulder. "You know what? I also have another surprise for you."

"What is it?"

"You and me are going on a little trip," he replied.

"You mean I get to go home?" Mel asked.

"Not home, but we'll be together, and we'll have a lot of fun. In fact, we need to leave now, so let's put some of your clothes in your duffle bag." He opened the small closet in her room and retrieved the bag. "Here we go. You might want to go to the bathroom first and I'll pack for you."

"Okay. Be right back." Mel walked to the bathroom and closed the door.

Danny's smile faded as he walked to the window and peered out. "Still clear." He wasn't stupid. He knew Sue would call the FBI when he saw the look on her face.

"You about ready, Mel?" he asked through the bathroom door.

"Almost."

Danny returned to her bed and zipped up the bag. He walked to the door and peered into the hall. Clear so far. A back exit onto the small grounds of the facility was at the end of the hall on the first floor. Mel's room was two floors up. He'd been here enough times to know where every camera was, including the elevator and he was prepared to jam the signal as he'd done before.

Mel emerged from the bathroom. "I'm ready. Where are we going?"

"Just follow me. It's a surprise." Danny slung her duffle bag over his shoulder and led her to the door. "Grab your walker."

"Okay."

The risk of pushing her too hard weighed on his mind. Each step was hard enough for her to take and forcing her to continue when she felt tired meant she could succumb to a fall and injure herself. But he'd already timed this out. He hadn't gone there every day just to see his sister. Five minutes with Mel in tow and he could be at the back exit where a locked gate would lead them to the front parking lot. He'd parked near that gate. Danny learned that it had been on a timer and opened for landscapers between the hours of 11am and 1pm. It was 11:45 now.

He followed Mel while she used her walker and he led her to the elevator. When the doors opened, Danny jammed the signal to the camera and stepped inside. It also happened to jam everything in the hall, but it wouldn't last long. Just long enough to see them reach the first floor. "We're on our way, Mel."

She peered at him. "Thank you, Danny."

"For what?"

"For never leaving me."

22

All the signs pointed to the man they now knew to be Danny King. The train station car bomb utilized the same materials as the other attacks and ATF Agent Chris Stallard was about to present the evidence to the BAU team.

He laid out the proof inside the ops room while Surrey examined it. "Reid figures this was a trial run because it's different from his other attacks. What do you think?"

Stallard pressed his hands against his thick waist and nodded. "It's the only damn thing that makes any sense to me. Why else change up your M.O. so much unless you had something else in mind? That said, we're about to learn that for ourselves just as soon as Tillis and his people bring in Mr. King." He paused a moment to gauge the others. "By the look on your face, Agent Reid, you don't think that's going to happen. You know something the rest of us don't?"

"It was a mistake to reach out to Danny King. My mistake. I got lucky it didn't cost any lives. He's smarter than I gave him credit for, and he knew the authorities were behind the messages.

The train station attack was retribution." Kate sighed. "The thing is, the woman at the facility grew suspicious when I told her that I wanted to talk to Danny. Afraid, even. I have a feeling when Danny walked in there, he probably saw that same fear. Given all that's happened, we have to consider the idea he had a plan to get his sister back, and we might've bumped up his timeline to make that happen. We should prepare in the event Tillis walks away empty-handed. If the train station was in fact a test run, then I think he'll go after the people who took his sister from him."

"Then tell me, Agent Reid," Stallard began. "How the hell do we go about figuring out who they are?"

"We go to the state. Social Services, most likely. Find out who's on the pending guardianship case," Kate replied. "We know where he lives too, so we can search his house. No chance he'll be going back there anytime soon, but that could also shed some light. If Tillis loses Danny, he'll be on the run with his sister. His options will be few, but I have no doubt he'll look to the state for revenge."

"Based on the train station attack, he's learned just enough to be really dangerous now," Surrey cut in.

"Okay, so we get the names of the people on King's guardian-ship case, round them up and get them someplace safe. I can have a team sweep the Social Services building as a precaution. Surrounding buildings too. I have no idea how King would've had time to plot this out, but like you said, we don't want to underesti-mate him again," Stallard replied.

"Tillis needs leverage right now in the event he doesn't bring in the bomber. This has to steer clear of media attention. No easy task when ATF decides to sweep a government building," Duncan added.

"I'll do my best to ensure a media blackout for as long as I can," Stallard replied. "If I don't hear from anyone, I'll assume King slipped by us and will keep pushing forward."

Agent Tillis walked through the doors of ManorCare Assisted Living alongside two other agents. With his suit jacket open to reveal his weapon, he approached the front desk. Subtlety was beyond his comprehension. "I need to see the manager of this facility. We need to ensure your patients are locked down while we run a search."

"I'm sorry, who are you?" The woman peered at his credentials.

"We received a call that had been placed here regarding a man we're looking for. He's visiting one of your patients, Melanie King. Ma'am, it's critical that everyone remain calm. We don't think the man will harm anyone here, but we need to find him."

Sue appeared from the breakroom holding a cup of coffee. "Oh. You're here about Danny?" Her eyes revealed alarm, though she held the mug with a steady hand.

"Are you the one who called?" Tillis asked.

"Yes, sir. Danny's upstairs visiting his sister. Second floor, room 237. Should I..." she reached for the phone.

"No." Tillis held up his hand. "Just stay here, keep everyone calm. Your manager needs to be made aware of the situation and you'll need to keep your patients in their rooms. Can you do that for us?"

"Yes, of course. She's just out back. "I'll go get her."

"This has to happen now. Make the call to your security and let them know to remain calm and keep the patients safe."

Sue nodded quickly. "I will."

Tillis glanced at his agents and waved them on. "We do this quietly. I don't want any dust ups." He led them to the elevator and pressed the second-floor button. "Garcia's waiting at the exit to the road in case our boy decides to sprint out of here."

The elevator doors opened, and the three agents stepped out. Tillis looked at the sign. "Room 237 is this way. I don't want King to panic, okay? Just keep him calm. If he's with his sister, I don't want to risk her becoming his hostage." Tillis arrived at the door and pulled his gun. "Be ready." He turned the handle quietly and opened the door. "Danny King. FBI."

The room was empty. Tillis continued inside with his gun ready. "Check the bathroom. "Danny King? FBI. You can't get out of here, so how about we make sure your sister stays safe?"

The agent pushed open the bathroom door and aimed his gun inside. "Clear."

"Shit." Tillis lowered his weapon. "Spread out and check the common areas, the back, everywhere. If that little shit is gone..." He picked up his phone. "It's Tillis. We're about to search the place. Keep up your guard and look out for the white Ford Focus." He looked back to his agents. "Garcia's on alert. Let's move. Go check the common room downstairs."

"Got it." The agent headed down the staircase at the back.

"You go up and clear the floor," Tillis added.

"You want me to go into the rooms?" the agent asked.

"No, he won't go into a room. He'd be trapped. "Just make sure there isn't a fire escape or another exit to take him down to the bottom. I'll search the grounds at the back. Go. Now!" Tillis ran to the stairs that served as the fire exit and hustled down to the main floor. He jogged to the desk. "What's out back?"

Sue peered at him. "Picnic tables and a garden. What's going on? Where's Danny?"

"That's what we're trying to find out. Keep everyone in their rooms." Tillis hurried to the glass door at the back and shoved his way through. The bright midday sunlight hit his eyes as he used his hand to shield them. Outside, a few patients were on a stroll, some rested on the chairs. He walked out onto the greens and surveyed the area. "Shit." Danny was a young blonde-haired man and would've easily stood out among the people out here.

Tillis moved through the grounds and reached the fence along the back of the property. A truck was parked outside the open gate. "No. God damn it! He's gone. Son of a bitch is gone!"

∾

MEL TURNED TO HER BROTHER. "Why did we go out the back, Danny? Where are we going now? Home?"

"Not yet, Mel. Look, I promised I'd get you out of there, right? That's what I did. You don't ever have to go back to that place ever again. I won't let them take you from me."

"Are you going to get in trouble for this?"

He glanced at her and saw the look of uncertainty in her eyes. "No. No, of course not. We're family, Mel. It's those guys who will get in trouble. Not us. Just because you fell that one time doesn't mean they could just say I wasn't taking care of you."

"I'm sorry, Danny."

"What for?"

"I was stupid, and I fell. My stupid feet tripped me up and if that hadn't happened. If I hadn't got hurt, nothing would've changed, and you wouldn't be in trouble."

"This isn't your fault. Please don't say that." Danny peered at the road ahead. It wouldn't be long before they realized he had taken Mel. Once they did, it would be too risky to stay on the road. But Danny had planned for this. "You remember that place Mom used to take us to?"

"The place where Grandma and Grandpa used to go for the summer?"

"That's right. We can be there in about an hour. What do you say?"

"I don't understand why we can't just go home."

"Because we can't, Mel," he snapped. "I'm sorry. I don't mean to yell. We can't go home. Not yet. But I can get you settled in and you'll get to see Grandma, then I can go and take care of a few things. It'll be just a little too much work for you if I take you along. You think you can hang out there for a while?"

"Is there a TV?" she asked.

Danny smiled. "Of course there is. So, does that sound like a plan?"

She nodded. "Yeah."

"Good."

TILLIS PACED HIS OFFICE. "That damn car is registered to his sister. Once we got the last name, it was pretty easy to pinpoint the information. I've asked PBP to keep eyes out for it. Son of a bitch slipped right out from under us." He turned to Kate. "What about the threat to the case workers?"

"It's just a hunch that's the route Danny will go, but I don't want to risk ignoring the threat. We're still waiting on the all-clear from Stallard for the building. The three workers were located and Stallard will get them out of there in the event Danny put a target on their backs."

"I don't know how this doesn't become the lead story on the 5 o'clock news tonight," Tillis replied.

"The train station attack is our diversion," Surrey began. "It's our best cover right now. The police, ATF, your people. They're all tied up with that attack."

"Where can he go and how do we find him?" Tillis paced the floor. "Let's look into any connections this kid has to distant relatives. Friends. Anyone he thinks he can trust enough to turn to. He has his sister to consider, so I think he'll be mindful of her limitations. Danny King is in a bind and he can't do this alone. It's time we capitalize on that."

"We'd discussed getting into his house in the event he slipped away. It's time to make that happen," Kate said.

Tillis swiped his keys. "No time like the present."

Surrey pushed up from the table. "Hang on. One of us needs to stay on top of Stallard so we can get those people out of that building."

"Let me handle that," Duncan replied. "It's best you and Reid stick together. You're on the same wavelength, so I'm not getting in the middle of that right now. Not when we need everything at our disposal. I'll get a car and keep in touch when I have them. You guys just figure out where he went." She disappeared into the hall.

"You people ready or what?" Tillis stood in the doorway.

Kate grabbed her things. "How far to his house?"

"Twenty minutes, tops," Tillis replied.

The agents followed Tillis into the lobby. It seemed Kate and Surrey had shared the same concern as they regarded one another before Kate began, "Hey, should we consider getting ATF out there? Can you arrange that with Stallard?"

Tillis stopped at the doors and turned back to her. "Considering what we know about Danny King, we'd better be ready for a homemade welcome mat."

DUNCAN MADE the drive to the Social Services office, which was about thirty minutes away. She reached for her phone and placed a call to Fisher. His line rang. "Come on, I need you to answer." A moment later, she heard his voice.

"Eva. 'Bout time I heard from one of you. What the hell's going on?" Fisher asked. "Do we have King in custody?"

"No. He fled the assisted living facility just before Agent Tillis arrived."

"Shit. What's the plan now?" he pressed on.

"Reid and Surrey are with Tillis and are heading to Danny King's home. They're hoping to find a clue as to where he might go. Local police have a BOLO out on the car. I'm heading to the government building where ATF is sweeping to be sure King hadn't planned on blowing that up too."

"Christ, what *isn't* happening there?"

She scoffed. "No shit. This whole thing blew up on us today. Literally."

"I thought we had the situation under control, Eva? Last night, you established contact with him. Kept him occupied in hopes he'd reveal something."

"Yeah, well, that didn't work out the way we planned. Reid blames herself. Says King got scared and planned his escape because he saw through the stunt."

"Is that what you think? Did she screw up on that call?" Fisher asked.

Eva closed her eyes for a brief moment and took in a breath. With her hands tightening around the wheel, she managed her reply. "It was my call, Cam. I thought it was a good idea to make contact. Everyone was concerned he would track down another victim. We had no leads, and this was my answer. Reid took the hit for me. What's happening today is on me."

Fisher was quiet for a moment. "You took a shot and it missed. It happens, Eva. You can't put that on your shoulders. Reid made the call and it fell flat. Whether it really caused him to go and blow up a car at a train station, I have my doubts. He was going to do that regardless. You have to take the hit and move on."

She pulled into the parking lot. "Listen, I'm here. I'm going to find Agent Stallard. I just wanted to give you a head's up on the status. I'll be in touch." Duncan ended the call and stepped out of the car.

If Stallard was trying to keep this quiet, he'd failed. Duncan spotted two ATF vehicles parked alongside the building. The parking lot was empty. And no doubt that whoever had been evacuated posted it on social media. It had been more than an hour and it was only a matter of time before the first news van showed up.

Duncan walked toward the entrance and noticed Stallard. "Are we clear?"

He turned back to her, slightly startled. "Well, aren't you as quiet as a church mouse?"

"You have to be in my line of work." She smiled.

"Same here." Stallard held her gaze.

She noticed his stare linger and cleared her throat to break the awkward glance. "So, can we get the three staffers? We need to get them back to the field office just as soon as possible."

"Uh, right, yeah. We're clear here. Nothing found. I'm sending my guys out before the press shows up. I haven't spoken to those people directly yet, so I'm glad you're here to back me up. Let's take care of that now." He opened the door. "Ladies first."

Duncan walked inside. She was a beautiful woman and was used to men treating her differently. It was hard enough to be treated as an equal in this line of work, but she rarely took offense. It was in men's nature to be chivalrous. Well, most men's nature. She played it down. Sometimes it worked. Sometimes, she would get the look that Stallard gave her.

He followed her inside. "Everyone's around back of the building several feet away. We can cut through. I'll let everyone know it's safe to go back inside. You can wrangle the three caseworkers and try to avoid questions from anyone else."

"You got it." Duncan had the names of the employees and a picture of them. Their government photo IDs were available in the database. She spotted a woman who appeared to be the one she needed. "Excuse me, are you Liz Farley?"

She turned to Duncan. "I am. And you are?"

"Can I speak to you for just a moment? Duncan pulled her aside. "I'm sure you've been concerned by what's happened this morning."

"Yes, it's frightening."

"I know. Ms. Farley, we have reason to believe you could be in danger and until we get to the bottom of this, we'd really appreciate it if you'd come back to the FBI's office with me."

The woman cast around her gaze with uncertainty. "Me?"

"Yes, ma'am. I can elaborate once we get you out of here. It's not just you. I'm actually looking for Greg Hughes and Kimberly Hightower as well."

"I work with them." Liz pointed toward the crowd. "That's Greg there. And over there is Kim." She turned back to Duncan. "We're all in danger?"

"We're doing everything in our power to keep you safe. That's why I'll need the three of you to come with me."

"I see. I can bring them over here."

"Thank you." Duncan watched as the woman hurried to her colleagues. The look on their faces meant they were about to panic. She was going to have to do damage control and fast. Duncan wore a reassuring smile as they approached.

"What's going on here?" the man asked.

"Are you Greg Hughes?"

"Yes. Liz said we have to go with you. Why? I don't understand."

"You will when I get you three out of here. We should go now." Duncan started back toward the building and spotted

Stallard. "We're good here. I'm taking them back to the field office."

"Got it." He turned to them. "This will all make sense very soon, folks. Thank you for your cooperation." Stallard looked at Duncan again. "I'll see you back there. I've still got to get these guys back inside."

"See you soon." Duncan walked into the building with the employees trailing.

"Wait, can I go back into my office and get my stuff?" Greg asked.

"I'm afraid not." Duncan didn't elaborate and continued through the hall.

He looked at his co-workers when Liz spoke up. "It's okay Greg. We're going to be fine. You can call your wife when we get out of here, I'm sure."

He patted his pockets. "Shit. I don't have my phone."

"Is it upstairs?" Liz asked.

"No, I left it in my car, and I was going to get it earlier when all this happened." He caught up to Duncan and tapped her on the shoulder. "Ma'am, I left my cell phone in my car. It's just out front. Can I at least get that? It's not in the building."

They reached the front entrance and he pointed through the glass doors. "Right there. The blue sedan. Please. I have to call my wife and let her know what's going on. I was supposed to meet her for lunch today and it's almost that time."

Duncan pushed through the doors and looked at her car that was only feet away. "I'm afraid not, sir. Please, just follow me to my car." She pressed the remote to unlock it and heard the footsteps behind her. "Mr. Hughes?"

He'd started to jog to his car. "I'll just be a minute. Hang on."

"Mr. Hughes? No. I need you to come back here."

Liz tapped Duncan's shoulder. "I don't understand. Why can't he go get his phone? I thought the building was all clear and everything was okay?"

Duncan turned to the women. "Just get in the car, ma'am. Please." She turned back to find Hughes had reached his blue sedan. "Mr. Hughes?" She shouted and ran ahead. "Get away from the..."

The heat struck her first, then the energy wave. Duncan was blown off her feet and came down hard on the concrete. Blood trickled from the back of her head and down to her shoulder. With blurred vision and ears ringing, she saw black smoke rise in the air.

Duncan tried to look back to see that the women were safe, but a faint feeling swept over her. She gasped for air and her eyes closed until she felt a hand slap her cheek. Her eyelids fluttered open, and a hazy figure hovered over her with moving lips and no sound.

"Wake up! Duncan, wake up!" Stallard tapped her cheek. "Come on. Keep your eyes open. You can do it." He gazed back at the scene. The two women were inside the car, peering through the window, screaming and crying. And as he gazed out to where the smoke billowed, he saw the blue sedan on fire. "Oh, God."

23

The narrow two-story home where Danny King and his sister had grown up was shrouded in overgrown shrubs and tall grass from a wet spring. Dry rot under the eaves and missing roof shingles made evident the family's financial struggles. The drawn curtains and a vacant driveway were pretty good indicators that no one was home.

"I see ATF coming up behind us." Agent Tillis peered through his rearview mirror. He rolled down his driver's side window when one of the agents leaned in. "Afternoon."

"Sir," the agent replied. "I'll have my team get started on a perimeter sweep. Checking for tripwires, things of that nature. Then, we'll work on access to the interior. This will take some time and I'll need you three to stay put until we clear the place. Are we good?"

"We're good. Thanks, man."

The agent nodded and turned around. "Okay guys, let's get started."

When he walked away, Tillis heard his phone ring in the center console and answered the call. "Tillis, here." He shot a look at Kate. "What? Is anyone hurt? Is she okay?"

Kate's heart jumped into her throat. She whipped back at Surrey, who appeared just as in the dark as she. "What's going on?"

"Got it. No, we'll head down there now. ATF is at the King home with us and preparing to sweep the place. We'll see you down there. Thanks, man." Tillis ended the call. "A car bomb went off at the building where Agent Duncan had gathered the case workers. I'm sorry to say that she was injured in that explosion."

"Oh my God." Kate's eyes reddened and her lips quivered. "Is she okay? I have to see her."

"Just chill out a second." Tillis held up his hands. "Stallard's getting her onto an ambulance now and he'll go with her to Pittsburgh General Hospital. She's hurt, but he says she's doing okay."

"Thank God. How did this happen? I thought Stallard's people cleared the building," Kate pressed on.

"They did. You were right about the case workers being King's next targets. After the building was cleared, Duncan ushered the staff to her car. One of them asked to grab his phone from his car in the parking lot. She insisted he stay with her. He didn't listen. When he reached his car, Duncan went after him. It blew up seconds later. He's dead."

With impassioned eyes, Surrey touched Kate's shoulder. "Duncan's okay, Reid. She's okay. That's the takeaway."

"But I don't understand. If the car was rigged, that must've meant Danny was there and was watching them. He uses a remote detonator."

"I only know what Stallard just told me." Tillis stepped out of the car and reached the agent in charge. "Hey, we have to go. There's been another explosion. Do me a favor and stay here to clear the home? Keep the neighbors back. These houses are too damn close, so if you find something, evacuate them. And for God's sake, watch yourselves. This asshole is all over the board right now."

"It's under control," the agent replied. "I'll update Stallard."

"Thanks man." Tillis returned to the car and slipped behind the wheel. "Let's go."

Kate grabbed her phone. "I need to call Fisher. He has to know what's going on."

"We should wait to see how she's doing," Surrey began. "You heard what Stallard said. She's doing all right. That's a good sign. Get the facts and then tell him, otherwise you'll only worry him."

"Yeah. I guess you're right." Kate leaned her head back on the headrest. Her eyes stared up at the car's roof. "He must've been there waiting for them. But how could he have done this with his sister there, and so fast? He wouldn't want her to see him for who he really is."

Tillis glanced at her while he drove. "Stallard and his team are all over this, Reid."

She gazed through the passenger window and blotted her stinging eyes. The two had relied on each other and had grown close in recent months. Duncan backed Kate all the way where Quinn had been concerned. And their closeness had become especially evident since Nick's departure. Duncan deserved far more credit for her work on this team than she got and that was going to change if Kate had any say.

"This is it." Tillis pulled up to the emergency entrance. "We'll find someone with answers."

Kate stepped out of the passenger side and Surrey caught up

to her. "She'll be fine, Reid. Duncan will be fine. You have to stay positive."

She replied with a measured grin that quickly vanished when they entered the lobby.

Tillis hurried to the front desk. "FBI Agent Tillis. One of ours was just brought in. Eva Duncan. We need to know how she is and if we can see her."

The nurse checked her computer. "Yes. I'll call up the doctor now."

He shook his head as he focused on Kate and Surrey. "What I want to know is did ATF check the other vehicles?"

Agent Stallard approached from beyond the corridor, apparently having heard the question. "I instructed my team to check the cars. The other two had explosive devices as well. I don't have all the details yet, but it appears that the one that did go off was somehow signaled when the guy used his phone."

"He had already cloned it," Kate said.

"That's my best guess." He nodded as the doctor approached. "I think that's the woman you want to see."

Kate spun around. "How is she? Can I go see her?"

"You must be Agent Reid," the doctor replied.

"Yes."

"Ms. Duncan has been asking for you. She does have a concussion. Minor contusions and lacerations on her face and head. She's rattled. The blast temporarily caused her to lose her hearing, but it seems to have returned to near normal. Otherwise, she'll be just fine."

"Then I can go back?" Kate pressed on.

"Of course. I would prefer one at a time if that's all right with everyone."

"You go," Surrey replied. "I'll get the download from Stallard."

Kate followed the doctor into the hall when they arrived at the door. "She's right through here. Ms. Duncan, you have someone here to see you."

Kate watched as she struggled to pull herself up in the bed. "Don't. It's okay. How are you doing?"

"I'm okay. Just have a nasty headache," Duncan replied.

"I'll have the nurse give you some more pain meds." The doctor left the room.

Kate took her hand. "What happened?"

"Something I should've been prepared for, given who we're dealing with. I screwed up—again."

"You didn't screw up. Stallard said the guy took off to his car. You tried to stop him. This isn't on you. If anything, ATF should've swept the cars first. Stallard knows King's M.O." Kate shook it off. "I'm just glad you're okay. Do you want me to call Cam?"

"No. I'll call him. Really, I'm okay. You need to get me out of here today, Kate. Somehow, Danny King leapt right over us, and we have to know how far he's gone. The other cars..."

"Stallard's team checked them out. We were at King's house when he called and told us what happened."

"Then you should get back there. Seriously. We can't afford to lose him. He's off the rails now that he knows we're closing in."

"I had to see you first. Now that I know you're okay, then we need to head back there. ATF had to clear the property and they're keeping everyone away. So, we should be able to get inside now."

"Then go. I'll be fine. I'll be such a pain in these doctors' asses that they'll bend over backwards to release me." Duncan laughed. "Just stay safe. Please."

DANNY STOOD at the door of the cottage tucked into the woods. He kept Mel steady with one hand while he knocked with the other. "Grandma said she'd be here."

"We haven't been here in a long time. Not since Mom died," Mel said.

"I know." Danny's attention was captured when the door opened. "Hi, Grandma."

"Danny. Mel." Her wide smile deepened the wrinkles at her eyes as she peered over her glasses. "My beautiful grandchildren. Come in. Come in."

Danny helped Mel lift her walker over the threshold and guided her inside. The place smelled just as he remembered, musty with a hint of coffee. "I'm sorry I didn't give you a lot of notice that we were coming."

"Don't you apologize. My grandchildren are welcome here any time." She closed the door.

Danny let his gaze roam around the small living room. The furnishings were a little more worn. The carpet was worse for wear. He could see his grandmother struggled to care for the place on her own. After losing her daughter two years ago, she'd lost her husband a few short months after that. Danny hadn't brought Mel back here since. He wasn't the same person after his mother died. Now, he hardly recognized himself at all.

"How about I get Mel settled in and then I can go and pick up food and stuff? I need to take care of a few things, Grandma. Do you think you'll be okay here with her?"

"Well, of course. I would love nothing more than to catch up with my granddaughter."

Danny eyed her obvious frailty, knowing this was his only option. At least Mel wouldn't be alone. "About what happened after Mom died..."

"Don't think about it. It doesn't matter now. What matters is that you're here. I can see to Mel for a while." She held his gaze with her soft, but tired brown eyes. "Just take care of whatever you need to take care of, Danny. We'll be just fine."

He took Mel gently by the arms. "You'll be okay here for a while?"

"When are you coming back?" she asked.

"Not until late," Danny replied. "But I'm doing this so we can be together. That's all that matters, right?"

"Yeah. That's all that matters," Mel replied.

"Good. Then it's settled." He peered at his grandmother. "I'll be back soon."

"Okay, sweetheart."

He stepped into his car and started back into the city. They knew exactly who he was now. Danny had nothing left to lose, so he might as well finish what he started.

THE PERIMETER of the house had been cleared and the ATF team leader waited at the front of the home. Tillis pulled up to the curb. "I need you both here with me right now. I'm sorry about what happened to your colleague, but..."

"I know what I have to do. You don't need to be concerned about me." Kate got out of the car and hurried up the steps, leaving the others in her wake. While the outcome could have been much worse, Kate bore responsibility for what happened to Duncan. Whether it was warranted hardly mattered. Once Fisher learned of the incident, she pondered whether he would jump on the first flight here, or if he would let Kate see this to its end. If it was Nick in the same spot, the answer would've been clear. And Kate would soon find out if Cameron Fisher was going to do the same.

"We're good to go in?" Tillis approached the agent.

"It's clear," he replied.

Kate was about to speak when Surrey grabbed her arm. He shook his head and led her several feet away. "Before we get in there, I know you're pissed about what happened to Duncan. I am too." He released her arm, but his eyes remained fixed. "Just remember who we're dealing with. I know these guys are good, but this kid; he's not concerned about anyone else except his sister. Just be careful inside. We're close now. We just have to dot the i's, you hear me?"

"I appreciate your concern, Surrey, but people have died because we aren't doing our jobs. More could've died today too. This is on me. I pushed King over the edge. I forced him to make a move and I didn't anticipate the results. It's up to me to fix this."

"My God, Reid. Do you ever tire of blaming yourself? How's that cross on your back feel, I wonder?"

Kate pulled back at the unexpected swipe. "Excuse me?"

"I get that you're some kind of super sleuth. And hey, I've seen your work. I don't dispute the title. You are a hell of an agent. The way you develop your profiles... Look, all I'm saying is not everything is on you. We are a team here, aren't we? We all put in our two cents to help Agent Tillis and this is where we're at."

"But I'm supposed to be the lead on this case," she replied.

"And you have been. But if you don't figure out how to separate yourself from a case, how to step back so you can see the whole picture, you're not going to be the best. Despite your best efforts. And you have to let shit go, Reid. I know that you've been struggling with the Lehmann case and yet, you do nothing to resolve your issues. You just push it in so no one else can see it. You want everyone to think you're bullet-proof. Trust me, you're not. Just like I'm not and neither is anyone on our team."

Kate folded her arms in defiance.

"I can see you don't agree. That's fine. You don't have to. But mark my words, if you don't let this stuff go, get help for it—I guarantee you that you won't be the BAU's lead profiler in two, maybe three years, max."

"Then where will I be, Agent Surrey?" Her tone hardened.

"In my opinion? Probably dead."

Tillis walked toward them. "We're burning daylight. Let's get in there, folks."

24

Cameron Fisher didn't rise to anger easily. The former NYPD detective hadn't been built that way. But when he got the call from Duncan, anger that derived from a feeling of helplessness arose in him. He marched through the BAU halls. Sweat soaked through the underarms of his dress shirt. One of his own was in the hospital, and it just so happened to be the woman he loved.

He arrived outside Walsh's office. "We're going to Pittsburgh. I've requested the plane. Just waiting on Cole's approval."

Walsh stood from his desk. "What happened?"

"Duncan's in the hospital. Another car bomb. She's okay but she has a concussion, cuts and bruises. One more dead. It's time we get our asses up there and help our team. It's looking more and more like the serial bomber realizes he has nothing left to lose. And I don't think he'll have any qualms taking out anyone who gets in his way."

"I'm ready when you are," Walsh replied. "What's the status of Reid and Surrey?"

"They're about to search the bomber's house. They're hoping to learn where Danny King fled to." Fisher started out of the office. "Be ready in twenty."

Walsh waited for him to leave when he picked up the phone. "Scarborough, it's me. Fisher and I are headed to Pittsburgh. Shit hit the fan. Duncan's in the hospital..."

"Oh my God. Is she okay?" Scarborough asked.

"She'll be fine. Have you talked to Reid today?"

"No. She texted me a quick update. Nothing specific. Listen, if you're going there, I'll need you to keep eyes out. Kate's being watched."

"What?" Walsh asked.

"I told Fisher that I got a text and image from an unknown. It said, 'another bomb and your girl isn't here.' They're watching her, Levi."

"What the hell? When was this and why didn't you tell me?"

"Early this morning. Fisher said I was being paranoid and that they weren't following Kate."

"I call bullshit." Walsh peered through his office window. "They know she's working that case and now Duncan's in the hospital? Something's off. We're leaving in twenty. I'll get a lay of the land and touch base when I know anything."

"Levi, you have to stay hyper-vigilant. Don't give these guys the upper hand. I might be way out in left field about this, but I think they might be using the serial bomber case to find a way to keep us quiet."

Walsh rubbed the top of his head. "I have to pull some stuff together before we go. Listen, man, I'll keep you posted. Kate can look out for herself. I need you to remember that."

"Yeah, well, I thought Duncan could too and look what happened to her. I'm calling Kate now. I have to know she's okay."

"Whatever you have to do, man. Talk soon." Walsh ended the

call and gathered his laptop and carrier bag. He wondered if Kate knew they were coming or if Fisher was about to blindside her. Either way, she wasn't going to be happy. This was her show and by the sound of it, everything's gone south. "Damn it." If it turned out Quinn and the people he worked for were using the serial bomber case as cover to do what they needed to do to shield themselves, then this wasn't going to end well—for any of them.

Walsh pulled the strap over his shoulder and started into the bullpen near the elevators. He checked the time. Five minutes to spare.

Fisher emerged from the corridor and headed toward the elevators, walking right past Walsh. "You coming?"

He hurried to catch up. "Right behind you."

They stepped onto the elevator and started down to the parking garage. Walsh eyed his boss, seeing the obvious concern on his face. "Hey, man. Duncan's tough as hell. She'll be fine."

"I know. I just can't figure out how this went from some reject planting shitty little homemade bombs on the cars of rich people to targeting government workers, including our people." Fisher turned to him. "That doesn't just happen, you know that. That's not how these people work."

"If we could predict a killer's intention, we could stop them before they killed. We're good, but we ain't that good."

The doors parted and they hurried to Fisher's car. "The plane's waiting on the tarmac of the airstrip. We should be there within 90 minutes."

Walsh climbed onto the passenger seat of Fisher's SUV. "Did you tell Reid we were coming?"

Fisher pressed the ignition. "Duncan knows. I need Reid to stay focused on finding the bomber."

Walsh looked on as they pulled out of the garage and headed toward the airstrip on the Quantico compound. It was only a few minutes' drive. "I heard Scarborough filled you in on the message he received."

"I'm aware. Look, I get Scarborough's a friend and Reid's husband and I share his concern. I do. But we can't let this conspiracy talk get out of control."

"Out of control?" Walsh asked. "We're being silenced, man. It might be a stretch to think these assholes had anything to do with the bombing investigation, but why send the picture from the train station crime scene? Someone wrapped up in it was there and knew that Reid wasn't. Aren't you concerned about that at all?"

"Course I am," Fisher snapped back. "But are you seriously trying to sell me on the idea top brass is willing to possibly kill innocent people to keep their secret? That someone helped a fugitive escape because he was the grandson of someone who was once important at the Bureau? Come on, man. Don't fall into that trap."

Walsh shrugged and peered through the windshield. "I don't know what to think anymore."

"Think about catching this bomber because we're here." Fisher pulled to a stop. He jumped out and walked toward the plane that waited on the tarmac.

Walsh hurried to catch up to him. Maybe he was right. Duncan was already injured. He wouldn't let anyone else on their team suffer the same fate. And he knew that if anything happened to Kate again, there wasn't a chance in hell she'd recover from it this time.

Kate stood before the plastic folding table in the kitchen of Danny King's home. "Must be where he worked."

Surrey used his gloved hand to pick up the phones inside a

basket that lay on the table. "The lives of his future targets right here on these phones."

"Hey Tillis, you might want to come see this," Kate said.

Tillis approached them. "What do we have here?"

"Can you get your forensics team to figure out whose phones these are? No doubt they're clones. We just need to know the numbers and who those numbers belong to."

"On it." Tillis grabbed evidence bags from his kit and sealed each of the three phones inside. "Anything else catch your eye? A map of where he planned to go?" His tone dripped with sarcasm.

"If only." She let her gaze roam. "Not much to call home. I'll start upstairs and keep my fingers crossed." Kate continued down the short hallway at the top of the steps and peered into the first bedroom. A double bed was pushed into the corner of the room with covers bunched on top of it. A crate was used as a nightstand and a small wooden desk and chair rested along the opposite wall. "Danny's room." She walked inside toward the desk. Her fingers grazed the carvings etched on the wood top. "What the hell happened in your life, Danny?"

It appeared that he'd cleared out any electronic devices. The desk was bare, the drawers were empty. Not even a pair of headphones. She opened his closet door to find a few shirts hanging. Nothing on the floor. "I don't know why I thought you'd leave something behind. You've been planning this for a while, haven't you?"

Kate moved to the doorway and peered inside a final time before continuing on to the second bedroom. A wheelchair rested against the wall. A small dresser and side table was placed on the opposite wall. The single bed lay beneath a window while flowered wallpaper adorned the room. "Melanie's room."

She searched the closet. Clothes, some shoes. It looked like most of it had been packed up when Melanie was placed in the home. She walked toward the nightstand and opened the top drawer. A couple of young adult novels, a pad of paper, a hairbrush. "Damn." There was nothing to offer even the slightest clue as to where Danny had gone.

A third bedroom lay at the end of the hall. Kate turned on her heel and headed in that direction. She opened the door to a waft of stale air. A hospital bed lay against the back wall with a chair beside it. On the other side was a tray table on wheels. The room appeared to have been left untouched since the mother died. Kate turned to see several envelopes stacked on the long dresser top. She sifted through them. "Unpaid medical bills."

It was clear Danny King had faced a slew of challenges in his young life. Kate considered for a moment that maybe the catalyst to his final descent hadn't been that he thought he would be caught. But that he thought he might never have his sister by his side again.

"Reid?" Surrey caught her by surprise, and she spun around.

"Whoa. This must've been the mom's room," he said.

"Looks like it. I was hoping I might find something in here. I don't know why I thought we'd get a hit. We already know King is smart. He's not going to make this easier on us. Our emphasis has to be the BOLO on the Ford Focus. We missed our shot, Surrey."

Kate followed him back into the hall and stopped at a door, turning the handle to open it.

Surrey eyed her. "It's a linen closet."

"Yeah. And there just so happens to be a photo album in here." She reached inside and retrieved it. "We wanted to learn if he had more family. Whatever family he has left will probably be in this album."

They returned downstairs to find Tillis standing in the middle of the living room.

"What's wrong?" Kate joined him.

"I just got a call from Senior Unit Agent Fisher. He's here. I mean, he's at the field office and headed this way. So is Agent Walsh."

Kate shot a look at Surrey who appeared just as surprised. "You didn't know he was coming either?"

"I had no idea."

"Duncan. He's coming because of what happened to her." Kate didn't want to admit it, but Fisher had made the decision she would've expected from Nick. He hadn't trusted that she could do the job after all. "He'll want to be briefed on where we're at," Kate added. "I did find a family photo album. We might get lucky enough to track down any remaining family members."

"Great. Let's take a look." Tillis huddled in.

The agents examined the photos while Kate flipped the pages. She stopped for a moment. "The father's out of the picture by the look of things, but that guy right there could be Dad. It's an old photo."

"Should we try to track him down?" Tillis asked.

"Let's pull the name from King's birth certificate and see what we find," Kate replied. "It's hard to say what role Dad played, but it definitely doesn't look like he stuck around while Mom was sick. Who knows if or when he might've taken off?"

Surrey walked away and continued to search the house, heading into the kitchen again. He pulled out the drawers and opened the cabinets. He raised his sights to the ceiling and took in a breath when something caught his eye. With a narrowed gaze, he looked closer. His face turned deadpan and without a word, he returned to the living room and stood inches behind Kate. "We need to get out of here."

"What?" She turned to him.

"What's going on?" Tillis asked.

In a low, urgent tone, Surrey continued. "Out. Now."

Kate closed the photo album and tucked it under her arm, heading straight for the door.

Tillis and Surrey were just steps behind her. Kate made her way across the street to their car and waited for them to catch up. She peered at Surrey. "You mind telling us what that was about?"

"He was watching us," Surrey replied.

"I saw what looked like a camera inside a smoke detector. If there was one..."

"There were more," Tillis added.

"Yep. He knew we'd get inside," Surrey replied.

"But the house was cleared of explosives," Kate pressed on.

"I'm not talking about explosives. If he learns how we plan to find him, we'll never get to him." Surrey added. "That photo album doesn't guarantee us anything, but I'd rather he not see that we have it. It might be too late. I don't know."

Kate regarded them. "Then he left those phones on purpose. We were meant to find them."

Wearing a baseball hat and sunglasses, Danny watched from the end of the street one block over as the federal agents and the ATF drove right past him. He'd grown up in this neighborhood and parked his car in a nearby alleyway, keeping out of sight until they'd decided they weren't going to find him.

He shoved his hands in his pants pockets and walked over the one block until he made it to the end of his street. From there, he noticed a car remained and smirked. "Guess you guys aren't as dumb as I thought." It made sense to leave someone behind in case he decided to show up, which he had. But he needed those cameras inside his house. It was the only way for him to stay a step ahead. Looked like he was out of luck.

Danny walked back to his car and stepped inside. He pulled off his hat and gripped the steering wheel. Mel waited for him back at the cabin. If his grandmother turned on the TV, it wouldn't be long before she figured out why he'd brought Mel to see her. Danny's face would be everywhere and soon. She was just the kind of crusty old bitch to call the cops and have them waiting for his return. It was time he faced facts. He took Mel to the old cottage where they'd spent many a summer night because getting back at the people who made him this way was going to cost him. He'd gotten Mel out of that facility, but if he didn't get out of this alive, she'd end up right back there and would blame him for it.

Danny keyed the ignition. "Fuck it. Just do what you came here to do."

25

The doctor finished writing in Duncan's chart and continued to study it. With a raised brow, she peered at her. "You still have a concussion. It would be best if you stayed overnight so we can keep an eye on you."

"I appreciate your concern, Doc, I really do." Duncan buttoned her blouse as her legs hung over the edge of the bed. "But I have a job to do."

Fisher stood before her with arms folded. "I agree with the doctor. I don't think you should leave yet. One night here isn't going to hurt anything. We'll get a handle on the situation and now that Walsh and I are here, we can pick up the slack."

"You know what? I'll let you two speak in private." The doctor left the room.

"I can't stay here, Cam. I can't sit here watching television while you all are searching for Danny King. I helped get the team this far, I have to see this to the end."

Fisher leaned in for a closer look at her head. "I don't know. You have a lump the size of a golf ball on the back of your skull,

Eva. The doctor doesn't think you should leave yet. She's the professional here."

"She's also not demanding that I stay. All I heard her say was that she didn't *want* me to leave. Not that I *couldn't* leave. Obviously, for you and Walsh to be here now means you see what's at stake. I'm checking out of here and you can't stop me."

He stepped back. "For Pete's sake, Eva, why are you so damn stubborn?"

"Because I've worked with you for the past five years." She grabbed her things. "Everyone's at the field office. We need to come up with a plan to find Danny King. He was right to say we didn't know what he was capable of. I'm not sure we do even now."

Fisher took her by the arm and helped her to the door. "I talked to Reid just before coming in here."

"How'd she sound?"

"Normal, I guess. Why?"

"Your being here is going to make her feel like you don't trust her to do the job she was hired to do."

"Her job is to profile, which she did. It was Tillis's job to track down the bomber. But like so many other times, we find ourselves a part of the investigation rather than contributing to it."

"What is that supposed to mean?" Duncan asked.

"It means we might be overstepping. It's too late now because we're in it, but..."

Duncan stopped and turned to him as they stood in the hall. "I don't understand. How many times have we helped the local agents and law enforcement with tracking down an unsub? Since when are you against that?"

"I'm not against it, I'm just tired of risking the lives of my team."

"The team's lives or mine?" she asked.

"Yeah, okay. I'm talking about what you just went through, but what about Reid only months ago getting taken hostage? And all this shit now with Quinn? Look, I'm just saying that since Scarborough, we've gotten our hands into a lot of risky situations."

"What shit with Quinn? What the hell are you talking about?" Duncan demanded.

"Nothing. It's not important."

She held his gaze. "This is our job, Cam. We need to get to the field office. Reid and the others are waiting."

THE SIGHT of Levi Walsh always brought a smile to Kate, even in the face of disappointment. "I'd hoped I wouldn't see you until this was over, but I can't say I'm not glad you're here." She pulled him into a brief embrace.

"I figured you three had things under control, but I think Fisher was worried about Duncan."

"I'm sure that's what it was." Kate smiled and patted him on the shoulder. "Anyway, we need to get you up to speed. When is Fisher due here?" She spun around at the sound of steps behind her.

"Right now." Fisher walked into the ops room with Duncan next to him.

"Eva, what are you doing here? You're supposed to be in the hospital," Kate said.

"I'm fine. I appreciate the concern, but I'm fine and I need to be here."

Tillis and Stallard made their way over. "I'm Grant Tillis, this is ATF Agent Chris Stallard. Looks like I have the entire BAU here at my disposal."

Fisher offered his hand. "Senior Unit Agent Cameron Fisher.

This is SSA Levi Walsh. I apologize if it feels like we're taking over. Just so you know, that's not our intention."

"Could've fooled me," Stallard muttered.

Fisher shot him a sideways glance. "With one of my agents hurt and a suspect still at-large, given what happened this morning, I felt it was in the best interest of the investigation to have all hands on deck."

"I understand and welcome that decision," Tillis replied. "We have a kid out there who appears to have his back up against a wall and he chooses to lash out by blowing things up. Just to get you up to speed, Reid, Surrey, and I searched Danny King's house until Surrey noticed a camera inside a smoke detector."

"He knew we were there," Surrey added. "We all think it was his intention to get back into the house and take a look. See if he could learn what we had planned."

"And did he?" Fisher asked.

"No. We kept an officer on sight in the event King tried to show his face. Tillis recovered additional phones that we're sure are clones of his next intended victims. That's where our focus needs to be at the moment. Learning who they are and how we can get them under our protection," Surrey replied.

"And what about the case workers?" Fisher continued. "The two who are still living, anyway."

"They're here. Both are pretty scared at the moment. We have people looking after them," Tillis replied.

"Then I guess that leaves me to get a handle on this morning's train station attack."

"That's where I come in," Stallard interjected. "We found signatures that matched the other bombings. However, it has become increasingly clear that King is learning."

"Learning? How so?" Fisher asked.

"Let's just say, he's experimenting. Trying to figure out how much damage he can do with the materials he has. He won't risk an attempt at buying anything else. He knows we're obviously getting closer to him since we figured out where he lives. So what concerns us the most now is that he'll use what he learned from that blast at the station to make a larger statement. A deadlier one."

"We have to find a way to preempt him," Kate said. "Maybe it's time to get his face out into the public. I'd hoped we'd find something at his house to offer a clue, but..."

"You did." Surrey picked up the photo album. "Reid had the idea to take a look at his family pictures. Figure out if he has any family he can turn to."

"That's right. We were just about to do that when you arrived," Kate added.

"Don't let me stop you. I'd like to get with Tillis on issuing a statement to the press along with a photo of Danny King. That could go a long way in isolating him," Fisher replied.

Tillis nodded. "I think we can arrange that. If you want to follow me to Forensics. We should have his personnel files loaded. They have a photo of him there. We'll see if that'll fly for the cameras."

Agent Stallard waited for them to leave the room before he turned to Reid. "Why do I feel like you aren't real keen on the fact your boss is here?"

Walsh glanced at her.

"What gives you that idea? I understand. It's part of the deal sometimes." She brushed off his concerns and turned to Duncan. "You're sure you're up to this?"

"Of course I am. Tell me what you want me to do."

"The identities of the people whose phones we have here. Gather them up, if it's more than just our case workers, and get them under protection. But let's also focus on learning how they're connected. We know his first three victims were connected through PivoTech before they fired him, then he changed up his M.O. and went after Jeff Hardy. Now we have the case workers. One of whom is already dead. The other victim is standing in front of me," Kate replied.

Stallard folded his arms and widened his stance. "We might be neglecting something here."

"What's that?" Surrey asked.

"One thing that's been bothering me about the whole train station attack is that it was far outside what our bomber had done before. I can say from experience, it's uncommon to target a single individual with a bomb, unless maybe you're the IRA, but here? That's unusual. Then to switch it up and go after a larger crowd, only to take out no one. Not one person suffered a major injury in that attack. Anyone else find that strange?" He shook his head. "Then we have the timed bombs on the case workers' vehicles. Now, that I get. He was targeting individuals again, albeit, using a different technique." He paused a moment. "I can see this is riveting information for everyone but let me backtrack to the train station. We did find two of his homemade devices, which leads one to believe it was our guy. But..."

"But?" Kate asked. "You were pretty sure we weren't dealing with a copycat."

"I was." Stallard nodded. "Maybe not so much now. I'm wondering if Danny King is part of a larger group. A support group, even. People who have advice to offer. Knows certain ways of doing things. Has similar views on the world. You see where I'm going with this?"

"Wouldn't be hard to find a group of like-minded individuals. Especially if you know where to look. And if Danny King is as good a hacker as he appears to be, then he knows exactly where to look," Walsh replied. "That would explain someone making a similar effort, say at the train station."

"That it would, Agent Walsh," Stallard added. "I don't claim to be an expert in that arena, but I'll bet a dollar to a dime you people would know just who to talk to about that."

Kate considered the notion. "If he did find a group, he might've used his company computer to engage with them. If that's the case, it's likely PivoTech would track the online activity of their employees. We could go back to them and demand the files."

"It would be one hell of a Hail Mary, but at this point, what do we have to lose?" Surrey replied.

"Even if he did use a company computer, which seems unlikely, none of this gets us any closer to finding him. That is our goal, is it not?" Duncan asked. "Why don't you let me pursue this with my friend in Unit 2? Same one who helped us figure out when the phones were cloned. I'll bet he could track down groups of that nature and root around for us."

"While you all work to that end, I need to head back to the shop," Stallard added. "I'll put my focus on this morning's blast. See if I can spot anything that could point to another suspect. Hell, I still can't rule out the idea there may be two of them out there." He started ahead. "Not that I want to throw a monkey wrench into this deal."

Kate waited for Stallard to leave. "With Fisher getting King's face out there, we should monitor any tips that come in. I'd still like to go through the photo album and start tracking down any family members. If he's out there alone with his sister, he won't be able to do anything. So, I think he'll find help somewhere."

❧

AT LAST CHECK, the time had been 4pm. Where the last two hours went, Kate had no idea. But as 6 o'clock rolled around, they still searched family records and photos of Danny King. Kate examined the information with Walsh. "Can I ask you something? Why did you guys really come here?"

"I already told you—because of Duncan."

"Levi, are you sure about that? Kind of feels like Fisher lost faith that I could close the deal."

"He hasn't lost faith in you or anyone on the team. A lot of things have come up since you got here."

"What do you mean?" Kate pressed on.

Walsh glanced at Surrey, who had his nose buried in a laptop searching records. "Nothing. Frankly, I'm glad to be here. We work better when we're all focused on the goal. I know it's crowded, but extra eyes never hurt anything."

Duncan ended the call as she sat nearby. "You're not going to believe this..."

"What is it?" Kate asked.

"That was Tillis. He's with Forensics. The cloned phones recovered from King's house? One of them isn't a clone. It's Danny King's phone," she replied.

"What? We have his phone? Did they get into it?" Kate asked.

"It was a number registered to him. That's all I know. Could've been some extra phone he kept laying around. I have no idea, but they're working on it now," Duncan replied.

"That seems a little convenient, don't you think?" Kate peered at them. "Something doesn't add up."

"According to Tillis, it's a pay and go phone, but it still has a provider. They're cooperating, which means we could learn where he placed his last call," Duncan said.

"That can't be his primary phone," Kate continued. "He wouldn't just leave it behind after taking the computers and whatever else in the house." She paused for a moment. "What if it's the remote?"

"What remote?" Surrey asked.

"For the bomb. Stallard said the first four attacks, he used a remote to detonate them. What if that's it? We should let him know." Kate picked up her phone to make the call. As she held it to her ear, her gaze landed on a photo inside the album. She dropped the call and peered at the image.

Walsh appeared to notice her expression. "You okay?"

"Look at this." She pointed to the picture.

Surrey walked toward her, and he and Walsh peered at the photo. Walsh shrugged his shoulders. "Looks like a family in front of a house."

"Not just a regular house, this looks like a cabin. There's a lake in the background too. Take a look at the blonde kid. That has to be Danny. His older sister standing next to him. And then the mother. At least, based on some of these other photos, I think that's the mother. No father."

"Then who's taking the picture and where is this place?" Surrey asked.

She removed the picture from beneath the plastic sheeting and examined it closely. Then she turned it over. "Well, look at that." Kate read the writing on the backside. "Grandma and Grandpa's cabin. 2010." She glanced at her colleagues. "Danny would've been about 12 or 13. His mom was still alive. They have grandparents and by the look of this, they're maternal grandparents. We need to know who they are and where the hell this cabin is. Danny King could be there right now."

26

I f there was anyone Nick Scarborough could trust with Kate's life, it was Levi Walsh. So when word reached him that Fisher and Walsh were headed to Pittsburgh, the weight lifted from his shoulders. What he needed was eyes and ears on the ground to keep watch over whatever scheme Goodman and his people, including Quinn, had concocted. Fisher was wrong to dismiss the notion that they were after Kate. He seemed to believe that Noah Quinn had some sort of moral line he wouldn't cross. That they all had a moral line—a laughable notion. The Bureau was like a cult in a lot of ways. Nick had been on the inside long enough to realize that. Fisher should have too.

He could admit that uncertainty surrounded the train station explosion. But there was no doubt the text and photo were intended to scare him into submission. It had worked. Kate was going to be safe with the team at her side, but it was time to acknowledge defeat.

Nick pulled out of the parking garage and into the golden rays of a setting sun. Agent Bryce's phone number was cued up and Nick placed the call.

The line rang and finally, Bryce answered. "Scarborough, listen I can't talk right now…"

Nick voiced concern at Bryce's hushed tone. "Hey, man, you all right?"

"I'm close. I gotta call you back." The line went dead.

Nick stared out onto the road ahead as he drove home, his mind spinning at Bryce's words. He wondered if the agent had been in danger, but it hadn't sounded that way. In fact, if Nick hadn't known any better, it sounded as though Bryce was smack dab in the middle of a possible breakthrough.

The rush of adrenaline sent a tingle down his spine. Something was happening and all Nick could do was stand on the sidelines.

THEY KNEW WHO HE WAS. They'd been to his home. They'd been to the facility that cared for his sister. Danny King wasn't safe anywhere in the city and never had that idea grown clearer than right now. Being out on the roads was a risk because if they knew everything else about his life, they sure as hell knew what kind of car he drove. Even though it was registered to Mel, he had to give the cops credit to put two and two together.

Danny parked in the back of the building designated for employees. The storefront was closed, and the lot was empty. Pivo-Tech's retail store in this location was small by comparison and only a handful of employees worked here. Danny and two others worked from home answering the tech support lines. He stepped out of his car and pulled down his baseball hat. The back lot was absent security cameras, but as he made his way to the rear entrance, a camera was mounted just above it.

Danny reached for his little black device that was wrapped in copper wire and black electrical tape. The electromagnetic field generated by the pulse could have been more elegant, but it did its job disrupting electronic circuitry, including the surveillance camera above.

With a store key still in his possession, Danny unlocked the back door and slipped inside. Emergency exit signs illuminated the otherwise darkened hall as he let the door close behind him. The alarm beeped and he hurried to the keypad only steps away. Standard protocol dictated a change in the security code and turning in the keys when someone was let go. His boss hardly cared about his own job and didn't think he would have bothered to follow standard operating procedure, but he was about to find out.

Danny keyed in the code. A moment later, the light turned green. "Dumb ass, Larry." His boss hadn't known half of what Danny knew about cyber security, computers, and internet protocols.

With the building disarmed, Danny was free to roam around. He'd waited until after 7pm to be sure the cleaners had gone home. Now it was just him and all he had to do was access his client files. That was the price to be paid to those who knew more than he did when it came to making the kind of impact he'd wanted to make. Danny had warned law enforcement, and yet they persisted. That wasn't on him.

TIPS HAD ALREADY BEGUN to pour in on sightings thanks to the evening news. The field office agents were already hard at work sifting through them. That left the BAU team to work on their existing theories in hopes of catching a break.

While Duncan pursued PivoTech to determine whether Danny had accessed the dark web via their servers, she had also enlisted the help of Unit 2's Villanova and his knowledge of underground groups that shared Danny's vision.

Duncan ended her phone call. "I got the name of three sites. If Danny King was going to visit a dark web domestic terrorist site, these would be it."

Fisher raised his sights to her. "Do you know how to access them?"

"Villanova is going to walk us through it." She sat next to him and opened the laptop. "How far have you gotten on the phones from his house?"

"We're waiting on Stallard to confirm if that one was used as the remote detonator. I wish I had more."

"Then we'll see if we can get inside these chat rooms," Duncan began. "There are a million out there, but these are the largest and they specifically discuss explosives. If Danny needed to learn from anyone, it would be these types of people. I also have a feeling, since the story's been all over the news, that someone in these groups will be talking about it."

Walsh peered at his phone from the other end of the table. "Hey, I just got those birth records."

Kate stood up and made her way to him. As she leaned over his shoulder, she read the email. "Mr. Al Monahan and Mrs. Grace Monahan. Ellen King's parents. I'm surprised she kept her husband's name."

Surrey joined them. "Are these two still alive? If so, we can pull property records to see if they own that cabin in the picture."

"I'll get on that now. Let me make a call." Walsh stepped out into the corridor to make the call, but before he could dial, the line rang. "Scarborough, hey man, what's going on?"

"Something's happening with Hugo Bryce in Boston. I called him a few minutes ago. He sounded like he was onto something. Said he had to call me back."

Walsh pressed his hand on his hip. "You mean, you haven't pulled him off yet?"

"I was trying to, which was why I called him. Something's happening and I'm sitting here on my hands waiting," Nick replied.

"I'm up to my eyeballs right now, man. What do you want me to do?" Walsh pressed on.

"Hell, I don't know, but this is making me nervous. Look, we know someone from Quinn's circle was there at the train station," Nick added.

"Right."

"You have to find out who that was. There has to be security footage that shows him. I have the angle from where the picture was taken. That'll narrow down the shot from the footage. Levi, you gotta find out who's watching Kate."

"We talked about this. You were going to end it before things got out of hand," Walsh replied.

"I know. But after hearing from Bryce. Damn it, Levi, something big is about to pop. I can't pull the plug until I know what that is," Nick said.

"You're playing with fire, brother. You know that." Walsh peered at the door to the ops room. "Look, we've got everyone and their mother working on this serial bomber case. Everyone's certain Danny King is going to give us another show. We're all trying to stop that."

"You're saying you won't help?" Nick asked.

"I'm saying we all think this could be his swan song, you hear me? People will die." Walsh took in a breath. "I get where you're coming from, Nick. Here's what I can do. Tillis is working with Pittsburgh police now reviewing DOT footage and running vehicle matches through the database. Maybe I can ask him to check out the footage from around the train station and see what he finds. No guarantees."

"Please. If you can do at least that," Nick pleaded. "Thank you, Levi."

"I'll call you back if I learn anything." Walsh ended the call and dialed Tillis's phone. "Agent Tillis, this is Levi Walsh."

"Yeah, what's up? You guys get a run on something?" Tillis asked.

"Not yet. Working on it though. Everyone's busting their tails on this."

"Okay. Why the call?"

"I need a favor," Walsh said. "You don't owe me one. I get that. But I'm asking because this affects someone at the Bureau. A friend of mine."

"How can I help?" Tillis continued. "Not like I don't have my hands full at the moment, but what do you need?"

"The train station blast this morning." He paused a moment. "Did you see anything unusual?"

"You mean besides the bombing?" Tillis asked.

"Yeah. I know how this sounds, but specifically, do you recall seeing someone just standing around looking, watching you guys work. Anything like that?" Walsh added.

"Several bystanders hung around, but the local cops taped off the area and kept them back. I don't understand. What exactly are you trying to ask me and what does it have to do with someone at the Bureau?"

"It's a long story, one that I'll tell you someday. But what I'm asking about is if you saw anyone who clearly didn't belong. Another one of us just hanging out, looking, watching."

"One of us? Another agent?" Tillis asked.

"Possibly." He listened while the line went quiet for a few seconds too long. "Tillis? You still there?"

"Yeah, I'm here. You know, there was someone hanging around. I told him he had to leave and started walking across the street to get him clear. Hell, we hadn't even cleared the scene yet and this guy just leaned up against his car across the street. And you know, he looked like a fed. I brushed it off because of all the shit we were dealing with but, yeah, I guess I did see someone out of place."

Walsh raised his lips into a crooked smile. "Any chance you can find security footage from the station that might show this person?"

"Probably. But I gotta tell you, with hunting down King, I don't think I can pull..."

"It's for someone we both know," Walsh cut in. "I can't tell you who. Not yet. But I need to protect this person. And I need your help to do it."

His sigh was audible. "Let me see what I can do. I can probably ask one of the local guys to check it out. I'll just say it's part of the search."

"Thank you," Walsh replied.

"Someday, you'd better tell me what this was all about," Tillis said.

"I will." Walsh ended the call and for a moment, forgot why he was out here. "Oh shit." He dialed another number. "Hey, it's Walsh. Listen, can you dig up any more vital records for Al and Grace Monahan? Death certs if they exist."

"You need it now?" the man on the end of the line asked.

"I do. I wouldn't ask if it wasn't important. I can hang on," Walsh replied.

"Okay. Give me a minute."

Walsh listened as the man typed on his computer. His thoughts raged on at the idea these guys, Quinn's guys, were watching Kate. He knew Nick had to put an end to this, but that wasn't going to be easy for him. Nick was driven to the truth and especially when it involved Kate. In his heart, Walsh knew that Nick wouldn't give up until he made Quinn and the others pay for what they had threatened to do to Kate. The question remained, what would be the price?

"Okay, I think I got it for you."

"Are they both deceased?" Walsh was jolted back into the moment.

"Al Monahan died in 2014. Grace Monahan is still living," he replied.

Walsh cast up his gaze. "And when did Ellen King die?"

"Hang on." He typed again but came back quickly. "2019."

"Okay. Thanks, man. Send me the certs via email, would you?" Walsh asked.

"You got it."

He ended the call and returned inside. "The grandfather is dead. Grandma's still alive and kicking."

Kate exhaled sharply. "Finally. Let's find out what property she owns."

Surrey rubbed his smooth chin. "Assessor records should show that. I'd like to get my hands on her social security number too. The more details we can gather, the better our odds of finding King."

Walsh picked up his phone again. "On it."

∾

Nick returned to his apartment. He paced the room with his phone in his hand, waiting for the call from Bryce. It had been more than an hour since he reached out and still nothing.

He finally returned to the sofa with a bottle of water in his hands. Walsh hadn't gotten back to him and neither had Bryce. His nerves were shot and for the first time in a long time, the thought of having a drink crossed his mind.

"Stop." He rubbed his forehead as if to scrub away the idea. Nick glanced into the kitchen. Kate wasn't a big drinker, but there was always a bottle or two of wine in the fridge. No hard liquor. No Jack Daniels, which was Nick's favorite. Jack had seen him through a lot of situations in the past.

Powerless to take his eyes off the refrigerator, he could almost taste the wine on his lips. The light acidic burn on his tongue. His hands rubbed hard against his thighs until he finally pushed off the couch. Standing in the middle of the living room, Nick continued to stare into the kitchen. "I just need to calm my nerves." He closed his eyes. "Famous last words of every alcoholic before going on a bender." Nick took a few steps closer and reached the breakfast counter. He moved into the kitchen and stood in front of the fridge, his fingers wrapping around the handle. When he pulled it open, his phone rang in his pocket. Nick let go of the door and answered the call. "Holy shit, Bryce. I've been waiting to hear from you."

"Sorry about that," Bryce replied. "Hey, are you sitting down? Cause if you're not, you should be."

27

Inside the PivoTech retail store, Danny perched on the stool at the customer help station. Through the front window, a streetlamp burned in the empty parking lot. The large sign at the entrance illuminated. He set his gaze to the window and thought about Mel and how she was doing with Grandma Grace.

There had been a reason why Danny hadn't been back to see the old lady since his mom died. As a kid, their mother would take them to the cottage. He had some fond memories, but most were of the many arguments his mom got into with her parents, until Grandpa finally died. How they had insisted his father wouldn't have left if she'd only let Mel be taken into a home sooner. That his mom had no idea how to take care of Mel. And how without a man to care for them, she would always struggle. Danny scoffed. He was young at the time, but remembered Mel crying a lot.

The thought of leaving his sister there sickened him. But out of the two evils, Grandma was the lesser. And who knew? Maybe there was still a shot for Danny to see this through to the other side. He could do what he set out to do, go and get Mel and drive the hell out of the state before anyone knew what he'd done. Maybe.

Danny returned his attention to the computer in front of him. He knew how to penetrate the firewalls that protected the company's servers and easily slipped into the files he needed. Not only his customer files, which were accessed with his own credentials, but the files of everyone who had purchased or otherwise utilized PivoTech's services at any time in the last 12 months. Anything before that was archived at corporate. Names, addresses, credit card information. It was all there and ripe for the picking.

Danny had cut a deal in a place filled with threatening people and dangerous ideas. Few knew how to access this place, but for him, it had been child's play. While he had to learn his way around the system, there were plenty of people who helped him cultivate the knowledge necessary to reach his goals. Now, he looked to them again, but nothing in this life was free. Danny knew that better than most. Still, these people would protect him because he knew who they were too, and he had become just as dangerous.

His codename was Kingmaker and information was his currency. The trade-off had benefited both parties. They got financial data on his clients. He learned how to hurt those clients.

Kingmaker took screen shots of the data and through a series of backdoor commands, logged into the group where he'd struck the deal. He sent the message to Dante358. *"No doubt you've seen what I can do. I'm not finished yet. Need to make them suffer. Six? Timers, Different locations. Need spotter. NAME YOUR PRICE."*

Dante358 knew more about the city than anyone. And he knew explosives. Danny didn't know what he did for a living outside the web, but he suspected Dante358 was an insider at the city government level. Danny could do the dirty work, but he needed a strategy. He needed someone who knew where the police were, where to make the most of his efforts. And he was willing to hand over the financial lives of the people on the screen.

DUNCAN STOOD from the table and rubbed her eyes. "I need some water. Anyone want anything?" A few mutters of "no thanks" sounded as she walked out. Duncan continued out into the hall and toward the kitchen. As she reached the breakroom, her phone buzzed with an incoming call. "Duncan, here."

"Are you in front of a computer?" Agent Villanova asked.

"No." She turned and started to jog back toward the room. "What did you find?"

"I'm sending it to you now. I got a hit on red-flagged language in a chat room. Don't know for sure, but it could be your guy or someone talking about him."

Duncan hurried back inside. "Where at? What site?" She returned to the chair and pulled the laptop in front of her while Fisher looked on with curiosity.

"I'm sending you the details now. Like I said, I can't be sure but..."

"Thank you. I'll take a look." Duncan ended the call.

"What was that about?" Fisher asked.

"Villanova thinks he picked up someone either talking about King or King himself. He's sending me the logs now and the site of the chat room."

Kate perked up at attention. "If he's online, is it possible to find out where he is? He must have an IP address."

"I don't know. Let me see what he's sending first." Duncan waited until the email appeared. She opened the log and cast the image onto the wall monitor. "This is it."

"It looks like a bunch of code," Surrey replied. "I don't know that much about this stuff."

"Luckily, I do." Duncan stood again and walked to the monitor. "This here, these are the flagged words. That's how our guys know when there's chatter. They key in parameters that cue up certain language." She continued to peer at the screen. "I see the website. But I don't know how to access the dark web."

"Can your guy help?" Fisher asked. "This could be happening in real-time. We might have a shot at finding him."

She picked up her phone and returned to her chair. "Hey, it's me again. I think you could be right. Can you walk me through how to access this site?" She nodded. "Great. No, I'm ready when you are."

The rest of the team huddled around Duncan. Kate stood nearby and nudged Surrey. "Until we get confirmation of the property records, this might be it."

"Fingers crossed it's that easy," Surrey replied.

Walsh heard his phone in his pocket and glanced at the caller ID. "Damn. Bad timing, man." He rejected the call.

Kate peered at him. "You okay?"

"Yeah. It's nothing."

Duncan keyed in the commands. "Okay. I'm there. What's next?" She nodded and kept typing. "Yeah, I see that on the screen. Oh, this is it. I'm in. What do I do now? Yeah, okay. Thanks." She ended the call. "He's going to monitor things on his end, but he says if that's our guy, he can locate his IP address if he isn't using an onion router. I won't bore you with the complexities of all that. Point being, if he's using a proxy server, all bets are off."

"So even if we determine Danny King is active on this site, we most likely won't get a location on him," Surrey replied.

"But we might learn what he has planned," Kate added.

"Agreed." Duncan peered at the screen. "I'll put this on the wall so you guys can have a better look."

Kate walked toward the front of the room. "And this is in real-time?"

"This is happening now." Duncan scanned the content. "I'm trying to see which one of these guys is Danny King."

"That has to be him." Kate pointed to the monitor. "King-maker. Original. Look at his comments."

Fisher approached the front of the room and stood next to Kate. "Yep, gotta be our guy. This is Danny, the Kingmaker."

Nick stood on his balcony and leaned over the railing. He gazed out over the bay and the waters glistening under the light of the moon. The soft breeze gently rocked his moored boat that he couldn't remember having taken out in a while.

Walsh wasn't answering his phone and the last thing he wanted was to tell Kate what he had learned. What they had was real. According to Bryce out of the Boston field office, Richard Lehmann's belongings had been accessed by his ASAC. No doubt, to relay information to Quinn and Coletta and all the people working to protect top brass at the Bureau.

The phone was signed out almost immediately upon the arrival of Lehmann's body. He also learned that the Boston ASAC spoke to George Lehmann. It made sense now. Whoever had sent the message knew about the phrase Kate used, *See you again.* She'd told George Lehmann about it while in his captivity.

"Damn it." Nick pushed off the railing and returned inside. He had to try him one more time. "Come on, Walsh. I need you to answer, buddy." When he picked up, Nick prepared to speak, but was cut off.

"Scarborough, I'm sorry about earlier. Things are moving fast around here. I just got a call from Tillis. He found what you were looking for. I'm sending it to you now. Look at it. I'll wait."

Nick waited for the message to arrive. "Okay. I got it." He played the video and spotted the man standing in front of a car. "Son of a bitch." He returned the phone to his ear. "Then it's true."

"What are you talking about?" Walsh asked.

"What Bryce said. He got back to me, which was why I called you earlier. Walsh, that's the ASAC of the Boston field office. According to Bryce, he was the one who signed out Richard Lehmann's phone, among other things. Bryce found an original copy of the evidence log. Someone had erased the ASAC's name. Guess that's how they handle things in their circle. Just pretend it never existed. George Lehmann helped him to gain entry into the phone and when he did, he found audio recordings of conversations between the brothers. It's proof, Walsh. Proof that Richard Lehmann had nothing to do with the murders. It was all planned by George Lehmann after Kate broke free from him."

"Revenge?" Walsh looked back at Kate before walking out into the hall.

"That's what it looked like. It was a set up and I think Richard Lehmann believed he'd be released, which of course, didn't happen."

"I can't believe this." Walsh paced the hall. "So then Quinn used the Boston ASAC to get information against Kate because they knew we were close to learning about Carol Whitman's father."

"I don't know how the connection was made to the Boston ASAC. I'm assuming it's because Quinn knew him from his time there. Still, it makes me wonder if Quinn had been aware of the investigation."

"Like he'd been monitoring Kate?" Walsh asked.

"Has to be. He was just waiting for an opportunity and when one presented itself, he went after it."

"So this ASAC who was at the train station, is he still here? Are we being followed?" Walsh pressed on.

"That's the other thing. I could be off base, but after learning all this, I don't think I am," Nick began. "It's possible that the investigation has been sabotaged by Quinn's people. The bomb at the train station, that wasn't the bomber's M.O., was it?"

"Not his M.O., but the IEDs were the same," Walsh said. "Scarborough, are you trying to tell me that this insider group, who's looking to keep us quiet, might've planted the devices?"

"No one was killed, were they?" Scarborough asked.

"A few minor injuries." Walsh lowered his gaze. "Son of a bitch. That means someone on the inside here knew what we were looking at. I've talked to these guys. No way they have a mole."

"Someone said something, Walsh. And now you have to find the bomber. But you also have to look out for whatever this group decides to do next."

"How the hell am I supposed to do that?" Walsh asked.

"I don't know. But if you don't, there's no telling what steps they'll take." He paused for a moment. "Levi, you can't let Kate out of your sight. She's not safe."

As NIGHT SETTLED over the city, Danny was ready. He switched off the computer and started toward the back again, turning off the lights along the way. No one would know he had been there because on his way out, he stopped into the security room and erased the footage for the past few hours. It had taken time to pull it all together, but he was ready. As he walked to the door, he reset the alarm and left the building.

His car was cast in darkness with the nearest light about 100 feet away. The advice had been given and the price had been paid. A lot of people were about to have their identities stolen and Danny couldn't have cared less. Imagine a computer retailer being hacked. He laughed at the irony.

Danny opened the trunk of his car and pulled back the blanket. Everything was there.

He surveyed the dark and empty lot before slipping behind the wheel of his car. The entire plan would take roughly two hours. It would be decided then whether he would go back to see Mel. Everything hinged on his plan going off without a hitch. Maybe, though, he would call her just to hear her voice again.

"Hey, sis. It's me. How you doing?"

"I'm getting bored. Grandma made me eat something gross."

"Can't be any worse than that food they served you at the home."

"I guess not. When are you coming back? Are we staying here?" Mel asked.

"How's Grandma been treating you? Has she asked you anything about me?"

"Like what?"

"Oh, nothing. Listen, I just wanted you to know how much I love you, Mel. I don't say it often and I'm sorry for that. I'm sorry Mom's gone. And I'm sorry for not taking care of you the way I should have."

"What's wrong, Danny? You sound sad."

"No. I'm okay. I'll be back soon, don't worry about that. Just watch a movie and I'll be there before you know it. Then we can figure out what to do after that."

"Okay."

"I have to go." Danny ended the call and closed his eyes. On opening them again, he cleared his throat and wiped his eyes. "It's time."

WALSH RETURNED to the ops room where the team waited to learn if an IP address could be located. The online conversation had been saved and they knew King's plot to plant six bombs and where those bombs would be placed. Now, all they had to do was capture Danny at one of those locations.

"Tillis is on his way back and Stallard is heading this way too." Fisher returned his phone to his pocket. "That means, we'll be splitting up and heading out. We'll keep eyes out for King at each of the locations. The cops will stay out of sight as much as possible and Tillis's team will take the lead.

"He can't determine the IP address," Duncan began. "He just got back with me and said the VPN showed it came from outside the US. It was what we assumed, but we had to try."

"Doesn't matter now. We know where he plans to be," Surrey added. "We'll get this guy, and we'll get him tonight."

Walsh touched Kate's arm and nodded for her to follow him into the corridor.

"What's up?" Kate asked.

"There's been a lot of things happening outside your purview," Walsh began. "Scarborough and I, well, and Fisher too, we've been hunting down the one who threatened you."

"Nick filled me in on some of it before I left. I know you've been working with him, which comes as no surprise. Did something break loose? Do you know who threatened me?"

"Yes, but there's a lot to it and given what's about to happen, I don't have the time to go into great detail. But you should know that it involves Noah Quinn. What I brought you out here to say was that these people are coming for you, Kate. I thought you should know."

Quinn's name brought heat under her collar. "People? Not just Quinn, but people."

"Yes. This is bigger than we ever thought. But Kate, please, just listen to me for a second. These people have been watching you since you arrived here. The train station bombing? It doesn't match King's M.O."

Her face lost all expression. "No. Don't you dare tell me someone inside the Bureau planned that. No. Stallard already said..."

"I know what he said. Kate, these people have eyes everywhere. They knew what King used and they copied it. Didn't it seem odd that it was so random? That no one was killed? They planned it that way."

"Why?" Her face masked in rage.

"To draw you out. I don't know if they had something else planned this morning for you, or not, but the whole thing was to bring you out into the open."

"Jesus." She placed her hands on her hips and her eyes reddened. "What the hell is going on here? Why are they doing this?"

"I need you to stay close to me tonight. I promised Scarborough that I wouldn't let anything happen to you..."

"For God's sake. Are you kidding me? You don't think I can handle this?"

"This isn't the time to be stubborn, Kate. Listen to me. This is real. This is dangerous. You are a target and not of Danny King's. We'll find him tonight. But you and me? We're sticking together like glue until this is over."

28

Under misty dark skies, Kate stared through the windshield at the road ahead. She tried to break free from the relentless thoughts that swirled in her mind. How had this become about her? And more importantly, why? What made Walsh's revelations all the worse was that Nick knew about them. Fisher knew too, yet she had been left in the dark. Anger boiled in her stomach. All this because of Noah Quinn and his hatred of her. It didn't make sense. They wouldn't have staged the train station bombing. That was a step too far even for Quinn.

Now they hunted a serial bomber and had been given the upper hand thanks to the work Eva Duncan had completed. But Kate's focus was scattered. What had Quinn wanted from her and how did he propose to get it?

"Reid?" Surrey tapped her shoulder from the backseat. "You with us?"

"Huh? Sorry. I'm here," she replied.

Walsh cast her a sideways glance from the driver's seat.

"We're coming up on one of the sites," Surrey added. "I need you here with us, you understand?"

"I said I was sorry. I'm here. I don't need you telling me how to do my job."

"Last thing we need is a squabble between you two," Walsh said. "We have five other teams heading to the locations. One of us will come up on Danny King and we need to be ready. The kid will be highly unstable, and he'll be armed with volatile explosives. I don't know about either one of you, but I'm not going to die today." He rolled to a stop several feet before the Fort Duquesne Bridge. "This is one of the targets. I see a parking lot over there. Could be a spot where he would make his mark."

"I think he'll aim higher." Surrey pointed toward the public park near the bridge and the water's edge. "That area over there, near the gazebo and park. The messages discussed a place where there would be structures. We know he plans on using devices with timers. My gut tells me he'll set it for morning when dog walkers and joggers are out."

Kate surveyed the area. "He's out of his element. This wasn't how things were supposed to go for him. He's acting out of desperation and not his original purpose."

"What are you talking about? What about the train station? You thought that could have been a trial run," Surrey replied.

Walsh and Kate traded glances.

Surrey picked up on the exchange. "Is there something I should know?" He peered at them. "Hey, am I a part of this team or not? Can someone let me in on what the hell is going on here?"

Walsh peered over his shoulder toward the backseat. "We can't be certain the train station blast was Danny King."

"Of course it was. Stallard said it was," Surrey replied.

Walsh sighed before Kate cut in. "Walsh and Fisher think

people on our side of the fence planned the explosion and made it look like it was King to throw us off."

Surrey laughed. "Are you serious? Why the hell would they do that?"

"To get to me." Kate opened the passenger door and stepped out into the steamy night air. She surveyed the nearby park and waited for Walsh and Surrey to join her. "What the hell are we supposed to do if we find a device? I don't know about you guys, but I don't know jack about disarming anything."

"We're to call Stallard who will send his people out," Walsh replied. "Our job is to find King and stop him, hopefully, before he finishes the job."

"So we wait?" Surrey appeared content to let go the previous discussion, for now.

"We'll keep in radio contact with the others, listen to whether anyone spots him. It's hard to say if he'll be driving the same car." Walsh peered at them. "We know he's coming. We just don't know when."

AGENT TILLIS ARRIVED at the second of the six targets King had planned. Alongside two other agents, they waited inside his car in search of where they might spot Danny King.

"How long do we sit here?" Agent Garcia pulled up from the backseat. "I feel like we should be doing more."

"We just need to stay out of sight in case King shows up here," Tillis replied. "He'll turn up at one of the targets."

"I hope he turns up here." Agent Lee peered through the windshield. "I have a cousin who lives nearby. The thought that asshole would set off a bomb where people come to work every day pisses me off."

"We'll get to him tonight. One of us will," Tillis replied. He picked up the radio. "Hey, what are the chances he'll livestream this shit?"

Kate peered into the vehicle at the radio receiver before glancing to Surrey. "He has a point. King has lost all sense of reality at this point. I wouldn't put it past him to get his message across again."

"Who do we have to put on that?" Surrey asked. "Can they preempt it?"

Kate reached for the radio and pressed the button. "Tillis, this is Reid. If King broadcasts his activities, I'm not sure he'll use a former victim's account to do it and it doesn't appear that he has his own, but it's possible he has an account under a different name."

"What do you suggest then, Reid?" Tillis asked.

"If anything, I think he'll use a group," she added. "Can you get your computer forensics lead to find a link between the group on the dark web and one on social media? Probably Facebook, since that's what he's used in the past. I have a feeling those people will have something set up to better reach your average Joe. King-maker will be a member of that group."

Tillis pressed the radio receiver again as he sat behind the wheel of his car. "Got it. I'll get them onboard and have them keep us posted. What happens if he livestreams? We won't have the ability to stop it."

"Assuming we find the group, we'll use it to determine his exact location and whoever's stationed there will get eyes on him. Then, we get onto the stream and bring attention to the moderators to shut it down," Kate replied.

"They won't act fast enough. The damage will be done," Tillis added.

Kate shrugged. "Then blood will be on the hands of those responsible for allowing it to be livestreamed."

DUNCAN LISTENED to the conversation and turned to Fisher as they waited at the third location. "You didn't have anything to add to that?"

"There's nothing more we can do than that, Eva. My hope is that we'll get to King before he blows up anything, livestreaming or not."

She cast down her gaze for a moment. "Why did you and Walsh come here?"

"You were hurt. You were in the damn hospital. I wasn't going to just let my people fight this alone. You needed help."

"That's where you and I disagree. I was fine, Cam. You saw me. I let down my guard and someone died. I'll have to live with that for the rest of my life. But having you here, trying to save me..."

"That's not what happened, and you know it. Don't make this just about you, Eva. This is about the team and the team needed extra hands." He held her gaze. "I don't know where this is coming from."

"Cam, this is the first time you let Reid take the reins. And the first time you jumped in to the rescue, just like Scarborough did." Duncan sighed. "We had this guy. The work I did with BAU-2 helped get us to this point. We didn't need you here. Not this time." She looked at him and furrowed her brow. "What?"

Fisher shrugged. "I was worried about you, yes. You can think I'm an asshole because I was worried about the woman I love, but there is another reason we came."

Her eyes softened. "What is it then?"

"A few months ago, after the Lehmann investigation, Reid was threatened."

"Threatened? By whom?"

"We didn't know. Long story short, Walsh and Scarborough have been digging around in search for answers about how Theo Bishop escaped to Mexico. The passport logs that were missing?"

"Yeah," she replied.

"It turned out that someone inside the Bureau made that happen. They let the Mercy Killer escape. And then when our people started getting too close, Reid was threatened during the Lehmann case."

"Why her?" Duncan asked.

"Because whoever was behind helping Bishop's mother, Carol Whitman, discovered something about Richard Lehmann. They discovered he had no part in the deaths his brother accused him of participating in."

"What? Are you serious?"

"I wish I wasn't," Fisher replied. "We're here because those same people inside the Bureau who threatened Reid, one who we all know well, it looks like they might have been behind the train station attack. I didn't want to believe any of it. In fact, I owe Scarborough one hell of an apology. Walsh pulled me aside before we left tonight. He told me these guys had evidence that Richard Lehmann didn't help his brother kill anyone."

Duncan's eyes widened and her mouth dropped. "Why the hell am I just now finding out about this?"

"Because we don't know their intentions. Scarborough thinks the blast was used to draw out Reid. For what, God knows. But they aren't going to stop unless we drop everything. Give them a pass."

"You said someone we all know is involved. Who is it, Cam?" Duncan insisted.

He held her gaze with a serious mien. "Noah Quinn."

DRESSED IN BLACK, Danny arrived at the first of his six targets. He had to act fast and had taken the time to build each device ahead of time. Input from Dante358 suggested he add additional powder. He would then install the devices near a metal structure to ensure maximum blast radius and a large metal debris field with the potential for severe injury. He didn't have gasoline as a propellant now, so he relied on the use of filler, metal junk that would be propelled at a fair distance. The timers were the cell phones he'd taken from the store. Everything aligned perfectly.

The Strip District was a popular spot among locals. Street vendors, shops and cafes. And on a Saturday, it would be packed with people. Alongside the Allegheny River, the half-mile area was the perfect target. It was his most ambitious plan to date, but there was little else he could do to take a stand. He didn't think of the people who would be hurt. He only thought about Mel and how the system had hurt his family.

Danny stepped out of his car and stood beside it, peering out onto the Strip. He walked to the trunk of his car and opened it. Inside lay the devices, nestled in Styrofoam and individual boxes. He didn't want any accidents if he hit a bump in the road.

He thought he'd be more nervous, but his hands were steady, and his breathing was normal. With the box in his hand, he lay it on the ground and gently closed the lid of the trunk. People still milled about, though not many. He suspected it would pick up as the hour grew later. Two popular bars resided in the area, though they were down closer to the end of the Strip.

It would be best for him to get the device in place quickly and hurry to the next location. Danny was confident the police would be looking for his car and there was no telling how much time he had. If only he'd been a good car thief too.

He walked along the pathway that ran parallel to the river and toward the street vendors' area. Some of the stands remained in place, covered and uncovered. The perfect spot revealed itself. A food truck. Big enough to scatter a lot of debris with the help of its large gas tank.

With the device in place, Danny walked back to his car, unhurried and careful not to draw attention. When 9am, Saturday morning arrived, the street would be busy. It was the perfect time.

His car was in sight and he pulled the keys from his pocket, fidgeting to find the right one. On arrival, he peered around and finally, stepped inside. Relief washed over him. The first one was in place. And it hadn't been nearly as hard as he thought.

Agent Ramirez sat behind the wheel of his car. Instinctively, he hunkered low and nudged his partner. "Hey, is that the car?"

His partner, Agent Watford, shot a look in the direction. "Holy shit. Sure as hell looks like a white Ford Focus. And the suspect. I'm calling it in." He pressed the radio. "Hey, we got a possible sighting of Danny King. Vehicle matches the description. He's getting inside the vehicle now."

Tillis was the first to reply. "He's leaving?"

"Ten-four. He just closed the door of his car. We need the go-ahead," Watford replied.

"If he's already in his car, follow him. See where he goes next," Tillis said. "Stallard, your people should get down there now to sweep the place. Watford, you and Ramirez tail this guy but do not let him see you."

"Copy that." Watford turned to his partner. "Let's see where he goes."

Ramirez keyed the ignition and waited for the white car to drive by. Without headlights, he headed out toward the street that fronted the river. "Once he gets out farther, I'll turn on the lights. I need another car between us, so he doesn't see."

Watford glanced at him. "Just don't lose him."

KATE EYED SURREY as the three had returned to the car to wait. "They can't lose him. When he starts getting closer to his next location, the guys will be alerted and be ready."

"They know what they're doing," Surrey replied.

"That means he's already planted at least one device," Walsh began. "I hope to hell Stallard's people find it before Danny figures out that he's being watched. Kid might just decide to blow them up."

The radio cut in again. "Watford here. We're still tailing the suspect. He's heading southeast toward the downtown area."

"He won't stop there. It'll be too busy," Tillis replied on the radio. "Just keep eyes on him. We'll be ready wherever he decides to go."

From inside their car, Kate looked at Walsh. "We're southeast of their location. He could be headed here."

"Then we'd better keep our eyes open and our heads down," Walsh replied.

Stallard's voice crackled on the radio. "I have a team headed to the Strip District now. They'll find the device. He won't make his mark there."

Several minutes went by. The radio was quiet. Kate's nerves stood on end. She tried to push back what Walsh had revealed about the train station attack. But she couldn't see past Noah Quinn. If this was all true, Quinn wouldn't get away with it. Not if she had anything to say on the matter. Whatever Richard Lehmann was or wasn't didn't matter because the man still attacked her. She killed him in self-defense. It had always lingered in her mind that he might not have been involved and that George used him as leverage. And Kate bought it, hook, line, and sinker. She shook away the thought and felt a hand on her shoulder.

"You still doing all right?" Surrey asked.

"Fine," Kate replied. "I'm just ready for this to be over." She stared out through her passenger window and spotted headlights approach. "Hang on. That could be him." She picked up the radio. "Watford, tell me you're heading down Fifth Street right now. I see headlights."

"We're two cars behind King and yes, we're coming down Fifth now. We're heading your way Agent Reid. I hope you guys are ready."

Kate gripped the door handle while her stare penetrated the darkness. Spotty streetlamps illuminated the park and cast an eerie glow through the heavy air. "We don't know where he'll stop."

"I'm ready." Walsh turned the engine. "We'll follow him. And when he stops, we wait."

"For what?" Kate asked. "Levi, we can't give him an opportunity to grab hold of one of his bombs."

"I understand, but we also can't risk some sort of shootout with his car full of explosives."

"Probably something we should've hashed out before now, folks. How do you want to play this?" Surrey asked.

Kate eyed Walsh and he nodded. "We take the lesser of the evils."

29

The headlights grew brighter as Danny's car neared. Parked under a heavily canopied tree, Kate watched as it approached. "Be ready."

The radio buzzed in again. "We're at your 9 o'clock and coming your way. Suspect's car is passing you now."

"Tell them to drop back," Surrey said. "We don't need a bunch of agents coming up on him. It's too dangerous."

"Surrey's right," Walsh picked up the radio. "Walsh here. Fall back. It's our turn now."

"You got eyes?" Watford responded.

"Eyes on the suspect. Drop back now." Walsh shifted the car into Drive and rolled down the side street until he reached the intersection.

"He's going to the park, near the gazebo and café," Surrey added.

Fisher's voice sounded on the radio. "I want all teams to get to the park. All teams, make your way to PNC Park."

Kate tried to pick up the radio, but Walsh grabbed her hand. "What are you doing? Fisher just gave everyone the go-ahead to come here. Levi, you told them to stay back, and Fisher is telling them otherwise."

"Leave it. By the time they get here, this could be over anyway, and we may need them." Walsh picked up the radio. "We're trailing the suspect now. Be aware his car is loaded with explosives. I'd suggest everyone keep their distance until we have him in custody."

"Walsh, you can't go this alone," Fisher responded.

"We already are. Those on their way, I ask that you stay back and let us get the situation under control first. We don't need any dead agents tonight." He dropped the receiver and continued to follow.

Kate's breath echoed in her ears. She thought about Nick and Quinn and all that had happened. But Danny King was about to plant a bomb and she had to stop him. Kate had come across plenty of cold-blooded killers. King was different. He couldn't see past his anger and grief and distrust in the system. She didn't know how to talk down someone like that. If he was willing to kill people at random, not for personal reasons, not for his own gratification, but as a statement, how is it possible to combat that effort?

"He's stopping." Walsh turned to her. "Be ready."

"I'm ready. Surrey?"

"I can't be any more ready. Let's end this city's nightmare." Surrey checked his weapon.

Walsh pulled to a stop at the nearest location that offered cover. He opened his door and turned to them. "Now's the time." He stepped out and cringed when the interior light came on. "Shit," he whispered.

"He's facing the other way. He doesn't see us." Surrey opened his door and stepped out.

Kate swallowed down her nerves and tried to slow her breathing. "You're okay. He can't get to you."

Surrey eyed her and whispered, "What did you say?"

She shook it off and walked around the other side to join them. Her chest felt tight and sweat trickled down her neck. Kate wiped her hands on her pants.

"Jesus, Reid, are you okay?" Surrey asked.

"I'm fine."

Walsh examined her for a moment.

"I'm fine," she insisted. "Let's just go before this kid blows up everything." Kate started behind them. Her eyes suddenly burned as she blinked away the stinging. She wiped them with the back of her free hand while holding her gun with the other. Her hands trembled as they moved closer.

Danny King stood outside his vehicle, staring off toward the park. Almost as if he had been reconsidering his plan.

The agents moved in and it was lost on no one that King possessed a deadly explosive device. Kate stepped ahead of Surrey and aligned with Walsh. "I know him. I've been working this case for weeks. You need to let me talk him down."

He stopped and regarded her. "Tell me you aren't thinking about Lehmann right now."

"I'm not. I'm here, Levi. It's me. You know me," Kate replied. "This is my case. Don't take it from me. I know who King is. Who he really is and why he's doing this." She looked at Surrey with eyes that pleaded for his support. Surrey had been an ally but had also gone against her before. Whether for good reason or not, it didn't matter to her in this moment. She spotted the hesitation in his face and locked eyes with him.

"Reid knows him. She's got this, Walsh. I'll back her up."

Walsh appeared reluctant. "I do know you. Better than most." He tossed a nod. "Go."

Kate started on. As they closed in on him, she readied herself for what was about to come. Danny King would fight it because he had nothing left to lose. His sister would be taken from him and he would face prison. Turning someone away from death when prison awaited them wasn't going to be easy.

She looked back at Walsh, almost asking for permission. He had been like a brother to her, and she'd learned a lot from him. She loved him, and his life was just as much at stake as hers. He offered a gentle nod and she moved forward.

Kate trained her weapon on him. "Danny King."

The young man shot around with the box in his hand, appearing startled. Realization masked his face. "Let me guess, it was you. Not some reporter. You texted me the other night, didn't you?"

"Put down the box, Danny. We tracked you inside the group chat. We know your plan and it ends here." Kate raised her gun just a little higher to solidify her point.

"Just you three? I thought I'd draw a bigger response than that."

"More are coming if you want to wait it out," Kate added. "But it's just us right now."

He scoffed. "I knew this was coming. That's why I thought I might as well go big or go home, right?"

"Somehow, I don't think that's true. I think you wanted this, Danny. You wanted us to stop you. You don't want to leave Melanie on her own," Kate pressed on.

Danny's eyes darkened. "What do you know about Mel?"

"I know she needs help. I know she can't take care of herself, which was why she was in a home."

"She was in a home because the fucking State didn't think I could take care of my own family."

"I know. And I know that you've shouldered a lot in the past few years. Your mom. Your sister. I understand why you felt the system failed you. It did." And as if from nowhere, her hands jerked the gun before she quickly steadied them again. It was only a split second. Kate's face masked in shock as she was forced to recall the moment she stood before George Lehmann with a gun to his head, just as she was doing now.

Walsh jumped to her aid after spotting her recoil. "Put down the box, son. That thing goes off by accident, you'll be the one who ends up dead."

Kate regained her composure and kept her eyes fixed on King. "He's right. It's over, Danny. We'll go get Melanie and make sure she's safe."

"You don't even know where she is. Only I do."

"I know she's at an old cottage your grandmother owns," Kate began. "She must be really scared right now not knowing where you are or what you're doing. So, how about we put this to rest and bring her back."

"Well, I guess if you know where she is, there isn't much point in any of this." Headlights appeared to catch his eye and he glanced beyond Kate.

Walsh turned his head and waved them back. "God damn it."

"Well, now. I think things just got interesting." Danny nodded. "The more, the merrier, right?"

"Keep them back," Kate said to Walsh, without letting down her guard. "He doesn't care about his life now."

"The lady's right." Danny smiled. "My life is over. It's only Mel's life that matters to me. All this time, I tried to make things better for her. But in this world, you either screw people over to get what you want, or they screw you over. There is no in-between. Someone needs to fix that. I tried."

"You have a right to be angry, Danny. But you killed innocent people. You could've killed a lot more at the train station, but you didn't," Kate replied. "I have to think that's because a part of you knows there's still good in this world."

"What the hell are you talking about, a train station?"

Kate lost all expression. Her eyes darted for a moment to Walsh. He had been right. The train station was her own damn people, including Quinn.

"Why would I choose prison? Either way, I've lost my sister." Danny opened the box and picked up a cell phone inside.

Kate thrust out her other hand, leaving her gun trained on him. "Danny, don't."

"Step back, Reid." Walsh grabbed her arm.

"Yeah, Reid. Step back or you might get hurt." Danny swiped the screen.

"Wait. Don't do this, Danny," Kate insisted.

"Why not?"

His eyes bored into hers and for the first time, she saw a frightened kid. "Because it would hurt Mel. A lot, I imagine. I don't think you want to put her in any more pain than she's already been forced to endure."

Walsh continued to glance back and make sure the other agents weren't getting close. He spotted Fisher step out of his car with Duncan next to him. Behind them, Tillis rolled up. There were too many of them here now and this kid would get spooked. He already teetered. It wouldn't take much to push him over the edge.

"She deserves a better brother than me."

When he looked down at the phone, Kate knew this was it." Danny!"

The explosion threw a bright light and forced Kate to stumble back, nearly falling into Surrey. They tangled into each other as he struggled to regain his footing.

Walsh shuffled back and used his arm to shield himself. "Get down!"

Debris flew inside the energy wave and Kate huddled on the ground, her back to the blast.

Fisher knelt down with Duncan by his side and when the worst of it ended, he stood. "I have to get up there." He ran toward his team. "Is everyone okay? Is anyone hurt?"

"I'm okay." Kate slowly got to her feet. "Surrey, are you okay?"

"Yeah. I'm good."

Fisher offered his hand to Walsh. "Come on, man. It's over." When they stood again, they watched the flames burn Danny's body as he lay on the ground. The grass around him singed and flared up, but soon extinguished in the sultry air. "Christ." He turned back as Tillis approached. "We need the Fire Department here now."

MELANIE KING WOULD SOON GET a visit from Social Services and find herself spending the rest of her days in the care of the State of Pennsylvania. Her grandmother had been too old to care for her. The local agents cleared the remaining locations and as a precaution, the areas were cordoned off for hours.

After the final briefing, the team boarded the plane and headed back to Quantico in the middle of the night. Kate buckled her belt and peered through the plane's window when Walsh sat down next to her. She turned to him and revealed a tender grin.

"What happened back there?" Walsh asked in a hushed tone.

"What do you mean? The kid blew himself up. Didn't

livestream it. Didn't kill anyone else. He knew it was over. We saved a lot of people tonight."

"That's not what I mean," Walsh continued. "What happened to you back there? You flinched, Kate. You trained a gun on a man's chest and you flinched."

She looked away. "He didn't know anything about the train station, Levi." Kate turned back. "Were they going to kill me? Is that why they were there?"

"I don't know. I don't think so. They wanted us to see what they could do."

"So they get away with it again. They could've killed someone." She shook her head. "I knew Richard Lehmann was innocent, Levi. I felt it the moment Surrey and I brought him onto that plane. If he hadn't attacked Surrey..."

"Then he wouldn't have been killed," Walsh cut in. "Kate, I'm sorry about all of this. You were targeted because of the Lehmann case. It was their best shot at shutting us down."

"And Quinn?" Kate held his gaze. "Am I supposed to forget that he's somehow involved in all this?"

"You want the truth? Yes. Kate, it's not worth what they're willing to do to you and to Nick."

"To Nick?" she asked.

"I fully believe this was a ploy to get to him through you. It's what I would expect from Quinn. He wasn't running the show, but I have no doubt he put in his two cents."

Kate pulled the elastic band from her hair. "What the hell am I supposed to do, Levi? Fold?"

"If you want them to stop, then yes. You fold. We drop the whole thing, and everyone gets on with their lives. No one loses their job. That's what I suggested to Scarborough."

"What did he say?" Kate asked.

"I don't think he'd made up his mind. That might change now,

I don't know. But if it doesn't, Kate, then you have to convince him. Ultimately, it's you he's been worried about. Same as me. The way you were targeted during this case." He turned away for a moment. "Scares the shit out of me as to what they were willing to do to keep their secret. Don't jeopardize this opportunity. You've worked too hard for it."

"I know, but..."

"But nothing. Quinn wins if you're out—if Nick's out. I don't think that's what you want." Walsh stood again. "And Kate, I think you should consider talking to someone."

"What do you mean?"

"You're dealing with things I can't imagine. And back there was the first I'd seen any hint that you might not be handling it well. The next time could cost your life or someone else's."

KATE FINALLY ARRIVED HOME. She walked inside the apartment to see Nick standing on the other side of the door. "You're still up."

"Of course I am." He pulled her into an embrace. "I should've told you, Kate. I'm sorry. I just didn't want to pull you out of the game."

"I know that you didn't trust me to put the job first. That's what I know, Nick." She pushed him away. "They followed me, and I had no idea. Do you know what they could've done?"

"It was a scare tactic," he added.

"You sure about that? Because I'm not. And now I have Levi telling me we need to scrap the whole thing. Let Quinn and the rest of them off scot-free. Nick, I don't think I can do that."

"Then it won't end." He turned on his heel and leaned against the back of the sofa sectional. "It won't end until we drop it. The Mercy Killer is dead. We got justice for his victims.

Maybe Walsh is right. I won't let them force you out or me, for that matter."

She folded her arms in defiance. "What do they have, really? Richard Lehmann attacked my partner. Tried to kill him, then he came after me. So what if he wasn't guilty of murder. And, frankly, I'm not entirely convinced of that. I think Quinn and his people got to George Lehmann and made him change his story. So what do they have? Why can't we fight it?"

"Oh, man, Kate. I—they're too big. Too powerful. It'll cost you everything you've worked for. Me? I've been the rising star and now that title belongs to you. This is what you've worked for. You took the lead in this case."

"Yeah, and Fisher came running to the rescue."

"Because he was worried about Duncan and he knew they were watching you. It's his job to protect his team. Just like it's mine," Nick replied.

Kate dipped her head and sighed. Nick was right. If she pushed this, nothing would happen to Quinn. He was protected. But her? She'd lose everything. And so would Nick. So she could be selfish and push this to its bitter end, or she could let it go and hope that someday Quinn got what he deserved. The question was, who was more important in her life, Nick or Noah Quinn? She looked up at him again. "Okay. We drop it."

"Really?" He pushed off the sofa and took her by the shoulders. "This is the best we can do, Kate. Those guys aren't worth it. I think I've finally realized that. You're too valuable to the team and there are plenty of bad guys out there left for you to find."

She relented. "Yeah. Maybe so. Listen, I'm exhausted. I need some sleep."

∾

NICK WOULDN'T KNOW and she'd be back tonight. So in the pre-dawn hours, Kate started on the long drive. She'd called into Fisher already and explained that she just needed to get her head together and that the final paperwork would have to wait until Monday. The King investigation took a toll. That was what she told him.

The George Washington Bridge came into view. It was Saturday and the drive hadn't been as long as she had expected. By mid-morning, Kate was about to cross over into Manhattan. She knew where he lived thanks to a friend at the New York Field Office. Kate had worked with colleagues all over and had amassed quite a contact list since joining the BAU. Maybe Nick had been right. People inside the Bureau knew who she was. Her talents preceded her. Kate was a rising star, and it was time she remembered that.

She arrived at Quinn's apartment building. He should be alone. From what she knew, he hadn't had a serious girlfriend. Shocker. The man was an egotistical son of a bitch. Who the hell could put up with his manipulative tactics? Kate pulled to a stop at the curb and gazed up at the grey stone building. How could Nick possibly have expected her to give up? After all the bullshit Quinn had pulled.

Kate stepped outside and closed the car door. Her throat tightened and her heart pounded. "You have to do this. You have to confront him. He can't get away with it."

She'd spent the entire drive weighing the consequences. Quinn would be fired and would never find another job in law enforcement if she told them what she knew. His friends inside the Bureau could've killed innocent people. How was that okay? How could Nick and Levi be okay with that? Maybe it didn't matter that it could end her career too. But as she considered it, in her heart, Kate knew she'd done nothing wrong in the Lehmann case. It would be an uphill battle, sure, but she was one of the good guys. Weren't they supposed to win?

She squeezed her hands into fists but couldn't move her legs. Quinn was inside his apartment; she was sure of it. "Just knock on his door. Tell him you know. He won't have the guts to stop you." It didn't matter that people more powerful than Quinn could hit back. She'd stop them too if that's what it took.

Her lips began to quiver as she stared at the building. In her head raged a war. A battle of right and wrong, of self-preservation or self-destruction. "You'll destroy everything," she whispered. "Nick won't understand." Tears welled and as they spilled down her cheeks, she wiped them away with a harsh hand. Kate took in a full, deep breath. "No. Just stop. You have to stop now. He's not worth it."

She stepped inside the car again and eyed the building. Kate dropped her head into her hands and sobbed. "I can't. I can't do it. He'll leave me. He'll never forgive me." After a few moments, she slowed her breathing and worked to calm herself. A final glance at the building and Kate drove away.

THE EVENING APPOINTMENT had been a special request. The return to D.C. left Kate clear on what she needed to do. And now, she had arrived.

The door to the office opened as Kate sat in the waiting room. "Agent Reid? Come on in."

Kate stood from the couch. "Thank you for seeing me tonight. I'm sure you'd rather be doing something a little more interesting on a Saturday evening."

"Not at all. Please come inside and take a seat." The doctor closed the door behind her and returned to her desk.

Kate sat down and labored to find comfort on the overstuffed chair.

"It's okay, Agent Reid. You can relax in here." The doctor placed her elbows on top of her desk. "So tell me, Kate. May I call you Kate?"

"Sure."

"Why are you here?"

Kate looked down at her feet and shrugged her shoulders. "I don't seem to be handling things very well."

"What kind of things?" the doctor pressed on.

Kate thought on the question for a moment. "My life hasn't been easy, Doctor. While I try not to talk about it, try not to dwell on it, my past is always there, waiting for me to bring it into the present again. And I've noticed it has a tendency to affect the decisions I make in my life and in my job."

"Can you elaborate?"

"How much time to you have?" Kate laughed.

"However much you need."

Right," she continued. "Well, okay. Recently, as in just the other day, I had my gun aimed at a man. A kid, really. And my team, who was right behind me, I almost—I almost made a mistake that could've resulted in their deaths, and my own."

"I see. That sounds like a very serious mistake if that's what it was," she replied.

"Oh, there's no doubt about that. I was pulled out of the situation and into another one and in that split second, everything could've changed."

"This other situation must weigh on your mind," the doctor said.

"Very much so, yes." Kate sighed. "Then today, I made a decision that went against my better judgement."

"And how did that go?"

"It's why I'm here with you now," she replied.

"Of course. Kate, I've read your file. All of it. There's a lot to digest. But there's still one thing that's bothering me. You didn't answer my question and that is why are you here?"

Kate's eyes reddened and she tucked her hair behind her ears. In a frail and fractured voice, one she hadn't known still existed inside her, she continued. "I'm here because...I need help."

The doctor smiled and nodded. "Okay then. Let's talk."

THE END

ABOUT THE AUTHOR

Robin Mahle has published more than 30 novels in the mystery/thriller genre. She also writes historical fiction as <u>Christine Chase.</u>

It is Robin's fast-paced style of storytelling combined with tense action and thrilling twists that bring her readers back for more. So be sure sure to subscribe to her newsletter to keep up on all the latest releases, sales, and giveaways. Go to robinmahle.com and sign up today!

Robin lives in Coastal Virginia with her husband and two children.

If you enjoyed Ms. Mahle's work, please share your experience by leaving a review on <u>Amazon.</u>

ALSO BY ROBIN MAHLE

www.ingramcontent.com/pod-product-compliance
Lightning Source LLC
Chambersburg PA
CBHW060535180626
46817CB00002B/578